The Chocolate Rose

LAURA FLORAND

ACKNOWLEDGMENTS

With my many, many thanks to Laurent Jeannin, head pastry chef at the Michelin three-star restaurant at Le Bristol in Paris, and Pastry Chef of the Year (2011). This book would not have been half so vivid without his patience and generosity in welcoming me into his kitchens, in answering all my questions, and in sharing so many stories of what it means to be a chef pâtissier.

Chapter 1

T he notice of the lawsuit arrived two weeks after the cookbook came out. Jolie opened it, spotted the words "on behalf of our client, Gabriel Delange", and felt the bottom drop out of her stomach.

Oh, God. Jolie spread the letter by the cookbook, centered proudly on her desk. Her father's name, PIERRE MANON, stamped its big, glossy, silver cover, right above the most beautiful thing to ever come out of his kitchens: the Rose. Back when she was a teenager, every TV crew that filmed her father filmed that rose, every magazine article about him featured it on its cover: out of all the beautiful dishes from his kitchens, the most sublime. Pink and red gently streaked great white chocolate petals, the outer ones spreading into bloom, the inner ones still curved, reluctant to break free from the bud, protecting for one last second the heart inside. That heart glowed under those petals, a sliver glimpse of pure gold. It was heartbreaking to eat it, and yet if you didn't, it would die within minutes, the gold leaf collapsing as the Tahitian vanilla mousse it encased melted in the passionate heat of the raspberry *coulis* beneath it.

Only her words and the food photographers' images could catch such a thing and give it permanence, like catching a firefly's glow.

She remembered now her father's hesitation when she had insisted on the Rose for the cover, how he had looked away and proposed other things and then at last smiled into her eager eyes and yielded.

A lawsuit.

Oh, boy.

Brought on behalf of his former *chef pâtissier*, Gabriel Delange. A man she primarily remembered from over a decade ago as being tall and far too skinny, yet somehow managing to fill a room with his energy, until he was all a teenager stuck in her father's office could look at. She had had a tiny fourteen-year-old crush on him. Gabriel Delange, who had made his own way after her father fired him. Who had opened his own restaurant, made it his, won his own three stars, and gained international celebrity as the first chef pâtissier to ever do so on his own. Gabriel Delange, who now stated that the work featured on the cover of the book as well as twelve other recipes in its contents were his. And that since he had previously warned Pierre Manon against appropriation of his work, he preferred to settle this in court.

Although entirely French, her father had always had something of a pseudo-Russian villain's face, with straw hair and blunt bones. He could have been the enemy in any James Bond film, and his former underling Gabriel Delange had clearly cast him in the role, but the brilliance of his imagination, the sensual joy he took in pleasing others through food, belied it.

Now his villain face was subtly slackened, as if he had been drinking too much vodka. More on the left side than the right.

Jolie bit the inside of her lip, watching him rock a French rolling pin back and forth on the table under his hands. Maybe he found the gesture therapeutic. Any work with his hands probably was. It had been two months since he had been released from the hospital.

Most people would consider him lucky. His impairment was minor, leaving him, to most intents and purposes, fully functional. But his left hand was probably always going to be clumsy. Capable but clumsy.

"Lucky" was one of those cruel words, sometimes. Her father had given his all to being one of the world's top chefs. He had lost his wife and daughters to the career. He had lost himself to it. And now—the destruction of the essential deftness in his hands left him nothing. Nothing but himself.

And her.

"Am I getting the *glaçage* right?" She had chosen to make éclairs, because it was a pastry chef's job and thus something her father wouldn't have made with his own hands. His supervisory role, double-checking for perfection while she did all the work, should feel natural to him, not forced.

Pierre Manon gave her éclairs a dull look. "No, but what does it matter?"

What did it matter. From the Michelin three-star chef who had spent years recovering after he lost a star. Only in the past couple of years had he started to find his feet again, and that only thanks to Jolie's inspiration to convince him to write a cookbook with her. An inch or two of his pride had grown back with every recipe he taught her, as if their work together was just the perfect blend of rain showers and sun to nurture his wounded *amour-propre*.

"I suppose you're planning on doing the demonstrations without me now," he said, low.

"No! I've put them off." For over a month now. It wasn't great, to delay the publicity events for the launch of the cookbook, but life happened. She could hardly be out signing books while her father, the chef whose name was on the cookbook, was hospitalized for a stroke. "We'll do them when you're ready."

He made a rumbling sound. "You think I'm going to get in front of a crowd and let them see me like this?"

"Papa, I think people will admire you for recovering so well from a stroke and putting yourself back out there. Since we're arguing that we make your recipes accessible to the home cook, I think it might even give them courage. *If he can pull himself back after a stroke and do it, I can at least try, too.*"

Pierre Manon grunted.

Jolie hesitated, studying him covertly. "Maybe we could get one of your old pastry chefs to demonstrate the pastry recipes for us. That could be the theme for some of the demonstrations. People would love it, I bet. Everyone would understand that you're recovering from a stroke, Papa."

He thumped the rolling pin hard on the table. He didn't say anything.

She was probably stressing him too much already, just by mentioning his old pastry chefs. God, if she handled this lawsuit wrong she could *kill* him.

She finished icing the éclairs, too dispirited to even bite into one, then took him out for a slow walk in the Jardins du Luxembourg. It was a nice June day, balmy and easy. A bright feeling seemed to glow in the people who spilled into the gardens at the perfect weather, in the laughter of the children playing with little sailboats on the pond in front of the Palace, in the fresh hope of new lovers clinging to each other, in the easy comfort of lovers of longer standing who lounged in chairs by each other reading, in the old, worn happiness of a white-haired couple walking hand in hand, whose love for each other had been used and worked like fifty-year-old shoes into something so exactly fitted to them that those bright new lovers wouldn't recognize it in their high-heeled love. But oh, how they would be grateful for it, fifty years on, if they reached that perfect fit, too.

Jolie loved walking in the Luxembourg Gardens at that time of year. She hoped it did her father good. But she couldn't really tell. The door closing to his apartment afterward felt like she was locking him back into his chosen tomb, and she stood a long moment with her hand pressed against his door, her head bowed, heavy and anxious.

Then she lifted her head.

"I'm heading down to Nice," she told her sisters over the phone, striding out of the apartment building. "Papa doesn't even need to know I'm gone. I should be back by tomorrow evening. I'm sure Gabriel Delange can see reason."

Chapter 2

Jo knew the third time she missed the damn town that she was going to get there too late. Sainte-Mère. How many Sainte-Mères existed off the Côte d'Azur, and how many roads to those towns were under construction?

She should never have accepted a stick shift from the car rental place. If they had held an automatic for her *per her reservation*, she would at least be negotiating these cobblestoned streets, narrower than her car, without fearing she would shift gears wrong and end up in a wall. "I don't think I'm going to be able to get back before tomorrow morning, at this rate," she told her oldest sister on the phone. "I'll have to catch a late train. Cover for me."

"How?" Estelle asked.

"I don't know!" Jo cried, frantically trying to back down a near-vertical slope the size of a piece of spaghetti, in order to allow a car to pass coming the other way. "I'm sick or something and don't want to expose him. You can come up with something!"

It was twelve-thirty when she finally fit her car down the small spiral ramp that passed for the entrance to the parking lot for the old walled part of town. Plane trees shaded the little parking area, and she climbed a staircase from it to the *place* below Gabriel Delange's restaurant.

The scent of jasmine wafted over her as she stepped into the *place*, delicate and elusive, as the breeze stirred vines massed over sun-pale walls. A surprisingly quixotic and modern fountain rippled water softly in the center of a tranquil, shaded area of cobblestones. She stopped beneath the fountain's stylized, edgy angel, dipping her hand into the water streaming from the golden rose it held. *Fontaine Delange*, said a little plaque.

He had a city fountain named after him already? Well, why not? There were only twenty-six three-star restaurants in France, eighty in the world. He had put this little town on the map.

His restaurant, Aux Anges, climbed up above the *place* in jumbled levels of ancient stone, a restored olive mill. She would have loved to sit under one of those little white parasols on its packed terrace high above, soaking up the view and exquisite food, biding her time until the kitchens calmed down after lunch. But, of course, his tables would be booked months in advance. In another restaurant, she might have been able to trade on her father's name and her own nascent credentials as a food writer, but the name Manon was not going to do her any favors here.

The scents, the heat, the sound of the fountain, the ancient worn stone all around her, all seemed to reach straight inside her and flick her tight-wound soul, loosing it in a rush. *Stop. It will be all right. Your father is out of immediate danger, has two other daughters, and will survive a day without you. Take your time, take a breath of that hot-sweet-crisp air.* Relief filled her at the same time as the air in her lungs. That breath smelled nothing like hospitals, or therapists' offices, or the stubborn, heavy despair in her father's apartment that seemed as unshakeable as the grime in the Paris air.

She walked past an art gallery and another restaurant that delighted in welcoming all the naive tourists who had tried showing up at Aux Anges without reservations. A little *auberge*, or inn, gave onto the *place*, jasmine vines crawling all over its stone walls, red geraniums brightening its balconies.

She turned down another street, then another, weaving her way to a secret, narrow alley, shaded by buildings that leaned close enough for a kiss, laundry stretching between balconies. Jasmine grew everywhere, tiny white flowers brushing their rich scent across her face.

Kitchen noises would always evoke summer for her, summer and her visits to France and her father. The open windows and back door of Aux Anges let out heat, and the noises of knives and pots and people yelling, and a cacophony of scents: olive oil, lavender, nuts, meat, caramel. . . .

As she approached the open door, the yelling grew louder, the same words overheard a million times in her father's kitchens: "*Service! J'ai dit service, merde,* it's going to be ruined. *SERVICE, S'IL VOUS PLAÎT!*"

"—Fast as we can, *merde – putain,* watch out!"

A cascade of dishes. Outraged yells. Insults echoed against the stone.

She peeked through the door, unable to resist. As a child and teenager, she had been the kid outside a candy shop, confined to her father's office, gazing at all that action, all that life: the insane speed and control and volcanic explosions as great culinary wonders were birthed and sent forth to be eaten.

At least fifteen people in white and black blurred through a futuristic forest of steel and marble. Four people seemed to be doing the yelling, two chefs in white, two waiters in black tuxedos, separated by a wide counter and second higher shelf of steel: the pass, through which elegant plates slipped into the hands of waiters, who carried them into the dining rooms with—ideally—barely a second's pause between when the plate was finished and when it headed toward the customer who was its destination. A wave of profound nostalgia swept Jolie.

"*Connard!*" somebody yelled.

"*C'est toi, le connard, putain!*"

A big body straightened from the counter closest to the door and turned toward the scene, blocking her view of anything but those broad shoulders. Thick, overlong hair in a rich, dark brown, threaded with gold like a molten dark caramel, fell over the collar of the big man's chef's jacket, a collar marked with the *bleu, blanc, rouge* of a Meilleur Ouvrier de France. That *bleu, blanc, rouge* meant the chef could only be one person, but he certainly wasn't skinny anymore. He had filled into that space she had used to only imagine him taking up, all muscled now and absolutely sure.

His growl started low and built, built, until it filled the kitchen and spilled out into the street as a full-bodied beast's roar, until she clapped her hands to her head to hold her hair on. Her ears buzzed until she wanted to reach inside them and somehow scratch the itch of it off.

When it died down, there was dead silence. She gripped the edge of the stone wall by the door, her body tingling everywhere. Her nipples felt tight against her bra. Her skin hungered to be rubbed very hard.

Gabriel Delange turned like a lion who had just finished chastising his cubs and spotted her.

Her heart thumped as if she had been caught out on the savannah without a rifle. Her *fight* instinct urged her to stalk across the small space between them, sink her hands into that thick hair, jerk her body up him, and kiss that mouth of his until he stopped roaring with it.

That would teach him.

And her *flight* option wanted to stretch her arm a little higher on that door, exposing her vulnerable body to be savaged.

She gripped that stone so hard it scraped her palm, fighting both urges.

Gabriel stood still, gazing at her. Behind him, the frozen tableau melted: *petits commis,* waiters, sous-chefs, all returning to their tasks with high-speed efficiency, the dispute evaporated. Someone started cleaning up the fallen dishes. Someone else whipped a prepped plate off the wall, where little prongs allowed them to be stacked without touching each other, and began to form another magical creation on top of it.

Jo tried to remember the professional motivation of her visit. She was wearing her let's-talk-about-this-professionally pants. She was wearing her but-this-is-a-friendly-visit little sandals. Given the way her nipples were tingling, she would have preferred that her casually formal blouse have survived her one attempt to eat chocolate in the car while she was wandering around lost for hours, but no . . . her silky pale camisole was all she had left.

Gabriel's eyebrows rose just a little as his gaze flicked over her. Curious. Perhaps intrigued. Cautiously so.

"You're late," he said flatly.

"I had a lot of car trouble," she apologized. It sounded better than saying she had spent hours circling Sainte-Mère and Sainte-Mère-Centre and Sainte-Mère-Vieux-Village, utterly lost. Wait, how did he know she was late? This was a surprise visit. "I'm sorry. I know this is a bad time."

"*Bon, allez.*" He thrust a folded bundle of white cloth at her. She recognized the sturdy texture of it instantly: a chef's jacket. A heavy professional apron followed. His gaze flicked over her again. "Where are your shoes?"

"I—"

"If you drop hot caramel on those painted toenails, I don't want to hear about it. Coming to work without your shoes. I thought Aurélie told me you had interned with Daniel Laurier."

"Uh—"

Eyes blue as the azure coast tightened at the corners. "You made it up to get a chance. *Parfait. And* you're late. That's all I need. Get dressed and go help Thomas with the grapefruit."

Probably she should have told him right then.

But . . . she had been having a hellish two months, and . . . a sneak peek into Gabriel Delange's kitchens. . .

A chance to work there through a lunch hour, to pretend she was part of it all. *Not* in an office. Not observing a chef's careful, dumbed-down demonstration. *Part* of it.

She had spent the past two months dealing with hospitals and fear and grief, and he had just handed her happiness on a plate. What was an impassioned food writer to do?

Not the ethical thing, that was for darn sure.

Chapter 3

Oh, God, her fingers hurt. It was so much harder to be part of it than it was to work through a recipe slowly or to observe it. She did try. She was not without kitchen skills, not by any means. But the speed, the intensity, the amount of competing motion she had to dodge, and the sheer repetition of task surpassed anything she had ever done before. Jo hated grapefruit. She hadn't known that before, but now she hated it with a profound and utter passion. Maybe she should give up cookbook writing, become a microbiologist, and create a fungus that would wipe grapefruit trees off the planet.

She couldn't even *see* all the beautiful things being created around her. She couldn't look up from her task. Peeling and peeling and peeling, laying the sections out in glistening rows of pink for someone else's use, until her fingers stung, and the acid sank into the stings, and the cold of the fruit made her clumsy.

Gabriel stopped by her station just as she was sneaking her thumb between her lips to suck the acid off it, for a second's relief, and she glanced up to find his eyes on her mouth, his eyebrows lifting a little. Oh, *merde*, hygiene. She dropped a grapefruit and dove after it, right in the path of a sous-chef carrying a giant bowl of *financier* batter.

The *sous* dodged, the heavy bowl whirling him around as his knees slammed into her ribs, and just before both he and his forty-pound bowl came crashing down on her, someone caught him. "Umph," she muttered weakly, peering up at the new hand cradling the bowl, as another hand gripped the sous-chef's shoulder.

A broad, strong hand. Lots of little scars from nicks and burns. Dark brown curls of hair. . .

Gabriel slipped the bowl into its spot on the mixing machine, righted his sous-chef, sent him on his way, and gazed down at her a moment. Her body tingled in anticipation of a punishing growl. But he just looked at her.

Jo stretched a little farther—absurdly conscious of the angle at which her butt was sticking into the air as she arched to reach under the whirring mixing machine—and hauled out the yellow fruit. She waved the trophy at him brightly.

Gabriel sighed. "Please get up." He reached down to grab her arm.

Wow, Jo thought as she floated feather-light to her feet. That was one strong grip.

"Maybe you should try something besides grapefruit," Gabriel said.

Jo sent an envious look down the counters to his sous-chefs, concocting treasures out of—here a bit of foam being laid gently down on a bed of woodland strawberries. There a curl of jasmine over a strange, quixotic, Chambordian tower of chocolate. There someone was dipping something into liquid nitrogen, the vapor rising around him as if he were a sorcerer's apprentice.

"Filling molds." Gabriel took her shoulders and steered her to a bare counter space. A space very far from where the sous-chefs were finishing works of wonder and calling for waiters, "Service, s'il vous plaît! Service!"

"Just like this." He pulled a great pan of rectangular molds out from under the counter, took a large pastry bag, and squeezed batter from it into a mold. Her eyes tracked that big hand's gentle, precise squeeze with helpless fascination. "To just this level. And then the pistachios on top. Just this amount." He sprinkled a pinch and glanced from the golden batter, with its scattering of green, to her face, a little smile flashing across his face as if he was enjoying some secret he didn't expect her to know. "You can do that, right?"

He sounded as if he *should* be sure of her ability to do that, but somehow wasn't.

"Of course," Jo said, smarting. She was *Pierre Manon's daughter.* Even if her father had always made her stay in his office, out of the way, staring through the glass walls at all the fun. And she was a really good food writer. She was going to be one of the best food writers in the world. She was working on it. She just— usually got one-on-one attention from the chef teaching her a recipe. They worked through it slowly. She got to concentrate, and take her time and lots and lots of notes and photos, and *feel* things, not just peel, chop, drop. . . .

She glanced up. In the time it had taken her to think three thoughts, Gabriel had gone about his business, accomplished six impossible things—she could see their fantastical incredibility waiting to be taken up to the tables—and now reappeared beside her, pressing in close to allow a *petit commis* to pass. No one took up more space than necessary in a kitchen. She knew that. There was no reason for her to feel so . . . small. Completely conscious of his proximity. Wishing he would roar again.

How would that feel, that bass vibrating over her skin from so close? He needed to shave, but under that two-day growth were good, strong lines of jaw, an intense—

"I was thinking you could fill all the molds *today*," Gabriel said.

She looked back down at the four she had filled—in the time it had taken him to finish six desserts of such beauty and complexity she wanted to cry from pleasure just looking at them.

Her four filled molds looked absolutely perfect, too,

she tried to convince herself. She was going to scatter the pistachios on them soon.

"Are your financiers made from ground pistachio?" she asked. "Is that your secret?"

"Why don't we talk about my secrets later? Could you hurry it up? We'll need those for the next round of tables, and they take twenty minutes to cook."

Jo gritted her teeth and thought about telling him she wasn't his new employee, but a chaos of people blurred around her as a new rush of orders came in, and maybe she should just shut her mouth, help as much as she could, and talk to him later. Leaving him in the lurch in the middle of the lunch service might not be the best way to convince him not to bring a lawsuit.

So she filled the first sheet of forty molds. Quickly. Tried to fill quickly. She scattered pistachios, pausing a moment to enjoy the effect of the little green-brown bits against the gold, and glanced up to catch Gabriel's eye on her. She flushed, scattered more quickly, grabbed the huge pan and spun toward the ovens.

Smack. The tallest of his sous-chefs, just slipping behind her, took it right in the chest. It went flying, flipped once, and landed face-down beside Gabriel, who was blowing foam off his hand so that it floated, oh-so-gently, to land on top of a little flower made of peaches, like an angel's wing coming to rest.

He didn't stop blowing because forty financiers ended up splattered over his feet. He let the foam drift gently down, while Jo stood caught by that careful pursing of his mouth, that delicate, controlled stream of air.

Ooh. Could she just melt against the marble?

He slid the plate over to the counter where the tuxedoed waiters appeared, called, "*Service!*" and only then glanced at her and down at the pan. Her nipples tightened in longing for a roar, but he only sighed and shook his head.

Her heart deflated. She didn't deserve a roar?

Crouching at his feet, she started to clean up the mess.

She didn't know why her butt, thrust in the air, kept burning while she did that, because every time she glanced up, he was not looking at it at all.

Two hours later, Jo gave her knife a blurry look and thanked God in heaven that her mother had put her foot down when Jo wanted to leave school and become a chef instead of finishing her education. "Do something where you can live a normal life," her mother had said, like someone who actually remembered what a normal life had been, before her failed marriage to Pierre Manon. "And have a family."

What she hadn't also added was *Do something where you can be a little lazier*. Like sit down, take a break, not cut off your own fingers from fatigue. There was something to be said for spending half your time typing into a computer.

A hand closed over her wrist, holding it firmly. Another deftly removed her clumsy knife, setting it on the counter. "Come here," Gabriel said, quite gently.

Around them, people were taking off aprons and white jackets and slipping out into the street. Lunch was over, and the restaurant was closing until seven-thirty, meaning everyone had a break until five-thirty. She followed Gabriel Delange numbly into his office, smaller than her father's old office but with the same big glass windows that allowed him to see the kitchens when he was in it.

She was half-expecting a muted roar or at least a dressing-down, but Gabriel smiled at her. Her heart sparked in ridiculous pleasure. Had she passed the test? Was she worth being taken on as a *petit commis*? Wait a minute, she didn't *want* to be taken on as menial labor in his kitchen. That fantasy had died in the first hour of grapefruit sectioning. She wrote about this kind of thing, she didn't have to *do* it for thirteen hours a day. Doing it was brutal. She tried to loosen her apron strings and discovered her fingers had grown too clumsy to work the knot. Plus, they stung.

"I think we know this isn't going to work out," Gabriel said gently.

She was so absurdly disappointed that anyone would think she had just failed a major exam. She jerked on the stupid knot, surprised to find her nostrils stinging as much as her fingers. Okay, that was just insane. Maybe she was a little on edge, between the book release, her father's stroke, the lawsuit, and just getting hired and fired by one of the world's greatest chefs in under three hours.

"*Tenez.*" Big fingers brushed hers aside, and he dealt deftly with the knot.

It didn't bear articulating, even in her own head, what it did to her to have him so competently remove her clothing. Tension rushed into her body, a sudden longing for him to keep going.

He folded the apron neatly and set it on his desk. "But I was wondering—*tiens.*"

Her mind noted vaguely the switch from *vous* to *tu,* like a long verbal step forward into someone's personal space. His fingers brushed her fumbling ones off the tight buttons of the chef's jacket. She swallowed as heat ran through her. If he got that jacket off her, he was going to see her nipples peek straight through her silky little camisole. . .

"If you would like to go out." Gabriel peeled aside her jacket. His gaze flickered instantly to her chest and heated, his breath drawing in. His mouth compressed in a clear effort not to gloat over his soon-fallen prey.

Jo gaped at him. "Did you just *fire* me and ask me to dinner at the same time?"

"No, not to dinner. I never can ask anyone out to dinner. Or lunch. But I'm free for a couple of hours right now."

She was exhausted. And also . . . what exactly did that mean? Free for a couple of hours in the afternoon? That sounded . . . direct. Way too direct. "I think I need to correct a false impression."

"Don't worry," Gabriel said dryly. "I've figured out that you didn't work at Daniel's."

Jo clenched her teeth. "You know, I might have just been nervous! You could have given me the benefit of the doubt!"

"I tried. For three hours."

"So I'm not good enough to work for you, but you'll have sex with me this afternoon if I'm available?"

"Right. Wait—no. That is, you aren't good enough to work for me, that's certain, but. . ." While she heated with outrage, his blue eyes heated with something else entirely. "Were you contemplating straight to sex? I wasn't actually proposing—that is, I was thinking—but whatever you like, of course." He grinned, shifting his body as close in to hers as if they were still negotiating space in the kitchen, leaning in to dominate her. "Anything at all."

He was suing her, had just fired her without even giving her a proper chance, and wasn't even going to offer dinner. How could she possibly be so tempted to let him get away with this? "About that false impression. I'm actually *too good* to work for you."

A tiny, choked laugh that about blew her head off. "I doubt it."

"I'm not whoever you were expecting to start as a *petit commis* today. I write about food." She took a breath, bit her lip, and gave a wry, lopsided grin. "I'm Jolie Manon."

And she got that roar close up.

Chapter 4

I t started out as a growl that ran over every nerve
ending in her skin. It built to a roar that buffeted
her with its force. She tilted her head back into it the
way she would into a wild storm approaching. It made
her feel *glorious.*

"You're *this* Jolie Manon." He yanked a great silver
book out of the trashcan by his desk and pointed to the
tiny script of her name, so easy to overlook with the
PIERRE   MANON   and   Gabriel's   gorgeous   Rose
dominating the cover. "He sent his *daughter?*" The roar
blasted over her again, making her giddy. "To cover for
him? That pathetic bastard. He can't even deal with me
himself or face me in court. He's still using people."

"You like leaping to negative conclusions, don't
you? He—"

"Letting you stay three hours in my kitchens is not
me leaping to negative conclusions. It's me trying my
damndest to be reasonable and not just fire you so I
can go out with you. That, you have to admit, would
have been a terrible thing to do. But no, you deserved
to be fired. And your *putain de père*—"

He reached up to the shelf above his head and
yanked books and magazines down. "He called me. He
begged me to come from the Leucé to help him get that
third star. I was twenty. I said, I'll get it. And I worked
my damn butt off. My girlfriend dumped me. My family
forgot who I was except when they wanted me to make
a dessert for somebody's Communion. I lost thirty
pounds. *This*—" He slapped onto his desk a twelve-
year-old copy of the top industry magazine. "It was the
Holy Grail at the time to be in this. Whose name?" He

pointed to the title of the article, *Pierre Manon Catches His Third Star.* "Whose work?" He pointed to the exquisite Rose on the cover. "Here." He flipped open the magazine to a smaller image of the Rose in the table of contents. "Here." Flipped further. "Here. And here." A glorious full-page cut-out of that Rose and a close-up of a detail in the petals. "Where am I?" He pointed to a tiny photo of himself, very young, cheek to cheek with her father, both grinning for the camera. "That's it. My name is never even mentioned. Not even *my exceptional chef pâtissier* or *I owe it all to.*"

He jerked open her cookbook. "This, this is my technique." He pointed to one of her father's famous *mise-en-bouche*, a mint-green drop caught on a spoon. "I invented it for a dessert, it was gorgeous, he saw it and immediately copied it for himself. This, this, this. . . these are all mine. I created these. He got Grégoire and my old sous-chefs to keep making them after he *had me fired,* but he knows I created them. *This.*" Again the roar, an anguished roar, as he placed his palm flat over the glorious Rose when the page fell open to its recipe, in a vain effort to snatch it back. "*This* gained *him* more fame than anything he ever did. That *I* made. That *he* never touched. It's *mine.* And after he milked it and I got him that star, he made the hotel *fire* me, *after I got him a third star,* because I couldn't treat him like he was God on earth every second. And because he was so fucking jealous of a magazine article they decided to do on *me.*"

Jo stared at him uneasily. She had been a sophomore in high school back in the States when all this happened. She had discovered on her next trip that her father's new pastry chef wasn't nearly as cute as the last one, but that was as far as her awareness had gone. Her father had always presented all the work that came out of his kitchens as his, and until that lawsuit notice showed up in her father's mailbox, it had never occurred to her that this was not the case.

"That's kind of the tradition," she said cautiously. "French kitchen hierarchy. The chef cuisinier is on top, in charge of the chef pâtissier."

"Yes, well." Gabriel Delange gave her a tight, dangerous smile. "*Not* anymore."

He had opened this place a year after his departure from the Luxe, the first and only chef pâtissier to take charge of his own restaurant. The chef cuisinier at Aux Anges, his younger brother, worked for *him*. Here, in this place in the jasmine-scented sun, every *mise-en-bouche*, every *plat* was foreplay for that final orgasm, his desserts. That was what the critics said.

She wondered if she could wear a wig and dark glasses to get back in and actually experience that orgasm herself. She had some pretty good wig skills, if she did say so herself.

She and the college friend with whom she had written restaurant reviews for their student paper had never been famous enough to need them, but they had liked to delude themselves.

"I suppose you think it's traditional for a father to use his daughter, too," Gabriel said darkly, tracing a finger over her tiny name on the cover of the book she had written. "He probably raised you to think that way."

"Those *are* his recipes," Jo protested. "I just wrote them down."

Just. It was really hard to turn a top chef's art into something you could express in words, in instructions. To tell the stories around the food, sometimes ones from her father, sometimes of other people's encounters with it. She wouldn't have minded having her name a little bigger. Her second book, *The French Taste,* already contracted and partly written, was going to be a collection of recipes from different top chefs, and the *name* on it was going to be *hers.*

"They're not all his recipes," Gabriel said. "At least fifteen percent of them are mine."

"And he gave me co-author credit." In small letters. That had seemed logical at the time. Gabriel was starting to piss her off, casting doubts on her father and how much he cared about his daughter.

"Last I heard, the author was the person who did the writing. Did your father do any writing?"

"You must never have heard of ghost-writing," Jo said dryly.

"I've heard of it. I haven't heard of making *your own daughter* your ghost."

She set her jaw. "I've got co-author credit. This is a big step in my career, and I had to talk him into doing it. Lay off."

"Oh, did he play hard to get?" Gabriel sneered. "He loved doing that for the television shows. Especially after he lost that third star, without me. I don't think it was as much fun, being called onto television sets so they could see how well he was surviving his humiliation."

"No, it wasn't," Jolie said tightly. Those first three years after he lost that star had been one of the most ghastly periods of her life. If she hadn't still had the excuse of her college classes to escape to, to save her sometimes from her father's black moods, she didn't know what she would have done.

"So where is he? I thought our lawyers would fight it out and the media would be great for me, bad for him. I didn't expect him to send his daughter to handle his problems."

Jolie gave him a hard, cold look. "He had a stroke. Not long before the release." And if Gabriel was *happy* about that, she would cut his heart out with one of his own spoons.

Gabriel looked as if his head had just butted hard against a rock wall. "I—what? A bad stroke?"

"Pretty bad, yes."

Gabriel blinked and gave his head a tiny shake, as if trying to get a stunned double vision to settle back into one image. "Is he all right?"

Jolie opened her hands. "He survived. He should recover well, the doctors said. With good therapy. He'll probably always have slurred speech and more difficulty moving on one side, and there are all kinds of precautions to take to lower the risk of a recurrence."

"*Merde,*" Gabriel said very softly. "*Merde,* Jolie. I—I mean, I despise your father, but—*merde.* I'm really sorry." He closed a hand around her shoulder. For a second, she thought he was going to pull her in and pat her on the back. Maybe he did remember her a tiny bit from when she was a young teenager, grazing through his orbit. Or maybe he was just that shaken. He looked as if she had thrown his world upside down. "He's lost some of the use of a hand?" he repeated almost inaudibly, flexing his free hand open and closed, rippling the fingers, as if he had to make sure they still worked.

"I'm not going to stress him right now. I'll handle the lawsuit; I'm not even going to let him know about it. But I wanted to talk to you."

He hesitated. His blue eyes grew wary, and he released her shoulder. "I can find out if that stroke story is true. You're not just trying to soften me up?"

"No." Jo glared at him. "No. I didn't invent my father's brush with death and permanent brain damage to soften you up."

He curled his fingers around the edge of his desk and tilted his head back, gazing at the ceiling. He seemed to be trying to process. After a moment, he shook himself, like an animal shedding water. "You know, if you had told me right at the first that I was suing you, it could have saved me all that effort of trying to ask you out on a date."

Her jaw tightened. She lifted her chin. "Don't worry. As enticing as your offer of a couple of hours in the afternoon, no lunch, no dinner, sounded . . . the answer would have been no."

Chapter 5

D amn it, that was the last time Gabriel fired a woman just so he could go out with her. He should have known that wouldn't work out well. The daughter of the man he hated most on earth, too. Didn't that just figure?

She *hadn't* been up to his kitchen standards, that was true. But she wasn't hopeless. A couple of weeks adjusting to the intensity of three-star kitchens would have either led her to quit all by herself, loathing him for a brutal taskmaster, or forged her into someone almost capable of his team's most simplistic tasks.

Then he could have gone around leaning in close to her when her head was bent in concentration, making her drop things. Or seeing if her pupils kept dilating when she looked up at him. Or if she kept waving her butt at him. Unfortunately, the chef's jacket hid her breasts while she was working, but *something* had intrigued her nipples, when he first spotted her in that camisole peeking into his kitchen, and it certainly wasn't the cold. It had aroused the heck out of him, trying to guess what those nipples were doing under that chef's jacket every time he got close to her. And, *putain,* when he got that coat off, there they were, all tight for him.

That would make him evil, wouldn't it? Constantly brushing up against a woman who was dependent on him for her livelihood. Or looming over her. Or curving his hand around hers on a knife to show her how to cut something. Or. . . .

He sighed. Between extended, long-term sexual harassment or just firing her straight off, also for sexual reasons, how was a man supposed to figure out the right thing to do? Working with her in professional indifference was definitely out.

Not when she stared at him with such fascination in those pistachio eyes of hers. The inner golden-brown ring shrank every time she stared up at him, the pupil swallowing up all but the green. She had three tiny *grains de beauté,* flat little beauty marks, on her cheek under her right eye, gathered close together, like a miniature constellation of stars. Her hair matched the deep golden-brown color of the *financiers* when they came out of the oven. When she didn't know he was looking at her, her body seemed so strong and graceful that surprise struck him every time someone on his team stopped near her and made it clear how small she was. When she caught his eye on her, that strength and grace collapsed like a house of cards hit by a strong wind, leaving her scrambling after it as it fluttered away from her hands. Toward him.

He wanted to catch that fluttering strength and grace. Pick it up and gather it to him. Lose himself in it, kiss her, make sure she knew what good care he could take of it.

Except according to his every attempt at a girlfriend, he took lousy care of that kind of thing.

He pushed that thought out of his mind. You couldn't accomplish anything impossible by focusing on all the tries you hadn't gotten to work. Better to think about the present. Like the way she dug her teeth into her lower lip and focused with such intense, ferocious delight when she was trying to scatter pistachios just right. He felt so damn sorry for that lower lip, he wanted to prove to it that someone in its cruel world knew how to treat it right. And those painted toenails in her little sandals had about killed him. Exposed feet were so alien in a professional kitchen, it was as if she was wandering around naked.

Well. Not quite. But his mind found it astonishingly easy to start speculating on what she would look like, wandering around naked.

All things considered, trying to work with her in professional indifference sounded like a good way to ruin every single damn day of his life for the foreseeable future.

Unfortunately, it was astonishingly hard to meet women who *didn't* work for you when your social life was limited to five to nine in the morning, three to five in the afternoon, and Mondays and Tuesdays. He tried to keep an eye out when he was running or at the gym, but women just didn't seem to feel that flirtatious at five a.m.. Maybe he needed to get a dog, but that seemed a mean thing to do to the poor animal, given his working hours. Plus, did women really like being jumped on by dogs at five in the morning just so a man could introduce himself? He had even started giving serious thought to joining the women-packed, early-morning yoga class at the gym, before the cute daughter of his worst enemy showed up.

It was just a good thing he was suing her.

No, really. It had all kinds of perks.

He could see her again without having to figure out a way to convince her to go out on a date with him while he was firing her, for one. He might even be able to get his lawyer to get her lawyer to reveal her phone number.

His social life was so pathetic.

"This might take longer than I thought," Jo told her sister Fleur on a grunt of effort, hauling her overnight case up the narrow stairs of the *auberge* across from Aux Anges. She stumbled on a step, dropping her phone, and the weight of the case disappeared so suddenly that she tripped and fell forward onto the stairs.

"*Pardon,*" said a voice roughened by far too many growls that day. She arched her back to look up, pushing with her hands against the stair.

Gabriel Delange, her case in one hand, studied her butt with incredulous appreciation. "Do you think it's Freudian, how you keep falling in these positions around me? Thank God I fired you."

"I never actually worked for you," Jo pointed out between her teeth, scrabbling for her phone and pushing to her feet. He grabbed her upper arm with his free hand and hauled her up with that ease that made her feel as if her gravity had been shut off. Had he thought she was waving her tush at him *on purpose*? And if so, shouldn't he be *regretting* having fired her?

"That's right, you were just trying to steal more recipes."

"You are the worst man for jumping to negative conclusi—"

"Thinking you were waving your butt at me on purpose is not a negative conclusion. Which one is your room?"

Fulminating, Jolie shoved her key into the lock. It was old and took some jiggling, but she got it open just as Gabriel was reaching to show her how much better he was at turning a key in a lock, being a man and all.

He strolled into her room as if he owned any space he happened to be around and deposited her carry-on by her bed. Wait. What in the world was she doing, letting him into her room?

"Look at that," he said. "You've got your own little terrace and the most perfect view." The view of his restaurant was, indeed, beautiful: the haphazard levels of its ancient mill structure, its old sun-worn stones, the white parasols on the terraces, the palm trees in front of it, and the vines climbing over the walls. The fountain the city had built in his honor shimmered gently in the sunlight. When all was quiet, she might be able to hear it.

"I thought we said we would meet tomorrow morning to talk about ways to resolve the book issue."

Jolie braced her feet.

"*Enfin.* You said that. But you never know when inspiration for resolving a problem might strike me. So when I saw you coming into this hotel, I thought I would come get your phone number and also make sure I know where I can find you whenever I want you."

Find her whenever he wanted her?

Down, girl. That is not *a good thing.*

"Especially since, now that I've recovered from the shock of realizing you helped steal that Rose from me, I can't stop thinking about your willingness to go straight to sex. You don't go to bed early, do you?"

Jo gasped as if he'd just tossed her down on that white bed and curled over her with a lazy smile. A cruelly enticing image for a woman who didn't believe in letting men treat her like that. Although come to think of it, where had she come up with such an idiotic principle? "I never said I was willing to go straight to sex!"

He held up a hand. "I never said you did. I said I couldn't stop thinking about your willingness to go straight to sex, which is more like a guessing game. Would she be willing or wouldn't she? You can't blame a man for thinking things, when he's spent half the day gazing at your *fesses* in that position you favor."

"I do not favor—"

"I like it a lot myself," he volunteered kindly.

She gaped at him like a hooked fish. Oh, damn, *why* did every erogenous zone in her body have to dissolve at that information? Did he think he could just grab her up off the street and haul her to the nearest bed, no stopping even for a damn dinner date?

The cheerfulness faded from his face as their eyes held. His eyebrows went up a little, and then something dangerous grew in the place of that humor. A tension invaded his body, and the room shrank around him. Stripped of his chef's attire, he seemed even bigger somehow, the muscles and hardness of his body undisguised. He wore only a thin, fitted blue-gray T-shirt that highlighted his eyes, growing darker by the second. Jeans hugged his hips. No chef's jacket hid the way those broad shoulders tapered to a lean waist or disguised the profound confidence with which he moved. As if he mastered everything around him. And if any of his environs ever resisted his mastery, he would flex his full strength and stamp them down with a roar.

His voice dropped to a rumble. "We could see if you like it, too."

Damn it, that sounded so tempting. *Don't let him treat you like trash, for God's sake.* "You're behaving *atrociously.*"

Surprise flickered. Then his hand opened in resigned acceptance of her judgment. "I always do somehow. I've spent my life in kitchens, since I was fifteen years old. All the manners are at the tables."

"You didn't get arms like that spending your entire time in kitchens." The leanness, yes. The lack of fat, the abs, the long, supple muscles—that came from the adrenalin-intense work of a three-star kitchen. But the bulk of his shoulders came from serious weights. What was she doing, mentioning his arms? She *wanted* him to throw her down on that bed, didn't she?

Oh, yeah, she really did.

He glanced down at his folded arms, expression flickering between smugness and, oddly, embarrassment. "It was either that or the bookstore," he said cryptically. "And bookstores don't open at five in the morning. Besides, I had to do *something* besides sink into depression when I lost my girlfriend and then had all my work and self-sacrifice betrayed by your father in the space of a year."

More than ten years later, he still wasn't about to get over her father's role in his life, was he? "So you decided to become a beast?"

A tiny tick of silence. "A—beast?"

"You know—brute strength, unshaved, atrocious

manners, ready to rend sick old men, roaring."

He rubbed his chin involuntarily and looked surprised to find that much growth on it. Danger glinted deep in the blue eyes. "You like it when I roar." A little growl seeped into his tone as he brought his body in to dominate hers, the bed one easy push of his fingers away. "I saw it."

Definitely the most atrocious manners of anyone she had ever met. "You did not see any such thing."

His eyes flickered down over her silk camisole. Damn it, she needed to change. "You must get cold *really* easily, then." The little growl rumbled over her skin. "It's thirty-five degrees today."

Or, on American terms, in the high nineties. She glared, at a loss as to what to do with a man rude enough to mention the state of her nipples when their entire adult acquaintance had lasted four hours and was founded on his lawsuit against her.

Especially when her palm tingled with the need to test that three-day growth on his jaw herself. She wanted to lean just a little forward and see what those muscles would do in reaction to her weight. And how her own muscles would melt.

"Who wanted La Rose on the cover of that cookbook? I don't have any trouble believing Pierre could be that arrogant, but . . . *was* it him? Or was it you? Or an editor?"

"I pushed for it," she admitted uneasily. A big man she barely knew was looming over her in a hotel room, and she was afraid saying the wrong thing could end the moment. Okay, that was beyond stupid. "But—it *had* to be on the cover. It's so beautiful."

You wouldn't think this rough man who came on to her so strongly could have made that Rose. It wasn't good for her defences right now, to know that somewhere inside him was the heart that could produce that.

He drew a hard breath that brushed his chest

against hers. Her head spun. "If it had been my name on that book, I would have agreed," he said through his teeth.

She and her father had stolen that from him, too. When he did publish his own cookbook, and as a three-star chef it was a given that one day he would, he wouldn't be able to use his own Rose on the cover without looking imitative.

"I really am sorry," she said quietly. "It never occurred to me to think of it as anything but my father's creation." She had seen Gabriel make those Roses, when she was a young teenager, but her father tended to represent things as if Gabriel was just a handyman for Pierre Manon's genius.

Gabriel's mouth twisted hard. "No, I bet he never once acknowledged me, did he?"

No. He hadn't. Jolie rubbed the back of her neck. "I'll work with you to figure out fair compensation, if that helps at all."

He moved away from her abruptly to look out over her little terrace. *Darn,* said her body. *Will you hush?* her head told it.

"I'm not doing it for fair compensation. There isn't any. Besides, I know I'm never going to win that lawsuit. You can't patent a recipe. I just want the attention it will generate. I want people to *know* that it's mine, and how wrong I think he is to try to use it. Who knows, maybe it will even help change the way kitchen hierarchy works, in other kitchens besides mine."

Arousal faded before the sickness growing in her stomach. Maybe what he wanted was fair. Maybe she understood his furious desire to expose an injustice. But the publicity, the judgment of their peers, was what would kill her father. "He's just had a stroke," she said desperately.

His mouth twisted. "Despite my bestial manners, I did hear you when you said that, Jolie. I'm still thinking."

Chapter 6

M aybe he should get one of those rule books for dating, Gabriel thought as he gilded a glowing yellow dome with a torch that evening. A beast. It was true he was arrogant, sure of himself, determined to have exactly what he wanted the way he wanted it . . . and he didn't know why women yelled those things at him like an insult instead of a compliment.

And, fine, he didn't always bother to shave. But . . . *already* he was a beast? He had been so nice to her when she kept causing catastrophes in his kitchen, too. And he hadn't even blamed her when she told him *she* was the catalyst for stealing his Rose again. He had taken it as an involuntary and painful compliment, that the best thing she had seen come out of her father's kitchens was his.

What was he supposed to have done differently with Jolie Manon? He threw out a prepped plate because three grains of powder had fallen in the wrong spot, so obviously he noticed when her pupils dilated every time she looked at him. Or those nipples. Even men who had no appreciation of subtle detail would have noticed those tight nipples. Then she kept finding excuses to stick her butt up in the air right in front of him. . . .

It would have been rude *not* to let her know he was equally attracted. Right? It wasn't as if he was acting like that was his only use for a woman; she was the one with the one-track mind. He had *told* her he was willing to do whatever she wanted. *"Anything at all."*

How much more could a man offer to a woman, beyond anything at all she wanted? She had seemed to take that the wrong way, too, though. He didn't know why he always had that effect on women.

He brightened, as he pulled another plate off the wall. He still had one thing in his favor. Jolie might think he was an utter jerk and pretend she never wanted to see him again, but he *was* holding her deathly ill father hostage.

There had to be something he could do with that.

Jo woke slowly, disoriented. A low tap sounded again on her door, throwing her heart into overdrive. Strange hotel room, unfamiliar area of the country, and it must be after midnight.

She stared at the door. The fountain in the distance played a soft lullaby through windows open to relieve the day's heat. Two possibilities presented themselves: either a homicidal rapist had snuck into the hotel and chosen her room, or . . . somebody had just finished shutting down his kitchens and thought he would stop by.

The door didn't have a peephole. But faced with a lady or tiger choice, Jolie wasn't the type to stand around dithering. She was across the room in one leap, yanking the door open. "What the hell is wrong with you?" she hissed at the man looming over her with one forearm braced on the doorjamb, the other hand still raised to knock.

He stared down at her. His eyes ate her entire body up in one look, then ate it again, then fixated on her chest. Belatedly, she remembered that she was wearing only a cotton camisole sleep top and a lace-edged girly version of boy shorts. And no bra. "*Putain.*" He sounded strangled. "I'm not supposed to notice you're attracted to me, right?"

If she could have roared, she would have. As it was, her outrage strangled her. What a *loathsome* man. "I was dreaming. Not about you. It's *midnight.* What are you doing here?"

"I *asked* you if you went to bed early. Didn't you say no?"

She remembered how in the summer she would get into the habit of staying up until two in the morning, natural instinct for a teenager anyway, just so she could hang out with her father when he came in and talk to him as he unwound. "Midnight isn't early by most people's standards."

"I can't sleep after we close." He pushed his way into her room. "Too much adrenalin. So I had an idea."

Ooh, adrenalin to use up. She clenched her fists quickly. *"I'm not an outlet for your adrenalin,"* she hissed. What was wrong with her?

He stopped and stared at her. "Is that all you ever think about when I'm around, me throwing you down on that bed and having sex with you?"

Jolie's vision turned red. Yes, damn him. God, the man was such a beast.

"And you're going to think I'm rude if I tell you that I find nothing at all wrong with that and would be more than happy to oblige," he double-checked, energy running through his muscles. "I'm not supposed to reassure you that it's completely reciprocal or anything."

She opened her mouth and closed it a few times, strangling. Completely, utterly, outrageously rude, yes. "You're suing my father!" And her, but she was just the name in tiny font in this scenario. And she knew it damn well.

"I can see how that would be embarrassing for you, then, to have all those things I'm not supposed to be talking about happening to your body when I'm around."

And while outrage choked her, he shifted closer, a prowling grace in his movements. His closeness kicked her body into wild excitement. She should have felt afraid, but she didn't. Even though she barely knew him and he had just invaded her hotel room at midnight, while she wore two skimpy bits of cotton. How did he short-circuit her brain that way?

"Can I kiss you?" The purr burred down her spine. "So you won't take it as a rejection when I tell you why I really came here? Just because my mind is capable of working on more than one track, unlike yours, doesn't mean your current obsession is one-sided."

If she gave into the urge to smack that smugness off his face, she was never going to convince him to drop that lawsuit, was she? "I wouldn't get involved with a three-star chef in a million years. My mom warned me about men like you."

He scowled abruptly, defensively. "Yes? And what great insights into my character did she give you based on your damn father?"

"That you're temperamental, arrogant, you live on your emotions, and your work is the god you think everyone in your whole life should worship. None of that fits?"

His scowl deepened. "What's wrong with all that? Anyway, you *do* worship the same god. You're a cookbook writer! I should be your wet dream! You certainly *act* as if I am!"

Oh, she would so utterly kill him. She sniffed. Loudly. And wrinkled her nose. "Next time you come straight from thirteen hours of working like a madman in hot kitchens, you might want to take a shower before you lean in quite so close and tell me you're my dream come true."

He drew back, startled. It was impossible to tell if he flushed, in the darkness, but he rubbed a hand over his three-day growth again in what could have been a self-conscious gesture. "Good idea," he said finally. "Thanks."

And turned and walked straight into her shower, closing and locking the door behind him.

Jolie gaped at the white door. On the other side of

it, the water started running.

He had *locked the door.*

Not only assuming she might come in after him, but choosing to keep her out if she did.

That made her so mad, she almost declined to put her clothes back on, but decided that continuing to strut around nearly naked when he got out of the shower might not be the best way to make him respect her. Or to keep herself from getting involved with a chef.

Insisting on respect from a man instead of wallowing in his bestial instincts was a bitter, hard, thankless road.

Normally, a shower was one of Gabriel's key steps to relaxing after he left the restaurant. First the walk through the quiet, jasmine-scented streets to his apartment and that tired climb up his stairs, knowing that soon he could let everything slide off him. Then the shower. Then maybe some inane late-night show or browsing the Internet while he finally unwound enough to eat for the first time in thirteen hours and at last crash into his bed.

But knowing Jolie Manon was out there in her little white cami and boy shorts while her hot water was sluicing over him was enough to keep his blood pumping harder than when fifty of the same order came in at once and they only had plates prepped for half of them. Harder than the rumor that a Michelin reviewer was in the house, during that year before he got his third star. His second third star, the one that nobody else could steal from him.

Nearly as hard as when he had seen that *putain de livre de cuisine* with PIERRE MANON stamped over *his Rose.*

Warm water slid over his shoulders as he savored how much more luscious this heart-pounding was than any of those. *Putain*, but he loved pushing her and seeing what she did.

What might she be doing out there? Calling the police? Disappearing into the night while she had the chance? Waiting for him in a sexy pose on the bed, with her butt in the air?

He ducked to fit his head under the hotel showerhead, and his hand scraped over his face.

Hmm.

"Jolie!" he called through the door.

No answer. If she had chosen to disappear into the night, he was going to so enjoy chasing after her to save her. He could hardly let a woman run around the streets in that cami-boy short outfit.

Her pink *trousse de toilette* sat on the edge of the sink, so he stretched out a hand to the unopened bag of pink disposable razors. Not every man would have the guts to shave himself with a woman's disposable, but Gabriel had nineteen years experience working in starred kitchens, and his hands could do anything he wanted them to.

He tossed the razor in the trash, sniffed his T-shirt, hesitated, then finally pulled on just his jeans. She was probably going to complain about him appearing without a shirt, but there were only so many ways she could have him. All right, an infinite number of ways she could have him, but only one didn't include a day's worth of male perspiration. He hadn't carried a change of T-shirt with him this morning on the off-chance that a woman made of pistachios and sweet golden-brown would walk into his life and beg him to eat her up.

That was just so wrong, for a woman to look at you like that and then get mad every time you opened your mouth to actually do it.

He came out of the shower thrumming with anticipation. Damn, no butt in the air on the hotel bed. Jolie sat on the terrace, studiously ignoring him. In jeans and a short-sleeved top. And a bra on under that top, too.

Merde. That skimpy pajama thing had played a key role in all his visions of what she might do while he was in the shower. In fact, in the disappearing-into-the-night option, he had gotten to the point in the fantasy when bad guys circled around her and she threw her vulnerable body into his rescuing arms, and he picked her up and hauled her somewhere safe . . . and warm . . . and when he taught her exactly how vulnerable she was, instead of telling him he was a beast, she wrapped her trembling, fragile body around his in panicked gratefulness for the lesson.

It had been a great fantasy. He was quite sorry to relinquish it to real life.

She kept typing into a tablet, refusing to look at him. As he got closer and closer. As her fingers faltered all over the place.

He put one knee on her lounger and bent over her, placing a hand by her head. The tablet screen showed complete gobbledy-gook. He smiled, revealing his teeth. The better to eat her with my dear. Picking up her hand, he laid it against his smooth jaw. "This better?"

The shiver ran from her palm against his skin all through her body. She tried to look up. But her gaze got stuck as soon as it hit the waistband of his jeans. Her lashes took a long, long time rising up his naked torso to his shoulders. Her fingers, still held captive by his against his jaw, flexed infinitesimally over his fresh-shaven skin, an elusive scattering of rain on parched earth. He had to fight not to rub his face against that caress like a cat begging for more.

She wasn't breathing. He gave a low growl of triumph at the look in her eyes. "Dream come true, Jolie?"

She shivered all over, her eyes dilating still further as she tilted her head at last to look up into his.

His heart pounded with the desperate desire to kiss

her until that tablet computer slid off her lap.

But she didn't seem to like it when he was polite enough to show her how much he was attracted to her, too.

So let her wallow in it by herself for a little.

See if that improved her opinion of his manners.

He straightened and moved to the wall of the terrace, almost positive he heard a frustrated puff of breath behind him. Looking down over the fountain Sainte-Mère had built in his honor when the town's tourism economy quintupled after he got his third star, he took a moment to stretch. Hands locked high over his head, he arched his back into it, rolling his neck, his shoulders. What started as a deliberate calculation was such a relief after the past seven hours without a break that he sank into it, taking his time, muscles easing. *Putain,* but that felt good. It would feel even better if slim little hands added their pressure.

He glanced back at Jolie Manon, who had her knees pulled up so he couldn't even see her chest, staring at him. Her fingers rubbed slowly back and forth over her jeans-clad knees, as if she needed texture.

Don't hold back, chaton. I'm happy to be your texture.

He sat on the edge of the terrace wall, stretching out his legs, bracing his hands against its edge so that his torso was long, lean, fully exposed, the muscles of his arms and shoulders flexing a little.

Putain, but he liked it, when she had to bite on her lower lip.

He had so many things he could do with that mouth of hers. Make her lose not only her worries but her entire mind, tangling with him desperately in a—

A beast, though.

A *beast.* Was he really that bad?

Would one of those civilized men who paid a

fortune to eat at his tables sit here in front of that slim, vulnerable, adorably delicious little body, those eyes so wide and dark on him, and not do anything about it?

And just because some men were *des putains d'idiots*, did that mean *he* had to be? In order to live up to their standards? Something was screwed up, there.

"About that *other* idea," he said firmly, because, well—he would *like* to be a prince. If it was remotely possible and didn't require him to ignore her screaming body language indefinitely. "I think you should give me fifteen percent of the royalties. Since fifteen percent of the recipes are mine. Of your father's royalties," he added, as he saw her eyes flicker in calculation.

She bit her lip. Wait, had that not been a princely thing to say? Damn it.

"*Not* yours. You did the same amount of writing, whether you knew you were writing up my work or not."

She worried at her lip.

Putain, would she *quit doing that?* It appealed to every heroic instinct he had—and he had a lot more of them than she gave him credit for—the thought of swooping in and protecting that lip from her cruelty. Offering himself to her teeth in its place. . . .

He shifted, wondering what her head was doing with his increasingly obvious arousal. Anyone would think she would like it, *since he aroused her,* but apparently it couldn't be that easy.

"And I want subsequent editions to acknowledge me under each recipe that's mine. *Created by Gabriel Delange* works fine. For the remaining print run of this first edition, you can just insert one of those slips of paper that corrects errors. It's not ideal, but it's either that or make you destroy the entire run."

That lower lip got more punishment. Her physical awareness of him faded as her worry rose. *Merde. You're not the knight in shining armor, you're the beast, remember? She's never in a million years going to think of you as the hero.* Women never did. "I'm just starting out as a food writer," she said, low. "If I have to get my publishing house to do all that, they probably won't ever work with me again."

Gabriel sat still for a moment, his fingers pressing into that rough stone. He tilted his head back, closing his eyes, concentrating on the distant sound of his fountain, below in the square. "I'm never going to get any damn justice, am I?"

She said nothing. When he opened his eyes again, she had her arms wrapped even more tightly around her knees, and she was watching him with a mixture of worry and apology.

Bordel. "It is so like that *salaud* to have a stroke just before that cookbook came out."

"As if he did it on purpose!"

Yes, all right, she loved her father. *Le connard. He* got three daughters to love him, even though he didn't deserve it, while Gabriel lost his girlfriend of six years— sixteen to twenty-two—and had had a really lousy success rate when it came to long-term relationships ever since.

How did Pierre Manon always manage to manipulate his situation to get everyone else to give him their all, so much more than he deserved?

"Forget it," he said roughly, shoving to his feet. "Don't mess up your career with your publishing house. I'll think of something else."

He headed back toward the hotel door and paused in front of her. Her eyes ate him up, making him very conscious of his naked upper body, of the way his shoulders blocked out her moonlight. *Chaton, you don't have to just look. I know what I make might mislead you, but I myself am more than happy to be devoured like junk food.* "Do you have a boyfriend or something? Fiancé? Married?"

Her eyes went enormous. She tightened her computer over her breasts, a defensive shield, but he saw her throat work again. "No," she whispered.

He shook his head, feeling heavy, puzzled. Like some damn *beast* who had wondered out of the woods and gotten lost, baffled, in society. "Then I don't understand why, when you want me to kiss you so damn badly, you'll get so mad if I do."

He strode out before he could crack and try it anyway and heard her tablet smack onto the stone terrace behind him.

Fallen out of her lap as she lost herself in dazed arousal? Or just poorly aimed at his head?

Why was he so bad at this? Surely no other man had to sue a woman just so he could make her put up with him long enough that he had a chance to figure out how to talk to her.

Chapter 7

G abriel was standing doing bicep curls at the crack of dawn the next morning when he recognized the *financier*-colored ponytail and sleepy face of one of the women doing deep breathing in the early morning yoga class. Her eyes looked so heavy, he wondered why she had dragged herself out here.

So disciplined she sought out a gym the first morning traveling? Or had she lain awake all night, tossing and turning in hopeless arousal, and now needed the calming influence? He grinned wickedly, thinking of all the ways he could help—eventually—calm her down.

The class moved to all fours, and for about the fifteenth time in the past twenty-four hours, Gabriel found himself staring at that little butt in the air. This time clad in skin-tight leggings. She arched her back, her head and butt rising higher, then flexed it like a cat, butt dropping. Then arched it again. Oh, that was . . . that was . . . there was only so much a man could take, here.

One of the bodybuilders who spent half his life in this place walked by, with a sardonic look for Gabriel, who realized he had been frozen watching the yoga class for a good five minutes.

"I was ogling someone specific!" Gabriel muttered, shifting to a machine, which just happened to keep that little corner of the yoga room in view. "Not the whole class!"

The bodybuilder rolled his eyes and moved on to his own weights. Easy for him to be judgmental. Gabriel had caught the other man ogling *him* a few times, and occasionally the serious bodybuilder women, so clearly big muscles were where his sexual interests lay.

Gabriel on the other hand—in the class, Jolie flowed again, hips lifting higher, chest pressing to the ground, little body seeming to grow longer, her back one supple arch—Gabriel was all about *flexibility.*

Jo stopped at the top of the narrow stone staircase that led into the *vieux village* from the more modern town that draped below it like a skirt, which was where the closest gym had been. It was a perfect morning, just the first hour of dawn, the scent of jasmine releasing all around her from the brush of her hand along the vine that crawled over the old railing. Gabriel's fountain played softly in the empty *place,* shaded by the plane trees with their peeling bark. For now, it was cool, a brief respite before the day's heat began to bake down.

She felt strong, supple, centered, at peace, after the hour of advanced yoga. As if she could handle anything, even a beast, with serene assurance and without that ridiculous attraction. Really, stress must have awakened some biological instinct to search out strength no matter what the cost to herself. There was no other explanation for how much he had drawn her.

A hard body nudged hers very gently from behind.

"*Bonjour,*" a low voice rumbled in her ear.

She whirled to find him standing on the staircase, immediately behind her and face almost on level with hers. Her center flew right out of her body and got lost somewhere, her serene assurance swamped under a wild urge to grab him and kiss him and see just how direct and ill-mannered he could be.

His face zoomed in even closer, and her heart lurched in twenty different directions as if tumbled in a dryer, and . . . he pressed a proper *bise* against each of her cheeks. Her whole being pulled toward the press of his freshly-shaved jaw, until it was all she could do not to rise up after him as he lifted his head. Barely lifted his head. His eyes glinted very blue as he studied hers from only centimeters away.

She swallowed.

He drew a breath.

She bit her lip.

His gaze tracked that, darkening.

She backed up.

One of his fists clenched briefly by his side.

"Good morning," she said stiffly. "You don't sleep very much."

"You either." He looked quite pleased about it. "And here you thought the only thing we had in common was a lawsuit and mutual sex appeal."

She turned on her heel and headed across the *place,* determined to ignore him, and he struggled to fall into step beside her. He kept having to shorten his long, fast stride and bring himself back even. He wore another soft, fitted T-shirt, gray-green today, and jeans. His hair was wet, his scent fresh, clean, some light apple-scented soap, and was it just her, or did his arm muscles have even more fantastic definition than they had the night before?

"Are you going into work *already?*"

"Actually, I'm free for a couple of hours." He cut a hopeful glance sideways at her, his eyebrows rising in question.

She gritted her teeth. Just in case she wanted to invite him up to her room?

His eyes flicked over her expression, and for a second, he looked almost glum, rubbing one hand over the back of his neck. Then he shook the glumness off him. "Did your yoga teacher let your class out early? I thought I had another five minutes."

"Are you *stalking* me?"

He scowled briefly. "In my bestial way? I was working out." He showed her the gym bag slung over his shoulder. "You mean, you didn't see me? You didn't know I was watching you while you went through some of those poses?"

Yep, all peace, all tranquility, completely gone. In their place, a burning sparked small and then grew until it burned in every part of her body that she had flexed and worked and stretched. And it had been a pretty comprehensive yoga class. So thoughts of him burned through pretty much all of her.

"I can imagine what you were thinking while you watched, thanks." She headed up the streets of the old part of town. Probably better to explore their empty morning quiet than to head toward her hotel room with him following as if that was exactly where he expected her to take him.

Okay, maybe not *better,* but certainly *smarter.*

Pff. That's what you think, her body protested sulkily. *It's about time some psychologist did some Body Q studies to balance out all these dumb E.Q. and I.Q. things.*

"Can you?" His grin came back. "Imagine what I was thinking? We should compare notes. Just to see if our imaginations are compatible."

Compatible. With the imagination of the man who had invented that exquisite fragile Rose guarding a melting heart of gold? Her own heart melted out of her at the thought.

Anyone would have supposed that man would be— elegant. Courtly. Careful and refined. Poetic. Ready to lay his cloak at a woman's feet.

Not openly stating that she would love to have him take her doggy-style and they both knew it.

She glared at him as a curve and descent of the street led them into another little *place.* In this one, the fountain was much older, a worn marble face of a beast spouting water from his mouth into a tiny basin.

Benches curved in a half-moon around it, near walls completely covered with the thick glossy green vines and delicate white flowers of jasmine. In the early morning, the *place* was still in shadow and utterly silent, except for the water and their footsteps.

She stopped in front of it, and when he stopped beside her, she twisted so that she was on the other side of it and facing him. "You're lucky you're so hot," she said bitterly.

"I know," he said despairingly, shoving his hands into his pockets as he leaned a shoulder against the jasmine. "It doesn't bear thinking of, what my social life would be like if I was ugly on top of everything else. *Now* what have I said?"

"You are so—incredibly—*arrogant*."

"I *know*." He sounded exasperated. "But I don't see how I've been arrogant with *you*. It seems as if ignoring your signals indifferently would have been a lot more arrogant, but apparently I have no idea."

Her signals. She ground her teeth over the urge to take two great fistfuls of his hair, yank his head down *hard*, so that it hurt, and *bite* that sensual, arrogant mouth of his. And that would teach him for finding her signals so obvious.

"You treat me like I'm your . . . your . . ." She searched her brain for the kind of French vocabulary she had never heard as a girl visiting her father and his family in the summer. "*Pute.*"

Gabriel looked as if he had been walking along, whistling cheerfully, and out of nowhere found his face slammed with a skillet. Cartoonish. It took him a full minute to get any sound out at all. "I *what?*"

She pressed her lips together and glared at him, refusing to repeat the nasty word for a hooker.

He shook his head as if it was still ringing and sat down abruptly on the stone bench beside that worn marble face, the jasmine tangling wildly behind him over the stone walls. "I really do have bestial manners, then," he said, smashed.

She started to wish she had bitten her tongue. He looked—distressed. He looked as if he wasn't going to go around calling it as he saw it with her anymore, with that blunt accuracy that was so infuriating and so arousing.

"That's not how I'm thinking about you," he said after a moment. She hadn't known he could sound so subdued. She didn't like it nearly as much as she had thought she would. "Like a—*pute*. I mean, I don't"—his hands squeezed the stone of the bench—"what qualifies as treating you like a *pute*, exactly? The fact that I want to have sex with you?"

Would her body *quit melting* when he said things like that? "The fact that you *act* like all you have to do is snap your fingers."

He gaped at her. Indignation started to grow in his face. "Snapping my fingers is what I do with my staff. If they are really slow and I have to get pointed about it. I've never snapped my fingers at you. I talk to you like you're an equal. Because you *are*."

She folded her arms over her chest. Just in case her shirt wasn't thick enough and he was reading her attraction to him like a three-step recipe again. "This is how you talk to all your equals?" she challenged dryly.

"*No*," he said, as if she was dense. "But the others don't look at me as if they wanted me to haul them off somewhere dark and dangerous."

She was really going to have to kill him.

"It's incredibly arousing," he confessed.

Her eyes flickered involuntarily down his body—the way the T-shirt clung to the flat abs, and his arm muscles stood out from the tension in his hands, and the long legs stretched there, on that bench in that intensely peaceful space of jasmine and running water and ancient stone. The realization that he was telling the truth jolted through her: he was aroused. It was just the two of them, hidden here in the early morning, and he wanted her. If she walked up to him, if she leaned down into him, he would—

"I could probably behave better if you would quit looking at me like that. Maybe. It might be too late," he admitted. "I've kind of gotten the idea in my head at this point."

"So you're behaving like this because I look easy," she said bitterly.

His eyebrows drew together. "What? I never said that at all." He hesitated. "*Enfin*—you can be. Easy. If you want to be. I won't think less of you." He snuck a hopeful glance at her. "I don't *disrespect* you because you want to have sex with me, you know. If that's where the *pute* thing came from."

She gritted her teeth, torn between the overwhelming desire to hit him and the one to completely give in, to be just—easy. Just go with it. Just get hauled off to somewhere dark and dangerous and growled at some more. *Working with chefs does not mean you have to get sexually involved with them. You idiot. You don't have to perpetuate any cycles.*

"But I'm behaving—what is so wrong with the way I'm behaving?—anyway, whatever I'm doing, I'm doing it because you look like something delicious."

Her lips parted.

So did his. "Just this sweet, buttery, golden-brown, pistachio-kissed deliciousness, like I could just bite my teeth into you so gently—" His hands were shaping the air as he talked. His tongue touched his teeth, and his teeth came slowly together as if they were sinking into something. "And you're right there, just—right there, as if you *want* me to. And then I hit some electrified forcefield every time I try. It makes me feel like one of those dogs with the collar and the invisible fence." He gave his wet, shaggy head a shake. "And it makes me *starving*."

Starving. Her soul seemed to run right out of her

body like the rippling flow of the fountain, into the palm of his hands. To think of this man starving for her.

He squeezed his eyes shut. "Oh, *putain*, you're doing it again."

Damn it. She took a hard step back and ran into the jasmine-cushioned wall, the vines grabbing at her hair.

He opened his eyes. And stared at her pressed back among the dark green vines and stars of white. She felt—caught. Held still for him by vines of jasmine. If he cornered her against that wall and kissed her, she would not manage one word to fight him off.

"Good *God*." He sprang to his feet, shoving his hands in his pockets and striding away to the edge of the curving walls.

The light slowly grew in the *place*, and a door opened from an old building with sea-blue shutters, a bent woman with white hair coming out with a little dog. Gabriel took another hard breath, focusing on the old woman like a lifeline.

"*Bonjour, Gabriel.*" Her eyes flicked with bright curiosity over Jolie.

He dipped his head. "*Bonjour, madame.*"

The old woman kept walking, slow and careful but leaving them to their peace. Some of the tension eased out of his body.

"I've got another idea. About how you can make up for stealing my Rose," he said over his shoulder, without turning to look at her. "But maybe we should talk about it later. This afternoon? What are you doing for lunch?"

She rubbed her arms, knowing she should move out from the shelter of the jasmine. But it smelled so good around her, and the effect on him was so enticing. She kept imagining him turning, prowling back toward her, sinking his hands through the vines on either side of her head, lowering his mouth . . . maybe she could slip her hands into the vines, hold herself prisoner to him. . . . "I thought you never took anyone out to lunch or dinner," she said with as much stiffness as she could manage.

"Oh, I wasn't asking you to lunch."

Her mouth set. She straightened out of the jasmine.

"I'm *working*," he growled defensively. "You of all people should know what a three-star restaurant takes."

Yes, she remembered her father's hours. Before he lost that third star, without Gabriel there to keep it for him, sank into a depression, and quit, which was at least better than literally falling on his big butcher's knife, as some chefs did.

"But what are you going to eat?" Gabriel asked.

A vague wave of her hands. "I don't know. There must be some good restaurant around here."

He turned back enough to give her an incredulous look.

"Where I don't need reservations six months in advance and an inexhaustible fortune." Jolie rolled her eyes. Didn't he know she would be lapping up everything that fertile brain and those supple hands could produce, if she could?

Straight, strong eyebrows drew together. "You're not paying in my restaurant. I may not be able to take you out, but, *putain*," his eyes glowed with a strange, vicarious hunger, "I can *feed* you."

Gabriel Delange. Feeding her.

If she threw herself across that little fountain and kissed him, would she be sending mixed signals?

Or sending consistent signals for the first time?

"I don't want you to turn away someone who has a reservation," she said reluctantly.

His expression changed. "You mean you want to sit at a table?" Was that *wistfulness* that crossed that strong, dangerous face?

"Where were you thinking I would sit?" she asked, confused. "Is there a bar or something?"

"I was thinking you could come into the kitchens." He hesitated. "It wouldn't be very comfortable, though," he admitted. "And you would have to eat standing up." That buoyant, animal energy faded. His hands flexed in his jeans pockets. He looked increasingly glum, resigned.

"In *your kitchens*?" Jolie lit like the morning sun, slipping over the centuries-old buildings at last to shine straight into their little alcove.

Gabriel's gaze caught on her face.

"Can I take notes? And pictures? Can I *write about it*?" Plunged into the heart of how he worked, of what he made. And not peeling grapefruit until her fingers screamed, but able to watch.

"You can do anything you want," he said slowly. He wasn't moving, except for his eyes, tracking over and over her face. "I told you. Anything at all."

Chapter 8

❝ So are you enjoying your vacation?" her father asked, sullen and slurred, when she called, and Jo stiffened with shock.

"My—"

"Your sisters told me." His voice dragged painfully.

"But I'm n—" Jo stopped. Of course, what *were* her sisters supposed to tell him about her absence from his side in his moment of need? Her perfectionist, narcissist father, so desperately short of the attention he craved. "It's for the book, Papa. Publicity."

"You've been doing all the signings without me?" he asked resentfully.

She rubbed between her eyebrows. "No, I— promised to do a little talk on food writing for a writers' group down here. How to make contact with chefs, how to work with them . . . I couldn't let the group or the publisher down. I knew Estelle and Fleur were going to be with you."

"No one complained about not having the real chef there?" he asked roughly.

"Of course they wanted you, Papa." An easy one. "But this particular talk was focused on the food writing itself, so we managed. I'm rescheduling the demonstrations until you feel up to it."

"Until I feel—" Her father made a harsh sound, like he used to when some underling's spot of sauce on a plate was a millimeter off. "I told you I can't do demonstrations like this!"

But it's my first cookbook! It's our cookbook. It deserves a launch! She bit her tongue. She couldn't stress her father right now. What if it drove him into another stroke? "Don't worry about it." She stared out at the white parasols on the upper terrace of the ancient mill.

Great chefs. Fascinating. Extraordinary. Impossible.

Maybe no one rose to greatness of any kind without being a narcissist. And no one rose to become a great chef without knowing how to make other people hungry. For more of them.

"When are you coming back to Paris?" her father asked morosely. "Or are you coming back to Paris? Too busy with the book, I suppose?"

"Papa!" His narcissistic life had peaked once. And then he had lost his wife and daughters, to a trans-Atlantic divorce. Then one of his stars. And two months ago, he had lost his skill, with the stroke. Her heart tore at her, at the utter devastation of his faith in himself, that arrogance he needed most of all. "Of course I'm coming back to Paris! I'm only here a couple more days."

She hoped she could talk Gabriel out of a lawsuit in two more days. Maybe instead he could take his vengeance out on her naked bod—she smacked herself on the forehead. Hard.

"I hate being so far away from you, Papa," she told him and hated herself for the fact that it was only partly true. She had spent most of her life far away from him. He had never been there for her. But that had been her mother's choice, of course, to move back to the States after the divorce. Her father's famous three-star restaurant in Paris was hardly transportable in pursuit, especially since her mother, with full guardianship, could have waited until he started up a successful restaurant in New York and then moved to Little Rock, Arkansas, if she wanted. Jo didn't think her mother would have done that; Brenda Manon had moved herself and her daughters back home to the U.S. because that was where her support network was, and her home country, rather than in an effort to get them as far away from her husband as possible. But then, Jolie's parents had probably sheltered their daughters from their most acrimonious battles, so maybe her father couldn't be so sure.

For Jo to choose to live her own life to her own benefit right now, when her father, who had never had any of them, so desperately needed her, would have been horrible.

"I love you, Papa," she said firmly, and he gave a little sigh of relief. He needed people to love him so much.

"Thank you, *pucette*," he said roughly. "You've always stood by me."

It was two when Jolie stepped into the alley. A matte-skinned, burly dark-haired man stepped back to let her pass before him, and she hesitated because he was the one carrying a big case of bottles and thus from her point of view should have right of way. And also, no woman really liked having a stranger his size behind her in an alley, even if the broad daylight and the proximity of so many helpful people with knife skills made that a little ridiculous. But he just raised his eyebrows and waited politely, in that very French way that conveyed he was physically incapable of pushing in front of her to go first, no matter what kind of load he was carrying, so she went on. The scent of roses wafted over her as she went past him, and she glanced around, trying and failing to find some sign of a climbing rose.

The first person she saw when she peeked through the kitchen door was Gabriel. Dipping his finger into some orange powder, he bent over a plate until he almost touched it and blew carefully, so that that the powder fell over the spiral of chocolate on the plate in a scattering of flame, and her body clenched. All around him, his team worked like speed demons—sous-chefs flying to finish plates, *petits commis* and interns prepping the components, all engaged in making the lunch menu's dozen desserts, requested via slips of paper waving from the metal shelf beyond him.

He slid the dessert down the counter to the pass, his lips relaxing from the pursed shape to reveal a grim cast to his face. Then he looked up suddenly and met her eyes.

He grinned, all the grim lines relaxing away. "You're late. Don't tell me you had car trouble again."

"I thought things would be slowing down a little bit if I waited until now. I don't want to be in the way."

His eyebrows flexed together. "You're not in the way. If I say you can be here, you can be here. You must be hungry." A stern look. "You haven't been snacking, have you?"

"No." She hadn't even eaten breakfast, in anticipation. "I'm starving."

His face suffused with so much delight that her mouth dropped open and she stood stunned. Why, he wasn't just dramatic, difficult, and compelling. He was *beautiful.* "Perfect." He grabbed her by both arms and pulled her inside. His eyes flickered to her mouth when the move brought her body so close to his. She took a breath.

But he dropped her arms and reached out to take the case of bottles from the man behind her, whom she had entirely forgotten. "Matt, *bonjour.*" He shook the other man's hand, once freed. "My cousin, Matthieu Rosier," he told Jolie, with absent politeness. "Matt, Jolie Manon."

"Manon," Matt mused, his brown eyes squinting curiously. "Didn't we burn someone named Manon in effigy once?"

"All my copies of his menus," Gabriel corrected, slanting a quick glance at Jo. "Not an actual straw figure. Drinking with my cousins has a very bad effect on my maturity level. *It was ten years ago, Matt, merde.*"

"*Pardon,*" Matt said with complete lack of sincere apology, grinning as he bent down and kissed Jo's cheeks. The scent of roses wafted around her more strongly, coming from his skin or clothes, and the gesture itself startled her; he must think she and Gabriel were personal, not professional acquaintances.

How right was he?

"Thanks for these." Gabriel touched the dark blue glass bottles Matt had been carrying, and Jolie saw that they were labeled *eau de rose,* stamped with a dramatic R inside a flowering rose and the words Rosier SA. "The rose harvest is all in, then?"

"We picked the last of them three days ago. Finally. We had such a damn cold winter, it made everything late." A kind of grumpy patience to Matt's voice, as if he was someone who really liked forcing everything into the shape he wanted it, and yet, as a man who dealt with nature, knew he had one opponent he just could not control.

"I wish I could have gotten out more than once to help pick," Gabriel said. "We all had to work in the rose and jasmine harvests when we were kids," he explained to Jolie. "These days, they have big crews come in, but I guess most of us still like to pitch in a little bit, on a Saturday morning or in my case a Monday one. There's something about spending a morning picking roses and ending up covered in the oils. The day after Matt's birthday, I think the whole damn clan is out there, hangovers and all. It's turned into a tradition."

"Speaking of which, if you hit on a new good wine nobody has discovered yet, pick me up twenty cases or so. No man's cellar should look as bare as mine does this week."

"Sure. In fact, why don't you go talk with Raphaël about it? He usually deals with the local wine-makers,"

Gabriel said, with perfect friendliness, but his cousin flicked a glance down at Jolie and laughed suddenly, for no reason.

"Raphaël. In the other part of the kitchens. Right." Matt mouthed something at Gabriel that looked suspiciously like *Bonne chance*, Good luck, as he headed off toward Raphaël's side of things.

Gabriel opened one of the bottles of rosewater and breathed in the scent of it, then proffered it to Jolie so she could do the same. As the scent of roses filled her again, she thought about the way he took pleasure in every scent and texture that entered his world and, at least as important, how his first instinct was to share that pleasure with her. He disappeared again for a second and came back with a white chef's jacket. "Here. You had better wear this again."

He slipped her arms in it for her, and little tremors spread through her body from where his hands touched. His movements so quick he could have had a woman's clothes off in the time it took her to take one heady gasp of his scent—would she *quit* coming up with these ideas?—he buttoned the jacket and tied her apron, tucking the apron strings under the roll he had made at the top of it, in the style every chef wore everywhere. His fingers brushed against her pelvis when he did so, through the thick layers of apron and capri pants.

"I must look like a big marshmallow in this outfit," she said ruefully, fighting the desire for more of those fingers.

"You look cute." His eyes flickered to her mouth again. Her heart jumped, but he only grabbed her and spun her to a spot at the counter right next to where he had been working. "Wait here. *Enfin*, feel free to move around if there's something you want to see. You can take all the notes and pictures you want." He started to move away, in that blur of speed at which he seemed to function, then paused, a superhuman stopping to exchange a word with a slow-motion mortal. His gaze ran over her one more time, and he smiled a slow, deep smile. "Thank you for coming," he said, and was gone.

She heard him calling to Raphaël, his brother and chef cuisinier, as he moved away into the savory side of the kitchens.

He had thanked *her* for coming? To be personally fed behind the scenes by the chef himself in one of the finest restaurants in the world?

But—wasn't he arrogant? Of course he was. And wasn't he most arrogant about his most famous accomplishments, his food?

A young woman reached past her with a murmured *Excusez-moi*, opening a steel cabinet above her head to reveal all kinds of plastic boxes and bottles labeled with everything from *cure-dents* to *colorant rouge*. A young man pulled open a drawer blocked by her knee. She tried to shrink, pulled out her notebook and camera, and let her pen start flying.

Gabriel reappeared in only a minute, smiling at her again. He really did look—very happy to have her here.

"I'm really in the way," she told him ruefully.

"You're not in the way." A little growl slipped into his tone, rubbing all over her skin. "I told you. If I say you can be here, you can be here."

A *petit commis*, reaching at just that moment for the cabinet above her, hesitated, eyeing his chef warily.

Gabriel closed his hands around her hips and shifted her a few inches to the left, allowing the *commis* to get what he needed. "You might have to move around a lot, though," he admitted. He sounded—wary. Anxious? Surely not. "There's not really anywhere you can stand that someone won't need to get through you once in a while." One of his thumbs flexed into her hip. "Unless you would rather sit in my office?" he asked reluctantly.

Her heart tightened. *Not* the office exile again. *Not* standing on the other side of that glass, watching perfection rise out of chaos. *Not* all safe and protected from his heat and growls and the scents and sounds around him. "Would that be easier for you?"

"*No.*" His hand flexed hard on her hips. "No, and I don't do easy. I do things the way I want them."

Yes. Just that Rose on the cover of her cookbook proved that. And every other thing he had ever done with his life.

And he had not been talking about doing *her* the way he wanted, so her mind could just quit going off on those kinky tracks. For crying out loud. Once a woman's body started down the dark side in its fantasies she could never get it back, could she?

He said something rough to one of his team, glanced back down at her, and got caught by her expression. A little smile kicked across his face and right in her belly at the same time. He bent his head. "I could probably do things the way you want them, too," he whispered and grinned. "At least, you seem to think so."

Jo glared helplessly. To absolutely no avail. He took a plate from a black-tuxedoed waiter and set it in front of her, and then it was all over but the sighing.

He fed her. The arrogant, rude, you-know-you-want-me chef. Sweeping in beside her. Sliding a plate in front of her. Excitedly telling her how he did it. Checking for her reaction. Leaving her to enjoy it while he kept working at the speed of a Tasmanian devil.

He never took one single bite himself. He was just too busy—constructing plates with intense speed, magical things that disappeared, swept away by the black-clad waiters moving through with their elegant grace. He threw himself wholeheartedly into the work, as if he was of no higher rank than his gifted sous-chefs, or as if he just could not help it; he *had* to make sure it was done exactly right.

It was like watching a superhero cartoon: a blur of motion and all the sudden a city had been built, a world saved—only instead of skyscrapers, his city was a fairytale wonderland. The only pauses ever in his motion were beside her. To offer her . . .

Caramel melting inside a shell . . . a glistening dome of chocolate, flecked with gold . . . the sweet touch of peach. She couldn't figure out why he seemed so—eager, careful, wary, almost shy—every time he slid something in front of her.

Silk slid over her lips. Tender, fragile textures melted on her tongue. Gossamer beauty broke under her fork. Sometimes he had to force her to break it, grabbing the utensil from her and dashing it into some fantastical treasure: "All at once, you have to eat it all at once, all the flavors together, before the hot cools and the cold melts."

Until she started to wonder . . . if she wasn't eating his heart.

An exquisite, complex, vulnerable heart.

A roar broke out, as she gazed down at the dessert he had set before her, its pale green shell shattered by her fork, the fresh, sweet red center of cherries spilling out like a wound. The roar wasn't directed at her, but she looked toward it, breathing it in.

The roaring beast shrugged his big shoulders, turning back toward her, and took his own deep breath when he saw her looking at him. "Do you like it?"

"You're beautiful," she said involuntarily.

His smile grew wider, a boyish delight. "You mean, this." He gestured to the marble counter, indicating her dessert and everything that had come before or been served to others.

"I said what I meant."

His hand froze in the middle of the sweeping gesture. It turned, pressing flat against the marble, and his head bent. She couldn't read his expression, as he stared down at his hand, so still. It was almost as if he was badly shaken, as if something was rising out of the shaking, warring inside him. At last he turned his head enough to give her a troubled, anxious look.

Her own expression grew troubled in response. What was she *doing*? Where was she going with this?

"I'm done for a couple of hours." He straightened and rolled his shoulders. His hands went to the white buttons on his jacket, and her erogenous zones all skittered like uncontrollable brats. "Shall we go talk about that Rose you stole from me?"

Chapter 9

H is path through town led them up a wide stairway lined with an ancient vine, thicker than his wrist, and along a pedestrian street so narrow he could stretch out his hands to touch both walls. Old arched doorways, painted in blues, greens, yellows, and burnt oranges, matched the beautiful sea-shades of the shutters above them. Wrought iron tables or old, distressed wooden ones with peeling paint stood outside doorways beside little chairs and potted flowers, creating inviting spots. Laundry hung above them from lines strung between balconies, like festival flags.

They came out onto a flat cobblestoned terrace area with a wide gravel space for *boules* over to one edge, old men playing against a backdrop of distant sea. Jolie itched to frame them in her camera, the blue of the famously azure coast, the plane trees, the silver ball flying through the air, caught suspended against a far-off dream. Instead, she let the image soak into her brain, joining Gabriel at a café table with a view over the sweeping skirt of civilization draped below the hilltown, all its crowded, heavily populated way to the sea.

Gabriel ordered coffee, and she asked for a Perrier. For all the opulent food she had been eating, she felt oddly light, fresh. He formed delight out of flavors, textures, beauty, never relying on an easy use of too much sugar or fat.

As they sat, the tension in Gabriel's muscles drained away from him slowly, his body growing heavy in the chair, as if he would never leave it again. But he would. Seven more intense hours at least tonight before he could sleep.

"Do you ever make your Rose?" she asked. "I didn't see it on the menu." Or in his kitchens. She didn't want to admit to him how heavily disappointment had squeezed her not to taste that Rose from his hands.

He shook his head. "I stopped making it after your father stole it from me the first time. It—hurt too much." He looked out toward the yacht-jeweled sea.

She rolled her napkin-wrapped utensils, remembering him a little more clearly from when he was twenty-three, so skinny his bones stood out and burning with passion. *I lost thirty pounds.* And his girlfriend. And won a star. And got the very lousiest reward possible.

Of course, so had her father gotten a crappy reward, years earlier, when his wife had divorced him and taken Jolie and her sisters to the other side of the sea. It took all of you, being a top chef. And all of everybody who loved you, too. As fascinated as she was by these starred creatures, she wouldn't want to be one in a million years. Nor trust her life and happiness to one.

Which made it increasingly terrifying that happiness seemed to spring out of her just being near Gabriel, great curling vines of it trying to tie her to him in an exasperated tangle.

"So I had another idea," Gabriel said.

She bit her lower lip and waited. His eyes flickered to her mouth and stayed there a long, frustrated moment. But then the waiter arrived with his coffee, and he curled his hand around the tiny white cup like a life preserver.

"You could write my cookbook for me. It's something I need to do, I just hate trying to sit down and put it into words. If I had words for these things, I would be writing about them instead of having to physically produce them. And I wouldn't be so exhausted."

Jolie smiled ruefully.

"No offense." He took a long sip of coffee. "I know you work hard."

"None taken." She wished she didn't have an absurd urge to tell him he could put his head in her lap and take a nap, if he wanted. She might work a full day, between research and writing, but she didn't work anything like as hard as he did. Besides, the research— going into chefs' kitchens, getting them to talk about their passion, tasting their delights and learning how to make them—that was all *play*. They indulged her, the way they wouldn't indulge their employees. In a way her own father hadn't indulged her. Food writing, she had discovered, put her on different terms—terms that pulled down that glass wall, that let her step into this world, live it, and, for the time she was working on a recipe with a chef, get an exceptional amount of his attention.

"I'm thinking of one that is just focused on desserts, but who knows, there might be interest in a second book that Raphaël and I could do together. But that would be for another time." Gabriel waved a hand, putting that second book into the future. The coffee was kicking in, the energy coming back to his body.

Energy in that body. That would be hovering over hers, teaching her. . . .

It hit her like the plunge down a roller coaster, giddy, screaming, arms flung waving in the air: *My third cookbook would be Gabriel Delange!! Omigod, omigod, omigod.*

And a jerk, on that roller coaster ride. One cookbook would put them in close working contact for at least a year. He had even thrown out the idea of a second one, two years.

And she found him so hot. So rudely, undeniably, arrogantly hot.

There was a road she could start down, and it wasn't a straight one. It curved neatly and smoothly right back around to a household of women with no father or husband there, to a broken family, to crying and tears.

She took a long swallow of Perrier to try to clear her head and instead got bubbles up her nose.

"You would be the author," he said. "I would be the title. We'll figure out the royalties." He dismissed those impatiently with a flick of his fingers.

"I'm in the middle of another project," she said slowly.

He frowned. "How long until that one is done?"

"My deadline is next January, but I could probably start working on yours at the same time. Actually, if you would feel comfortable working with me, I would love to interview you for this *French Taste* project, too, and maybe gather some stories and a contribution. It's kind of a wander through France, via its top chefs." She could probably survive that much contact with him, right? Without doing what her mother had always warned her against?

"Sure." A decisive move of his hand. "I would like that."

She sat blinking a moment, trying to figure him out. He had thrown her, here. From the exquisite Rose which was her first knowledge of him, to the rough, direct come-ons, as if she was stripping naked and doing a pole-dance for him, to the lunch in his kitchen, to this. "You do remember I'm Jolie *Manon.*"

"Yes, and I'm not supposed to rend your sick father with my lawsuit," he said dryly. "I've grasped that. Since you're willing to sacrifice yourself for him, this is what I want from you. I suppose you have some reason you can't give that to me either? Some way I would be a bad guy, a *beast,* if I insisted on it?"

"A bad guy to let me work with you on a cookbook?" she asked incredulously. "With *you?*" She might end up doing something that would be bad for her, but she could hardly blame him for that. It wasn't his job to save her from her own emotions; it was hers. "I can't even believe it. It's like a dream come true."

The cup stilled in front of his face. When it lowered, that grim dry look was gone, as was the fatigue, the blue eyes lit as if he had just been suffused with energy again. "A dream come true? *Vraiment?*"

"Really." She drew a breath, the next year stretching before her like her own personal fairyland. He could have dedicated his entire life to the search and not found a more perfect gift for her. Wait. He *had* dedicated his life to the search, from the time he was fifteen years old. He just hadn't known she would be the recipient of the gift, back then. Her eyes widened. "Really."

He sat forward, resting his chin on his hands, bringing his body much more intimately into her space. His eyes almost exactly matched that distant sea. "Good. I'm glad my manners are improving."

A dream come true. Gabriel didn't know how to talk to her after she said that. A cookbook. To take everything that was finest about him and ask her to put it into words, as she had done so beautifully for her father. Making his ephemeral life permanent, giving it that seal of immortality. Of—worth, somehow.

To ask her to make him immortal, too, and to have her react to that request as if he had given her the finest gift a man could give her. As if, to hand her *everything that was most beautiful about his life*, everything for which he had driven himself so hard, was, in fact, the most beautiful thing she could possibly ask for.

It—what was he supposed to do with that? He had wanted her from the first instant he had turned to see her small pistachio-and-gold self gazing at him with such fascination from his doorway. It wasn't that he had only wanted her for sex, because he wasn't an idiot. He had thought she was cute, and arousing, and *putain* but he would love to have a cute little girlfriend who looked at him like that. Not just for sex, but to have her—there. To smile at. And receive a smile back. To have her roll over in her sleep and put her arm over him, murmuring something befuddled but welcoming when he slipped into bed at one in the morning, instead of the bleak emptiness that currently greeted him. Sex sounded great—especially with her butt taunting him all the time. But it became, even in the fantasizing, a claiming process. A way of taking her and maybe managing to keep her.

He had known from the first that keeping her might be a hopeless case, because women stopped being nearly as fascinated and grew a lot more hostile and frustrated when they realized his working hours. But he couldn't stop himself from trying. He never could stop himself from trying for the impossible things that could be beautiful.

Still, it had started out mostly as fun. Arousing. Tantalizing.

And now—she had reached one of those slim hands of hers into him and closed it around his heart.

And she just held it there. How was he supposed to move around, continue to live calmly and strongly, while someone was squeezing his heart like that? He was afraid if he got up too fast from the café table or walked too quickly and outpaced her, it would get ripped right out of his body.

And it was *hard* to walk as slowly as she did. He supposed she had a nice long stride for someone her size. But he was used to consuming his day in a blur of speed.

Now he was getting ridiculous. She couldn't literally rip his heart right out of his body if he made the wrong move.

"Not that I can accept the offer," she said suddenly, her shoulders slumping.

Why the fuck did women always act so fastidious about his heart? What was wrong with it?

"My father's not doing so well after the stroke. Emotionally, I mean. I can't just leave him in Paris all alone."

Gabriel felt that wrench of appalled compassion for Pierre again—all alone, without even his hands to build dreams anymore—and fought it with a furious growl. "Look, he had a wife and three daughters." Which was more than Gabriel had ever managed to get in his life. If he hadn't poured so much of himself out for Pierre that his girlfriend *of six years* dumped him, he could— probably have his own ex-wife and daughters living on the other side of the world by now. "If no one is left who cares about him enough to stay with him besides you, it's his own fault."

Like it will be your own fault, that dark, wrenching compassion told him. *When you're all alone, and people don't even want to eat you up with a fork anymore.*

Merde, will you shut the fuck up? he growled at that inner voice.

Jolie's pistachio eyes had gone bleak. She looked down at her hands.

"You can visit," Gabriel snapped. "I'm not holding you prisoner. You'll probably only need to be here about half of each week." *See? See how nice and princely I can be?* Not that she probably appreciated it. She probably had no idea how begrudging and greedy he felt, forcing himself to let her see her father. *Salaud.* The last thing Gabriel wanted was to share something beautiful with *him.* He didn't even know if he was brave enough. If he was afraid she would rip his heart out of his body just by standing up too fast, what would a six-hour high-speed train trip do? Especially to see *Pierre Manon,* a man who knew how to steal everything beautiful out of another man's life for himself, and had the advantage of being her father, to boot. "It's not like I would have time for you Friday, Saturday, or Sunday anyway," he said roughly, and then kicked himself. As if she didn't already know, Pierre Manon's daughter, what lousy lonely weekends she would spend with a boyfriend like him. *Let's just rub it in, you bad-tempered idiot. You are so pathetic at being the prince.*

But Jolie's hands had curled on the table, as if she was closing them around something tantalizing. She looked back up at him, and her eyes were . . . hungry. Alive. The bleakness flushing away with energy. "Do you *mean* that?" she said. "You would really let me write a cookbook with you? I'm Jolie *Manon,* remember."

Yes, and it gave him a vicious, pure surge of victory to think of taking her away from her father, too. *Ha, you bastard, you can lose the most beautiful part of yourself to me, this time.* He had to squelch it. Remind himself that he wasn't *that* much of a beast, to let the old battle with Pierre soil the instinctive, delighted reaction he had had to her, long before he knew her name. She sure as hell deserved better from him than that.

But then, he always thought people deserved better of him than what he could do without trying.

"Pierre's daughter," he said. "I know. I saw what you did for him." *I would be delighted to have you worship me in words instead of him.*

She leaned forward, close enough to kiss. "And would you make your Rose for me?" she asked, hushed. "We could use it again. I could tell the story, of how you first created it working for Papa, and—"

He sat back hard in his chair, putting three feet between him and that kissable mouth. "No. Not the Rose." *And don't call him 'Papa'. That makes me feel— like strangling somebody. Myself, maybe.*

Her face fell, which was bad enough. But then she looked almost—relieved, which made his eyes narrow. Relieved, how? What was she escaping, when he didn't make that Rose for her? It had broken *his* heart. What power would it have over hers?

He so liked the thought of having power over her. It made his insides all greedy and grumbly and itching to pounce.

To roll her under him in a dark bed *and no one can save you from me, not even you.*

"So is it a deal? I drop the lawsuit, and you write the cookbook with me. I'll get one of my cousins to cough up an apartment you can stay in somewhere around here. Somebody must have something." In fact, wasn't one of his cousins heading off to the Rosier Fragrance Paris division for a year? Maybe they could trade.

Jolie narrowed her eyes at him. "Are you planning on holding a potential lawsuit over my head the whole time we're working together?"

"No. You need to call your agent, because I'm really looking forward to when I can hold a legal contract over your head instead."

Jolie tipped her Perrier to her lips and took a long swallow straight from the bottle that made him want to reach out and lay his hand against her throat, feel the muscles work as that coolness slid into her. "It does sound nice," she said dreamily.

Chapter 10

G abriel paid, his eyebrows flicking together when Jo started to pull out her wallet, his hand closing over the bill so that she had no hope whatsoever of seeing what was owed.

"You just fed me a three-star meal people fly around the world and book six months in advance to eat," she said dryly as they stood. "The least I could do is buy you coffee."

He grabbed her hand like he was afraid she would do something with it if he didn't. His fingers laced with hers and locked there tightly. She caught her breath as his slightly rough palm spread a rash of heat all over her skin. All he did was hold her hand, and she wanted to take all the lithe strength of her body and bow it around his. "You don't get to pay me back in kind," he said benevolently, strolling across the cobblestoned *place* to its edge, where they could see the town falling away below the old medieval walls, gradually growing more modern, from Renaissance buildings there at the base of the walls, to seventeenth- and eighteenth-century a little farther out, on through to the present, the farther it got from the six-hundred-year-old fortifications. "You're a woman. You have to pay me back with sexual favors."

She narrowed her eyes at him. He grinned, gazing out at the coast sloping into the sea. "Everyone knows that about dating."

She yanked at her hand.

He tightened his hold. "Sorry. Otherwise, I'm afraid you won't recognize this as a date."

It wasn't even humanly possible to free her hand just by yanking. His fingers were supple, warm, and strong as steel.

A shock of hunger and fear ran through her. His come-ons, she could ignore, refuse, dismiss as infuriatingly arrogant. This was something more serious. She liked it too much, but it could lead somewhere. "I thought this was a business meeting. Or maybe a blackmail session."

"Yes, I figured that out," he said, grimly dry. "That's why I'm making it more clear."

She pulled at her hand again. Could she admit, only to herself and to no one else, that the reason she kept pulling was that it aroused her so much when that didn't work? When she couldn't get it free?

His hand tightened again. "Will you stop? You make me nervous when you do that."

Nervous? His profile was still toward her, but it had, indeed, shifted to an expression more serious, not necessarily happy.

"Why nervous? Do you think I'm going to hit you or something if I get my hand free?"

He shook his head and didn't answer. His thumb rubbed coaxingly over the knuckle of hers.

She swallowed as that one tiny gesture turned every bone in her body to some soft, elastic thing with which he could do what he wanted. This was making *her* nervous. It had been easier, funner, and far less dangerous to just fight with a beast over sexual attraction. They were talking about working together now. They were holding hands. That made everything more loaded, brought implications in everywhere. "Shouldn't you be resting before tonight?"

It squeezed at her, his moment of utter fatigue at the café table, before he drank his coffee and got his second wind. Plus, he was probably safer when he was sleeping.

He slid a glance down at her. "Is this your way of

asking for us to shift to my apartment or your hotel, or is this one of those invisible-fence-dog-collar things?"

Okay, so maybe somewhere down under her question, she would have liked for them to shift out of the dry heat of this afternoon into the intimate, shadowed coolness of a room with a bed, but did he have to be so damn blunt about it? And did she have to love that bluntness quite so much? She gritted her teeth and yanked again. "I want my hand back now. Really."

His bigger hand hardened to something immutable. "No. Really."

On the *terrain de boules*, steel thumped into the dirt and then clocked gently against steel. Somebody gave an approving grunt, somebody a rueful curse. The scent of pine tingled around around them, oils from the trees that shaded the *boules* match baking into the air with the heat.

She thought about that trapped hand for a moment. And then she turned straight into him, stepped up onto the low stone wall that shielded them from the drop off the ramparts, and kissed him. Which, as far as establishing a working relationship went, was maybe not the best move, but *damn* was it satisfying.

He made a startled sound into her mouth, and his hand dropped hers so that both his arms could close around her, one hand pressing into her lower back, flexing her closer.

Delight swept through her, and she forgot her purpose. That strength holding her in, protecting her from the drop, the instant response of his mouth and his body. After the first second of surprise, he took her in as unquestioningly as if he had been expecting her to jump on him for some time. Her temper flicked at the idea and then got lost in the way his mouth shaped hers, his hold tightening as he deepened the kiss.

She could have kissed him forever, with that spice of temper and that long, luxurious pleasure. She hadn't known anything could feel so warm and so good. She hadn't known she should choose a private spot for this so that she never, ever had to stop.

But they had to break apart because they were standing in full view of half a dozen old men, two café terraces, and anyone who chanced to look up from the lower part of town. A lot of whom probably recognized Gabriel. It cost her, to tilt her head away, to try to catch her breath.

The blue of his eyes was burning. She couldn't hold his gaze. That blaze in it made her feel as if he was holding her out there over that drop off the ramparts.

She lifted her freed hand and waggled it, without nearly as much energy or flippancy as she had planned.

He stiffened, his hands hardening on her hips. His face went grim. Bleak even. What? "That was a horrible thing to do to me," he said flatly and released her. He turned, took one step, and stopped with a jerk to turn back to her. "Give me your damned hand back."

She stared at him, wishing she understood what in the world was going on in his head. She looked down at her hand and flexed it. It seemed small, suddenly, but capable for all that. A happy hand. She liked it. She had a lot of fun with it. It was hers, and not something she had ever understood how to trust to others. She looked at his hand, big, open, demanding, stretched toward hers, little calluses on the pads at the base of his fingers and on his fingertips.

Slowly, because the acquiescence seemed to deconstruct every part of her, fill the pieces with light, and put them back together in a shape she couldn't even recognize, she slipped her hand into his.

His closed snugly back around it, immediately. He, too, gazed down at their hands a moment.

The tension in his body eased, and a faint curve relaxed his mouth.

A strange, profound contentment filled her, all caught up with nerves and jittering sexual awareness though it was. She liked having her hand right there. She wished she hadn't just manipulated him with a kiss, because now she would have liked to lean back into him again and kiss him some more.

But . . . "Gabriel."

He smiled, with a sudden quick pleasure. Did his name on her lips make him that happy? That melted her again, and she almost forgot what she wanted to say. Oh, yeah. Damn.

"I really, really, really want to do this cookbook with you."

His hand flexed. His smile grew surer, deeper. "Thank you."

"I don't know if I can risk our working relationship for sex."

He stopped dead, his mouth opening and closing a few times. His hand tightened so hard on hers for a second, she made a little sound to remind him it wasn't a stress ball. He dropped it. That hand he had insisted so adamantly on holding. "*Tu te* fous *de moi?*" he said incredulously. Or in other words, *You've got to be fucking kidding me.*

"I *really* want to do this cookbook," she said pleadingly. *And how am I supposed to work with you for a year, and hold hands with you, and maybe do lots of other stuff, and not fall for you?* An arrogant chef who never stopped working and never stopped thinking he was the most important person in the room.

"Jolie. It's not mutually exclusive. The intention was quite the contrary, *je t'assure.*"

"But it might not work out. It probably won't work out. And then the cookbook would be *ruined.*" Working on a cookbook with *Gabriel Delange.* Shattered. Because she couldn't resist that combination of roaring bluntness and exquisite, wordless poetry, not even for the incredible chance of being able to concentrate on his *food* for a year. Not even for the chance to learn everything he was dreaming when he made it, to spend her nights thinking up the words to describe it.

"You need to look at the bigger picture, with your ambitions," he said urgently. "Never choose half of anything just to be safe, when you have a chance to have something whole and *perfect.*"

She bit her lip.

His fist clenched at his side as he focused on her mouth. "Why *wouldn't* it work out?" he asked hostilely, braced for attack.

She wrinkled her nose apologetically and touched her fingertips to her chest.

"You?" Gabriel looked startled.

"I'm not good at relationships." Wait—was he talking about her when he said *whole and perfect* or him? Or his vision of them both together? *Whole and perfect?* Her insides softened squooshily.

"*You're* not good at them?"

"What, you aren't either?"

"That's what everybody says." He sounded morose. "I try my best."

She searched his face, deeply curious now. In her experience, chefs weren't the most self-aware people out there.

"It's the hours." He shrugged big, surly shoulders, his jaw setting, arms folding. "And maybe my bestial manners, I don't know."

"Ah." Yes, the all-consuming nature of his work was a bit of a relationship-killer. Her own family certainly hadn't survived it.

"What about you?" he challenged sullenly.

"I don't know." Her eyebrows knit. "I'm just not that good at it."

He pulled them down one of those tiny alleys full of flowers and balconies, stopping before a narrow stone stairway that led up two floors to a tiny arched wooden door blocked by a profusion of red geraniums. He sat on the stairs and pulled her around to face him, standing her between his knees. "Jolie." His voice dropped low, gentle, that growling quality to it burring oh-so-softly over her, like the purr of a sleeping lion. "If it's sex you think you're not good at, I—might treat you better than you seem to think I would." His fingers rubbed gently over the insides of her wrists, over shiveringly sensitive skin and tendons and her pulse. She swayed at the caress, her body growing heavy, trying to beat her will and sink into him.

"I'm not really that worried about the se—"

"Kiss me again." He pulled her down into him, and her heavy body, subdued just by his touch on her wrists, had no resistance. "You might like"—his mouth brushed over hers, stroked her lips apart—"the way I manipulate you"—he pulled her lower lip so gently between his teeth. Released it. Took her mouth with a slow, gentle slide of his tongue—"better."

The stairs against her legs were awkard, the only purchase for her body his. She pressed her hands into his thighs, her torso sinking against his, the edge of a step digging into her shin.

He curved a hand under her bottom and pulled her in closer against him, taking her weight off that shin. Taking her weight off anything but him. She couldn't find her way out of the kiss, and she couldn't find her way to its center. It was a labyrinth of sensual delight, something she could stay caught in forever, getting ever more deeply lost in it. This time there was no one in the alley to see, only an orange cat on one of the balconies above them. It felt as if they could kiss here, sheltered by flowers and stone, until the end of time.

In fact, if someone told her that the world was about to end, this was what she would choose to do with the rest of her time: stay here and kiss Gabriel in the shadowed, flower-filled alley until the comet hit.

"You don't taste sweet and golden," he said with a surprised, rough laugh. "You don't taste"—he couldn't string a proper sentence, his words broken by strokes and bites and deep, deep kissing—"like anything—I've ever tasted—before."

He dragged her in still tighter. The other hand thrust into her hair, pulling it out of the clasp she had it in, stinging her roots with the urgency. She whimpered a little into his mouth, panicked, drowning, and he bit on her lower lip, so gentle and ferocious, stroked it with his tongue, and took her mouth again. He clearly liked discovering completely new flavors.

Her hands dug into his upper arms and kneaded them, pushing away even as she held on more tightly, trying to find her way up again. She was sinking into an ocean of him. She couldn't find a light to lead her to the surface, she could only find him, and she was running out of *her*.

He lifted her more and pulled her astride him, and she balked at being opened to him still more, at the pressure of his arousal against her sex.

She wrenched away, lost and panicked, panting, and he gasped at the sudden separation of their mouths. She wanted to fall back into him, to make amends for that separation, but at the same time, she squirmed, trying to pull her hips off his.

His fingers flexed hard into her bottom. And then he was lifting her off him, setting her sideways on his thigh. "I'm sorry." His voice was rough, hoarse, as he coaxed her head down onto his shoulder with a stroking hand. "That was—was that too much for you?" His arm curved around her waist, his other hand stroking her hair, but every few seconds, his arm tightened, his fingers digging deeply into her scalp, and he had to force them to ease up. "God, you taste delicious. *Putain.* Another attempt to prove I'm not a beast gets thoroughly fuc—scre—ruined." He laughed with a kind of despairing ruefulness, pressing his forehead to the top of hers. "But I wouldn't have minded either of the first two, obviously."

She really shouldn't let him keep stroking her hair like that, keep her tucked up safe in his body like that. Keep her tucked up safe *from him.* It was far more vulnerable, far more intimate, than the kissing could ever have been. More vulnerable than full-out, tangle-with-a-beast sex might have been. And yet it was as if his kisses had shattered all her defenses, and now she quite desperately needed his strength around her until she recovered. She couldn't bring herself to lift her head and slide off his thigh to her feet.

Why shouldn't she let him? Just because she had never felt so beautiful and precious in her life, did it mean she wasn't allowed to feel it now? It was such a dangerous feeling. A woman could learn to want it too much. A woman could give up part of herself for a feeling like that.

His stroking hand steadied slowly, fewer sudden flexings of strength he had to struggle to control. "This is nice, too," he murmured, the vibration of his voice in his chest tickling her ear. "This is really nice."

Jolie let herself sink more deeply into him, no muscles holding her back from him at all. For a little while longer, still, she tried to think. And then she gave up on it and tried not to think, since not thinking, just feeling, was so much more pleasant. She might have to revisit her conviction that all the best textures and tastes and scents in the world were in food. His textures—the hard resilience of muscle, the soft cotton of his T-shirt, the smoothness of his skin, the silk of his hair, the whisper of roughness of a jaw shaved that morning—were incredible.

"Really, really nice," he whispered to the top of her head as he pressed a kiss there.

Chapter 11

G abriel insisted on taking Jolie to the Nice train station for her trip back to Paris, a gallant gesture that very clearly put him out of temper. They had sat on those stairs for far too long, until a low-voiced argument filtering down from a balcony above had disturbed the mood. *You never pay attention to me anymore,* the woman had been arguing low, as if she was crushing tears. *What happened to all that romance at the beginning?*

You're never satisfied! the man had answered. *You want too much. Nothing I do is enough.*

The words had worked into their hold and wedged them apart, Gabriel growing brooding, uneasy, Jo unnerved, scrambling for flight. Anyway, she had to get back to Paris, as she told him. She needed to get her life organized, and above all see her father, if she was going to be spending several days a week down here. Gabriel scowled. Jo worried. Worried about how easy she had found it to curl up in the lap of an arrogant, rude, aggressive beast she barely knew and feel as if it was the most beautiful moment in her whole entire life.

It wasn't until they had passed a palm tree outside the Gare de Nice and entered the old Louis XIII building with its arch patterns in red brick and white stone, that it finally occurred to her. She looked up at him, suddenly, intensely relieved.

Gabriel looked from her face to the sleek silver and blue TGV behind her. "Happy to be heading back to Paris?" he growled.

"It's not the sex," she said confidently.

He gaped at her and then glanced around at the crowds. "Honestly, Jolie, can you think of *nothing* else?" He shifted in on her noticeably, much closer than a man should in crowds like that, but then, he had spent most of his life in packed, intense kitchens. "Not that I'm complaining," he rumbled, blue eyes glinting down at her.

"The reason I'm bad at relationships," she explained. "*I was not really thinking about sex!*" she hissed. Well, she hadn't been before he moved in on her that way. Now she was getting a pretty hot vision of being crowded by his body. Rubbed and roughed and handled all the ways he wanted. "It's because I like being who I am, I think. Not fitting myself around someone else."

His eyes narrowed, piercing. "Why are we talking about being bad at relationships right this second? And what do you mean, not fitting yourself around someone?"

Of course, ever since he had become head chef, that was all the people he saw all day every day had done, fit themselves around him. Before he became head chef, he would have done the fitting. He probably couldn't even grasp what she was talking about, the fact that she loved people, particularly food people, but she loved being alone, too. He wouldn't be able to understand that desire to do her own thing, to be busy in her own head without interference, a desire nourished perhaps in the hours she had kept herself occupied in her father's office as a child or in his apartment or roaming Paris while he worked.

"Guys just want so much space. And I run out of room for them. Or staying power, or something. I've always gotten sick of the guy pretty quickly."

His face set. His blue eyes glittered oddly against his grim face. "Are you telling me that you make a *habit* of dumping men who fall for you when you get tired of them?" Her boarding call sounded. "And you just the fuck told me that *right now*?"

She grabbed the handle of her case, laughing out loud with relief. "Well, at least I don't have to worry so much about working with you. I'm such an idiot to even think it. I would *never* end up down the same path as my mother."

And she hopped up into the train, with a happy wave.

Leaving Gabriel standing, riven to stone.

"You picked a fine time to move to the Côte d'Azur," her sister Estelle told her. "Jo. *I'm* busy in New York. Fleur's got a job in San Francisco. I thought you were going to be here in Paris for Papa."

Jo stuffed her hands in her pockets, her stomach clenching. Her father, all alone. Again. This time, without even his arrogance and his chef skills. "I'll be here three days out of the week. A twelve-hour round trip to spend three days with him every week isn't *enough?*"

"You were fixed in Paris! You could have been around for him *whenever* he needed you. I don't think a lot of your timing."

"It's funny how your guilty conscience only works on my behalf," Jo said sullenly. *Why did people always want so much of her? Why was she so stingy with herself?*

"Oh, so what do you want me to do? Quit my job in New York? I've already stretched it out here as much as I can. I've got to get back."

"What do you want *me* to do?" Jo asked. "Say no to this? *He's holding a lawsuit over my head!*" Thank you, Gabriel Delange. Otherwise, she could never excuse this, to herself or anyone else. Otherwise, she would be in Paris, fighting her father's depression every day.

Again the thought of her father, those three days without her, sitting at his table rolling that rolling pin bleakly, weighed down on her, grim and gray. *Oh, Papa.*

"He'll still be seeing his therapists, and I'll have someone come in every morning and evening to check on him." Even though he was perfectly capable of taking care of himself, a voice in her head pointed out.

Estelle zipped her suitcase with grim intention: *I'm out of here.* "And what are you going to tell him? About why you're spending half the week in Nice?"

"Sainte-Mère," Jo corrected. Although . . . did her father have to know the exact location? There were a lot of good chefs around Nice. She just had to pick one in rare contact with her father. . . . "Daniel Laurier!" she said triumphantly.

Estelle looked at her blankly.

"*You know,* the guy who took over Le Relais d'Or in Saint-Amour when he was nineteen? Dark hair? Intense? On TV all the time?"

"I can't believe you like chefs so much," Estelle muttered. "You actually know all the starred chefs by name? Didn't you get enough of that level of narcissism when we were kids?" She cast a guilty but bitter glance in the direction of their father's apartment building, a couple of *arrondissements* over.

Jo frowned, and plowed forward. "I'll tell Papa that I'm working with him. He won't have any problem with that."

"Going after a chef that's worth something, I see." Her father rolled that damn rolling pin. "I can't really blame you."

"Papa. I want to keep writing cookbooks. When I met with, with Daniel Laurier to ask about a recipe for *French Taste,* the idea just developed. Working with him is a great opportunity for me. You didn't think the only cookbook I would ever do would be yours?"

Her father shot her a glance and said nothing.

Ah. Maybe he had, in fact, wanted to be her sole

center of attention. He made her heart ache. And that heart stretched away from the ache toward the south and the scent of jasmine, in pure yearning to be free.

"Come on, Papa, help me with this recipe." She pulled one from his cookbook, a simple but delicious pea puree that he could do perfectly well, even with a hampered left hand. "Please?"

But he got up and left the room.

And left her with her aching heart. Yes, he was the one who chose to isolate himself, but that didn't make him any less alone.

"We've got Matt out there," Raphaël told Gabriel, stopping on the other side of the pass from him. Younger than Gabriel by six years, Raphaël had fewer of those molten streaks in his hair than Gabriel did, a darker brown. Raphaël had been working with Gabriel since he was twenty, when it had seemed more normal to him that he should come on as chef cuisinier to his famous older brother and still work under him. These days, their unusual hierarchy was starting to chafe. Gabriel didn't know what to do about it. He tried everything he could to share power equally with his brother these days, but old habits of control died hard. He was desperately afraid his brother was just going to up and leave him one day, and even more afraid that might be the best thing Raf could ever do for himself. *Fuck. Why were people's lives always better without him in them?*

"Oh, is that why he came by this afternoon? He wanted a table?" Gabriel was spraying the dome of a chocolate dessert last second with a blend of cocoa butter and chocolate so that it would arrive at the table glistening, glossy, perfect, reflecting every light in the room in its darkness.

It was beautiful, and yet for once, his heart wasn't really in it. Some nights, it was harder to keep forcing your heart out there for people to eat than others. *She dumped people.* She let men fall for all that pistachio and gold of her, and then she dumped them. She had probably boxed up more shirts and mailed them to clear the last remnants of a man out of her life than all his ex-girlfriends put together.

"He's got that, what's-her-name, Nathalie?"

Gabriel stopped. "*Bordel,* is this going to her? You know she's just going to run throw it up again as soon as she can get to the restroom." He stared at the beautiful work of art, utterly deflated. Damn it, the very last thing he needed was to think of some wannabe actress throwing up this bite of his heart, on top of everything else.

"I think she only ordered coffee," Raf said.

"What the hell is wrong with Matt?" *Only ordered coffee.* In *his* restaurant. If that wasn't a sign a man should get out of a relationship with a woman while he still had a chance to survive, Gabriel didn't know what was.

"She's beautiful?" Raphaël suggested cautiously, in the tones of a man who had no idea but was making a wild guess.

"Raf. Remember her at his birthday party? I've never seen *anyone* insist on sucking up more attention for herself. If Matt even stopped to joke with one of us, she started worrying her looks must be going and that was why he didn't love her anymore." He wished Matt had never tried working up in Paris this past winter for Rosier SA, on his quest for something a little more adventurous than running a valley of flowers in Provence, his life destiny as the Rosier patriarch's heir. In Paris, Matt had had to mingle with all those actresses and models with whom the luxury perfume houses packed their perfume launches, and it had turned out to be a very bad environment for a straightforward, wholehearted man who liked to fix things.

"I know. She's as bad as a top chef," Raf agreed,

shaking his head in disgust.

Gabriel gave his brother a disgruntled look. "Well, at least we're that way about our *food*. Not our actual bodies." Fortunately, because he probably had chocolate spray all over his face right now.

"So that makes us better than she is?" Raf challenged wryly.

Gabriel sent the dome through the pass and scowled at his brother. "It's not the same thing at all," he said firmly.

Raf shrugged. "You know Matt's an idiot. I think he tried to head-butt his older cousins into listening to him one too many times when he was little, and it did some damage."

"She doesn't even look at him! It's like she literally cannot see him, only whether he is looking at her."

"Yeah, but Matt's a big man. He'll pour himself out in the service of that need for a long time before he gets to the end of himself. Can we talk about something less depressing? How's *your* love life?"

"Fuck you, Raf."

Raphaël grimaced, with complete sympathy. "See, you need a girlfriend."

"Don't we all?" Gabriel said, even more tersely still. "If you've got any tips for getting a woman to put up with our hours, you just let me know, Raf."

Raphaël shrugged, sticking with that flippant cockiness he had been practicing as the younger brother for all their lives. "I'm trying to land them with great sex, myself."

A fractional pause of Gabriel's fingers on a slim stick of a white *biscuit* dipped, just the tip, into brilliant red strawberry *coulis*, to be balanced expertly on a curlicue of strawberry sorbet. "And how is that working out for you?"

A brief grim glimpse in Raphael's face of that same bone-deep loneliness Gabriel felt, and then he shrugged. Six years younger, that meant he had six fewer years of failure at relationships under his belt and correspondingly more cockiness. Or a determination to pretend so. "I believe I'm too big a fish for this small pond. Maybe we should think of opening a second restaurant somewhere more single women live."

"That will certainly help with the hours problem," Gabriel said sardonically.

"I could run that one," Raf said, and Gabriel looked at his brother a moment.

He had had even less sleep than usual, in order to take a woman to a train station and have her tell him with beaming delight how the fact that she would have no problem dumping him resolved all her issues. It was not a good time for him to try to deal with his brother's increasingly powerful, carefully repressed, desire to be in charge of his own place, to have his name lead. *Please don't dump me, too, Raf. Please don't dump me and make it clear that not sharing your life with me makes yours so damn much better.*

Raf grimaced oddly and swiped one of the macarons Gabriel was setting up, biting into its sweet caramel. "So, Pierre Manon's daughter looked cute."

"Don't even think about it, Raf."

His brother looked surprised and then laughed. "She seemed to be pretty focused on you, Gabe."

Gabriel couldn't help smiling at that, despite himself. She sure as hell had, hadn't she. The memory of her eyes dilating, as she let jasmine curl around her wrists and hold her trapped for him, kicked arousal all through him again.

She sees you, a voice whispered through him. *She's not like that Nathalie person Matt's got. She looks at you, and she likes what she sees.*

God, that was so deliciously enticing. Why the hell did she have to tell him she dumped people?

"So how is that idea of holding her father's life

hostage to get her to submit to your sexual desires working out?"

Gabriel huffed a breath and then growled at his brother, low and dangerous. "I am not exactly—we're *not* sleeping together."

"Oh, is that why you're so grumpy? How the hell did you screw up? She looked at you like she could eat you up. It was so cute. You kept feeding her desserts instead of you."

"We're going to work on a cookbook together!"

"You *would* consider that a good substitute for sex. Has it ever occurred to you that you might be over-obsessed with your work?"

"It's not a *substitute*. It's just—" He loved her fascinated arousal—even if she was a damn sadist about not following through on it. But it was more than wonderful to watch her melt at everything he fed her. Like he was a prince. "It's *bait*," Gabriel growled. "She said it was a dream come true."

"Poor kid." Raphaël shook his head. "That's how my nightmare started. Thinking that working with you would be a dream come true."

Gabriel tried not to wince. Raphaël had been young and bright-eyed, and maybe Gabriel had suckered him into this job. But he was so damn good at it. And Gabriel liked working with his brother. They hadn't killed each other, in over eight years, and before that, when he was Pierre's chef pâtissier in Paris, Gabriel had hardly ever seen him. He had missed most of his brother's adolescence, in fact.

Merde, he had missed most of his own.

"It's going to be an ironclad contract," he snapped. "She *has* to finish the cookbook with me." Has to. It made him sick to his stomach, to think of the woman who had been curled in his lap on those stairs deciding within a month or so that he was just a nightmare she had to get through. That she wanted to dump him but didn't have the choice.

Raphaël reached across the pass and punched him lightly in the shoulder. "I'm just teasing you, Gabe. Just try not to be too much of a beast to her. And remember, no matter how much she wants to get away from you, you can always hold her father's life over her head."

Chapter 12

Jolie's little balcony in the *vieux village* faced Gabriel's exactly, so that if each leaned far enough they could almost, almost touch each other's hands, three floors above the flower-filled pedestrian street. She wondered if any star-crossed lovers in the history of this town had ever fallen to their death as they pushed just that little bit farther to try to brush fingertips. If she and Gabriel had been children, they would have had a system to send a little box back and forth with messages and tiny presents. If they had been friendly neighbors, they would have shared a clothesline.

Jolie stood on her bare balcony in the old part of town, amid those shady, flowered stone streets not far from the restaurant, and curled her fingers around the rail, gazing at Gabriel, who stood with his own hands curved around his railing across the way, surrounded by pots of red geraniums. It had been a bit of a surprise, after he finished carrying her suitcases up for her and left, to have him pop out on the other balcony and grin at her. "You just happened to have a cousin who didn't need this apartment right across from you?"

He shrugged, noncommital. "The Rosier family, on my mother's side, is pretty extensive. And they've been in the fragrance industry here for centuries, so it's astonishing how many odd bits and pieces of property they have here and there."

Yes, but that didn't directly answer her question, did it?

She stretched her fingers out of pure curiosity. When he extended his own hand, about two feet rested between them. She leaned farther. He shook his head and dropped his hand back to the rail.

"You're no fun," she complained.

He laughed. "Do you want me to leap over the rail?"

Ooh. Yeah. Yeah, that would be hot, him bursting into her apartment in one monstrous lunge. . . .

His hands curled a little more deeply into the rail. His body shifted.

"It's a three-floor drop!" she exclaimed, panicked.

"That is about like you, to look at me like that with a three-floor drop between us. Trust me, I can jump this. Keep looking at me like that and you'll find out."

Her breath stopped. Her body melted.

He gathered himself into a spring.

"Stop!" she yelled, covering her eyes. "I'm not looking at you, all right? *And I'm not looking at you any particular way, even when I do.*"

"You know what I would do, if I did leap over there?" he asked conversationally.

The lips of her sex curled just from the question. "Uhh—"

His voice deepened. "Give it some thought, Jolie. A man who has just jumped across a two-meter gap, three floors up, to get to you."

She grabbed hold of the railing again.

"And it stays hot at night," he murmured. "You'll want to leave your windows open. Is that a nice thought to take to bed with you? That I might leap over that gap in the middle of the night?"

Hot damn. Was that ever a thought to take to bed.

"And do . . . something. Let's not go into the details."

"Why not?" she squeaked. And clapped her hand back over her eyes. She had not just said that.

The purring growl from him crawled all over her bones. "Because when I do leap over that gap, I want you to tell me every single thing you imagined me doing. I wouldn't want my own ideas to get in the way of your creativity. You seem to have a lot of it—where I'm concerned."

He was going to kill her. "You had better not leap across that gap! You could fall! Knock on the damn door!"

A little pause, and then a slow, slow grin. "Why, thank you, Jolie. I may very well take you up on that."

And, of course, her whole body just went *yummy.*

He watched her a second, his eyes glittering, but finally released his balcony railing with a sigh. "I've got to get back to the restaurant. The dinner rush will start soon." He half turned and paused, suddenly diffident, hopeful. "Come eat with me?"

It just undid her, the way he said that. All aggressive, all *yes-you-like-it* arrogance all the time— and when he invited her to enjoy his work, so exceptional that people flew in private planes halfway around the world to eat it, he was as shy and eager as a would-be-cocky teenager trying to coax a girl into watching his baseball game.

"Of course, I will," she said. "How could I resist?"

"We need a system," Gabriel told Jolie the next morning, falling into step with her in the soft pre-dawn. Fortunately, he didn't have trouble catching up with anyone, let alone someone half his size striding down cobblestoned streets with her head bent and a gym bag slung over her shoulder. Slowing down was more his problem. "Maybe whistles. *You know how to whistle, don't you, Jo?*" He switched to English for the quote, making his voice as breathy as he could.

"You so do not resemble Lauren Bacall in any shape, fashion, or form," Jolie told him grumpily.

"Well, then, you say it to me. And then all I have to do is whistle when I want you to come." He grinned.

Jo cut him a dark look.

"Down," he added limpidly. He took her gym bag and slung it with his over his own shoulder. "When I want you to come down from your apartment. So we can walk together to the gym." This was nice. He was used to the ephemeral, to seizing the moment, to pleasures that took all his effort and then disappeared in a mouthful, but still he didn't know if he dared think too much about how nice this was, walking through the pre-dawn streets. He had never dated anyone who got up as early as he did.

Jolie grunted. And she had been in such a good mood after he finished feeding her at the restaurant the night before. After she trailed, blissful and stuffed, back into the night to her new apartment, he had pretty much floated through the rest of the evening.

He peered at her. "Do you need coffee? I could have brought you a cup."

"By leaping over the railings with it?" she said snappishly. "Don't blame me when you get burned."

"Don't worry, I've handled hot things before." He grinned at her.

Jolie stamped extra hard on the paving stones, and he caught her arm agreeably when that made her almost twist her ankle. He would have liked to be holding her hand again. It was just a little unnerving to reach for it, though, given what she had told him about her penchant for getting sick of men. He had been dumped so many damn times.

With aggressive come-ons, at least you knew where you stood. Holding hands, you got—hopeful.

"You don't seem to have gotten enough sleep," he said. "Thinking of me?"

She shot him a glare hotter than hot caramel.

His lips parted as realization sank deliciously all through him. "*Merde*, you were." His voice dropped to a rumble. "Thinking of me. All. Night. Long."

That was the sweetest, most erotic victory that had

ever surged through his veins. She was going to *kill* him if she kept doing things like that.

She glared at him, livid.

"I thought we should date a little longer before I actually did come leaping over the balcony," he said apologetically. "Considering the way you reacted last time I knocked on the door at midnight. I wanted to, though. Does that make you feel better?"

"If you don't stop consoling me for not having had sex with me, I will kill you," Jolie said between her teeth.

He sighed. "You are so illogical. Isn't that what got you upset? What did you want me to say? That I didn't come by because I wasn't interested? That sounds a hell of a lot ruder to me. Plus, it's not even true."

"Nrggggh!" Jolie grasped a chunk of her hair and yanked.

"Here, let me have that." Gabriel freed her poor hair from her fist and linked his fingers with the misbehaving hand. *Putain,* but that made the whole walk better. And it had been so damn fun already.

Walking through the pre-dawn streets, the scent of jasmine barely awake, cicadas singing, while the cutest thing he had ever seen sulked because he hadn't invaded her apartment. It was so much more fun than every other morning he had ever walked by himself to the gym that he didn't know what to do with that much enjoyment.

"You know, all coffee does," he said, "is kick your heartbeat higher. So if you'll excuse me"—He flipped her against the nearest jasmine-covered wall so fast she was still stumbling when his mouth closed over hers. One kiss, hot, hard, and headily deep. She made a sound, her fingers sinking into his biceps, and he jerked his head up before he could completely lose his mind. "There." He took one of those hands digging convulsively into his biceps and placed it flat over his heart instead. "It worked for me. See? What about you?" His hand slipped over her heart, and it was hardly his fault that women's hearts were tucked behind their breasts like that, was it?

Jolie gave a little sighing sound, closing her eyes as she sank against the jasmine, surprising him into having to catch her arm to help her stay up.

Heat flushed his entire body. Wow.

That was so hot.

He glanced back up the street. Really, carrying her back to her apartment before Madame Delatour saw them like that and spending the next two hours inside it with her was all the workout he needed this morning. He bet he could let her practice her flexibility, too.

Lava-hot joy surged through him. Now that would be an *awesome* way to start a day.

Jolie got her hand up to circle around his wrist, just above the hand pressed to her brea—*heart*. She didn't seem to be able to do much with it, though, like force herself to pull it off. "About sex," she said.

He grinned with pure, hungry delight. "I love how you think about that even more than I do."

She tugged on his wrist in pique, but by accident he forgot to let her budge it. Her breast felt so damn good. And that glaze in her eyes even better. "If we—you know—do it," she managed.

If, right. That was so funny. Gabriel was smart enough not to laugh, though.

"We have to be professional about it," she said.

"*What?*"

She floundered. "I mean—just sex. And not let it interfere with our professional relationship."

He scowled at her. Their professional relationship was him feeding her and watching her melt in orgasmic delight. How the hell separate did she want them to get?

Her eyes pleaded with him. "You have to not get upset when I say I'm done."

He snatched his hand back, as if she had just crisped his palm black. You would think he would know after all those years playing with fire that getting burnt fucking hurt. "*You* say you're done?" he snapped, for something to say to make himself feel better. "What about me? Why don't I get to say it?"

She frowned. Well, good. At least it bothered her to have the idea turned back on her. It didn't seem to bother her that long, though. "I don't have any patience," she explained apologetically. "You probably have more."

No one, in his whole entire life, had ever accused him of patience, which was a weird thing, because there was almost nothing a man needed more of to succeed in his field.

Patience.

Persistence.

Passion.

And, all right, a healthy dose of fury when necessary. "No," he said flatly. "No fucking way."

She gaped at him. Damn it, there went his prince image *again.*

Well, tough damn luck. "If we have *sex*, and you dump me after you get all those orgasms out of your system, I get to get as upset as a I damn well please."

He didn't know how calming Jolie found her yoga after that, but he had one hell of a weight workout. It was just a damn shame the gym didn't allow people to throw some of those weights across the room when they needed to.

Chapter 13

He half-expected Jolie to duck out of their cookbook session that morning, but she showed up—in professional shoes, with round black toes, rolling and tightening an apron over a white chef's jacket, her hair all tucked up. *Putain*, but she was cute. He wondered if she thought that get-up quelled his imagination.

He smiled at her, the way a sabertooth smiles at some adorable little herbivore wandering into its lair, and welcomed her into his office. It was the first time since every able-bodied family member among the Rosiers and Delanges had pitched in to renovate the mill to his specifications that he regretted his office was glass-walled.

She gave him a very stern, very professional look. He wondered what he could do to get her to produce that stern, professional look when he was sitting on, say, his couch, all relaxed, just as she wandered into grabbing distance.

"Are you free?" he checked. "I forgot to ask about your promotional events. Just let me know when you need to be gone for one."

Her eyes slid away.

"You haven't gotten invited to do any promotional events?" he realized, startled. With Pierre Manon's name on the cookbook? "You need a better publicist. You want the number of mine?"

It outraged him to think Pierre would profit from it, but *merde*. Her tiny font name on that cover deserved something.

"Papa's had a stroke, all right?" she said tensely. An unhappier tension than the one he inspired in her, he could feel the difference right away. Nice to have the confirmation that he was so much better for her than her damn father. "He's not up to the demonstrations."

"Really?" Gabriel tried to quell the sick feeling of pity. That *salaud* was *not* getting pity out of him in addition to every other damn thing he had stolen. "Was the stroke that bad?"

She looked at his desk a long moment. "He could do demos," she finally muttered, low. "Not as fast, not as graceful, but he could manage. But he feels uncomfortable. He doesn't want people to see him like this. His nurses told me depression was normal."

Yeah, Pierre never could stand people seeing him when he was down. He had tucked his tail between his legs when he lost that star and crawled away like a dog. Gabriel had felt an acute sense of victory at the time. *I guess you should have valued me, connard.*

"But it's your first cookbook," it occurred to him, looking at that piquant face gone somber. Somber didn't suit her. "You must have been so excited when it came out."

She looked through his glass walls at the activity in the kitchens. "Papa's stroke was only a few weeks before the release. I kind of had other things than happy excitement to focus on at the time." She shot him a glance. "Sometimes I wonder, now, if he was stressing about what might happen when you saw that Rose on the cover."

Fuck. Gabriel felt a weird shock of relief at the timing. Because if Pierre was heading toward a stroke, and it had occurred *after* Gabriel sent that lawsuit notice, then . . . what a hellish thing to have on one's conscience. "You can't blame me for that, Jolie. I hadn't had any contact with him in ten years, at the time. Other than occasional subtle put-downs of his work in interviews, but come on. He's spent his life in top kitchens, he can stand that much heat."

She looked confused. "No, I'm not blaming you." Her head sank a little. "Maybe I'm blaming me," she muttered, very low.

"Blaming *you*? You couldn't have been more than fourteen years old."

"I pushed him to put the Rose on the cover," she reminded him. "I wanted it so much. It was always my favorite."

A quick flick of painful pleasure. That dessert had meant so much to him. Beautiful, famous, photographed by everyone. Proof in and of itself that Pierre Manon had been right to put his faith in him as his chef pâtissier, despite his youth, proof that he deserved more respect than Pierre was offering him, proof even to his girlfriend that he was really a beautiful man on the inside and she should be tolerant of the fact that she never saw him. And then. . . .

Jolie grimaced. "He hesitated. I couldn't figure out why he didn't want it, but I pushed him for it."

"Jolie. All the reasons that Rose made him uncomfortable happened well before you had anything to do with it and are his own fault. He could have owned up to it with you, right then. Said, 'No, I don't really feel right claiming this as my work.' If he had an uneasy conscience, he must have known enough to realize he shouldn't do it. If. Personally, I think he felt completely comfortable claiming it as his work, that he didn't give a damn at all about me and my reaction, and therefore his stroke didn't have anything to do with the cookbook at all."

She sent him a resentful look but didn't have the nerve to argue. *Yes, I do know your father better than you do, thank you. That's the difference between working with him sixteen hours a day as his chef pâtissier for four years and visiting in his office from time to time.*

Merde, no wonder she kept putting up that dog-collar-fence thing when he stepped close to her. She had her father's complete absence from her family as a glaring warning. On the other hand, at least if he got through that fence of hers, she was never going to be able to yell at him, *I didn't know what the life was like!*

No, she knew what the life was like, and so would skip the blame and just go straight to dumping him matter-of-factly.

Damn it.

"Maybe we should focus on your next cookbook," he said.

Her face brightened immediately. "Would you—could you—I know this is probably not the best moment to ask, but could you possibly show me your Rose?"

An image of that ephemeral, blushing fragility flashed through his mind, that delicate, vulnerable thing he had poured out to the world to try to win—everything. The gift of himself that had been used and abused, leaving him with nothing. "No. I thought *French Taste* was meant to be an amateur cookbook."

"I would just like to see you do it," she said wistfully.

"You had your father's version," he retorted, clipped. "No. Now, for your *French Taste*, how long do you usually spend working with each chef you're featuring?"

Jolie searched his face, her own slumping a second in disappointment. And he felt a pang, an urge he had not felt in ten years, to offer her a beautiful, delicate, hopeful Rose just so she wouldn't feel a second's disappointment in him.

He clamped that urge back, hard, covering it with a big, protective hand.

Jolie pulled on her professional attitude. "It depends on the chef and how much time he can spare at once. Simon Casset just spent the whole day with me. He said it was easier for him to focus on one thing, all at once. But I think Philippe Lyonnais wants us to work over several afternoons. He's going to show me some macaron recipes. Dominique Richard has promised to show me his *millefeuille* recipe, and I *might* include his *éclair au chocolat*, but I'm not sure yet. He's like Philippe, he wants several two-hour visits rather than one long one. And Luc Leroi can barely spare an hour at a time. He's exquisitely well-mannered about it, though."

Exquisitely well-mannered. Gabriel scowled. "There are a lot of exceptional French chefs who are sixty, too, you know."

"But the focus of this book is on the new generation. The chefs under forty. Didn't I mention?"

No, she had not mentioned that. *Dominique Richard*, for God's sake. If she liked being hit on by big aggressive men, Dom would be right up her alley. And if she liked princes, she'd probably be fantasizing about Luc Leroi all night. Instead of *him.*

"Simon's married now, you know," she said, an annoyingly thoughtful amusement in her voice. How transparent was he? "And Philippe's engaged."

"*Simon?*" The man who was so obsessive and one-track minded, he got off work to go train for iron distance triathlons? How had *he* had the time?

"It's really cute. His fiancée is so bouncy and so enthusiastic, and the expression on his face when he looks at her, it's just—priceless."

Simon Casset. Who pretty much defined geek. *Putain de merde*, Gabriel should never have stuck with the restaurant business. He should have opened some *salon de chocolat* with slightly more reasonable hours, even if you couldn't in a million years do the same kind of melt-at-a-glance work in it that you did in a three-star restaurant. *Simon* was married. And Gabriel didn't even have a girlfriend.

He was pretty sure Jolie wasn't going to let him claim her as a girlfriend.

"And Philippe's engaged now." She said it like she was patting a dog reassuringly on the head. It made this particular dog want to growl. "I just mention it in case you haven't heard."

He had heard, and he didn't need it rubbed in. He was the older than both the other men.

"None of them are in the restaurant business, though," she said, which was exactly what *he* was thinking, although his reasons were considerably more defensive. "So it's up to you, how you want to schedule interviews and the time to work with me. I'm grateful you're willing to contribute."

Was it unreasonable of him to be a little pissed off at her professionalism here? After all, he was holding her hand and kissing her in jasmine and promising to invade her apartment in the middle of the night. She could probably get away with expecting some personal favors.

Professional. He would show her professional. He gave her a slow smile. "Well, let's get started."

Chapter 14

❝ The trick is to find something of yours that a good amateur chef could have a remote hope of reproducing," Jolie said, trying to keep a professional tone. That slow smile of Gabriel's made her feel just a little—menaced. "It's almost incompatible with the idea of a three-star chef, but that's what I want to do."

"How about this one with raspberries?" Gabriel opened a big binder, flipping to a photo.

Jolie looked at the dessert. And then looked at him. The bottom layer was a perfect flat rectangle of red, kind of like a fruit strip that had grown up, gone to college, and become President of France. It even had gold flecks in it. The next layer was an exquisite marbling of red and white. Then a rectangle of chocolate. Then curves of chocolate cream as perfectly spiraled as a unicorn's horn. Then a red roll of melted sugar marbled with real gold leaf, like some fairy creature's cigar. And finally one fine arch of red that soared up into the stratosphere before bringing the eye back down to the layered base.

She smiled. "You're really cute, you know that?"

"*Cute?*" He looked at the photo, offended.

"Did I mention this cookbook is for *amateurs*?"

"You don't think they could do that?"

She laughed. He was more than cute, he was adorable. This man just got to her, every way there was.

"If we took off the arc?"

She shook her head.

"And the gold leaf?"

"And the half-molten sugar that you have to roll with your bare hands into a perfect cylinder?" Jolie suggested dryly.

Gabriel sighed. "This might be harder than I thought."

A moment ago her skin had been prickling with a sense of his sexual menace, and now she wanted to give him a hug. He charged her emotions like some super current. "You can do it," she said encouragingly.

His head lifted. "Of course I can do it. Who ever suggested anything else?"

He flipped through a book of photos of different desserts he had done, thinking.

"You could do your Rose," Jolie said again wistfully.

The page froze mid-turn. "For *amateurs?*"

"Well, no, but—you could show it to me, and I could take notes, and we could put it in *your* cookbook."

"Thanks, Jolie, but I don't care to imitate your father's cover." His jaw had gone very hard. "And I don't care to hide the Rose in my cookbook like a secret. So I think you—he's—effectively stolen that from me."

Jolie hung her head. She couldn't begin to tell him how much she loved that red-streaked white chocolate Rose flourishing around that secret, melting heart. Now that she knew the rough, wild man who had made it, she loved it even more. All the softness, all the beauty and wonder of him that he had ever put out there to the world was right there, in that Rose.

"You could make it just once," she whispered. "For me to just try." That would be—something wonderful in a way she didn't know how to say, to taste that Rose from his hands. Made for her.

His jaw tightened even further. He did not look at her. "I thought we were going to work on your *French Taste.*"

Jolie rubbed the back of her neck. And nodded.

"That's—of course. Let's do that."

She felt guilty about how long it took him to relax again, flipping through his photos. Eventually he did, though, as she kept grabbing pages to look at a dessert more closely, to exclaim. A smile slowly softened that hardened mouth, and then all at once, his usual ready grin flashed back, as if it just couldn't be kept away.

In the end he decided on a very simple—to him—*réligieuse au caramel au beurre salé*, a salted-butter caramel réligieuse.

"An exceptional take on a great classic." Jolie nodded in approval. "That will be perfect. We can maybe even share the *choux* recipe between yours and Dominique's éclairs."

Gabriel stopped mixing, his eyes narrowing.

"Or maybe not," Jolie allowed, grinning. "Maybe I can put both yours and Dominique's *choux* recipe up on my website and challenge readers to test them both and vote for which one is best."

"There's not much variation on the classic *choux* recipe," Gabriel told her. "But where there is variation, it's because my way is better. Now break the yolks into the *pâte* and mix. *Fort*, Jolie." His hand slid down her arm in one long stroke and closed around her hand on the wooden spoon. "Like this." With the barest exertion of his arm muscles, he took over hers, bringing her stirring to the rhythm he wanted.

Jolie stared at her arm in some surprise. She was used to it being quite a strong arm. Even with her knowledge of Gabriel's expertise and the obviousness of his muscles, she still hadn't quite been expecting her own arm to be overpowered so easily.

Heat flushed through her. Until she stood in his kitchen door and heard him roar, she had never in her life been tempted by the thought of being overpowered.

And now it was pretty much all she could think of: that power and passion bursting into her life. Vaulting across a three-floor drop into her apartment. Taking over her body.

"Don't stop," Gabriel rumbled into her ear, as his hand eased on hers and her own slowed. "You have to mix it hard until all the steam rises off it."

His body felt so hot and hard behind hers. Her nape prickled to be so exposed to him as she forced herself to concentrate on her mixing. The steam from the *choux* dough flushed over her face as a heavy warm sigh brushed over her neck.

All the hairs on her nape rose in pleasure.

"There." Gabriel pulled the pan off the burner and turned away a moment to correct a junior cook's plate preparation error that neither of his *sous* had caught. Even in the midst of his focus on her, he seemed to catch everything that happened in the kitchen. But in another sense, he barely seemed to notice the bodies brushing against them as his kitchen team continued their tasks. He was used to having people make space for him. For over a decade now, he had been the master of his domain, the one who heard *yes, chef* to anything he said.

Or—wait—her eyebrows flexed together, and she looked up at him. He would have been used to making space for other people, too, though, right? All his adolescence and adult life, working in a blend of many bodies, many motions. He ruled this space, but he had to rule it in a way that let everyone accomplish their incredible tasks, too, dozens of scrambling fairytale princes and princesses trying to fulfill the demands of a masterful monster. *Spin this sugar into gold. Count these grains of salt, fleck by fleck. Cross this molten chocolate with a boat made out of snow.*

Funny, no one ever wondered what drove the wicked monster to seek such impossible achievement.

"Meanwhile," Gabriel said, "start the milk infusing with vanilla, and start the caramel." He had two pans on burners, one with a vanilla bean floating in milk, the other with sugar over heat, before he even finished the sentence. "Keep an eye on those while you're making the heads and the bodies."

Jo grinned, filling a pastry bag with the *choux* dough. "I don't think having an amateur chef do anything else while trying to make caramel besides watch the pan like a hawk would be a good idea."

Gabriel looked around them blankly. "You *aren't* doing anything else. I mean—just squeezing dough onto baking sheets. Can't you watch a pan at the same time?"

Jo laughed. "You have to *slow down*. No one else moves as fast as you."

He frowned. Then he frowned harder. "What is that supposed to mean? Are you talking about—damn it, *I don't know how!*"

"Watch." Jolie caught his wrist. He stilled. "Just—watch me. I'm an amateur. Tell me what to do, tell me all your tricks and tips to make my technique better, but let me do it. Everything you see, every time you think, *oh, if she only knew how to do this,* or, *this is what she needs to know,* tell me, and I'll take notes and filter out the most feasible tips for readers."

He blinked at last at the word *readers.* "*Putain,* Jolie, you should have warned me right at the beginning that you weren't talking about sex for once. My brain nearly split. I can imagine quite a lot of impossible things, but you letting me give you tips to improve your sex technique is just not one of them."

"I hope you weren't talking about sex when you said you didn't know how to slow down, either," Jolie retorted dryly, before she thought.

He grinned—very slowly. And his hands flew. "No, see, Jolie, this caramel is going to melt fast, and has to be handled *fast.*" He tilted the pan over the burner as the sugar melted to gold. "And this milk is going to infuse slowly, and you have to let it simmer a long, long, long, long time." He held a palm over the pan to check its temperature. "And these *petits choux* here"— his big hand closed over hers on the pastry bag and tightened, nice and slow—"have to keep going in a steady, firm rhythm until they're all . . . ready."

She looked from his hand entirely encompassing hers, up that strong arm, to the body enclosing her, and then to his face. He leaned into her even more, his grin wicked. "And *I* can do all three of those things *all at once.*"

He was impossible. He was delicious. She so desperately wanted to bite that smug mouth of his.

"But in fact," he said soulfully, "I—and I don't want you to feel self-conscious about your one-track focus, I keep telling you *I don't mind*—but again, I myself was thinking about a broader picture than just sex. More the whole—" He made a big sweep of his arms around them, like he was enclosing them in a bubble, and then gestured back and forth between her chest and his.

"Has *no one* ever hit you?" Jolie asked. "That's so hard to believe."

"I think your father threw a pan across the kitchen in our last big fight, but I caught it."

"Did you throw it back at him?"

"It spattered me with hot oil, Jolie! Of course I did. He was out of control."

Funny, her strongest memories of her father from that same period were of the two of them slumped on a couch eating potato chips at one in the morning, their conversation drifting sleepily over all kinds of subjects—school, the latest political headline, food, what Jolie wanted to do when she grew up, how she had damn well better not marry a chef—until one or both of them fell asleep.

She had seen some of her father's tempers in his kitchen through the glass walls of his office—from which standpoint they had seemed bright and fascinating, like flashes of lightning and thunderclouds from the shelter of a securely grounded house—but she had never really experienced them directly. For what little amount of time he did see his daughters, he tried to give them his patience.

Patience. She looked up at Gabriel, who tried hers—deliciously. Like she wanted to beat her head against his chest all the time but would have fun doing it. "All I was *saying* is that you need to remember that other people go slower than you do."

A suspicion of a frown again, his eyes searching her face.

"Take your time."

His frown deepened. "I do know how to take my time when it's necessary, Jolie, but—"

"Just trust me."

He gaped at her and then let out a huff of a laugh. "That's hilarious. Thank you. No."

"I do know my way around kitchens somewhat," Jolie said stiffly.

He blinked again. "I keep losing track of what this conversation is about. All right. Cooking. Making something—beautiful." His hand shot out and whisked the caramel off the burner. "*Pardon.* I know I was supposed to slow down, trust you, and let you handle it, but burnt caramel really stinks."

"And *that* is why we need to make sure no amateur is trying to make a caramel while they have other things to think about," Jolie said firmly.

"Well, that's going to be a tough one for you, then, because you *always* have at least one other thing on your mind."

Chapter 15

B ut the *crème pâtissière* itself went better, Gabriel told himself. Less—argumentative. Well, he liked argumentative, and if Jolie didn't, she surely would have stopped arguing by now. But he had been aiming for something even more seductive than a good argument. Richer. More enticing. Like vanilla-infused milk being whisked into golden caramel, just so, his hand guiding hers, her happy face as he taught her how to avoid lumps. As she tasted the golden rich cream. Oh, so *that* was why he had picked this recipe. It had reminded him of her. How would a pistachio-caramel réligieuse work?

"And fill each little nun *just* the right amount," he said, compressing a grin out of all but the twitching corners of his mouth, as he used the tip to make a hole in the bottom of the *chou* and squirted cream into it until it was entirely full.

Jolie looked at his face suspiciously. "Are you sure I'm the one who always starts thinking about sex?"

"I knew it!" he exclaimed self-righteously. "I knew your mind was going down that track again! *Non, mais*—Jolie. Focus."

She considered the trays full of *choux* that waited for them. "You must have a lot of stamina," she said thoughtfully. "You have to fill a hundred of them with that stuff."

She killed him. He choked, tried not to, and then laughed so hard that he accidentally squirted the damn cream all over himself.

And that made *Jolie* crack up. She laughed so hard she sat down on the floor, and he had to thrust an arm out to keep one of his sous-chefs from running into the unexpected obstacle.

Oh, God, she was *glorious*. She made him so happy.

He dragged her up, so giddy with it, it was all he could do not to—not to do *everything*. Not to stuff himself inside her, for one. He ran his hands up her arms to frame her cheeks and bent down low. "I should make you eat that off me," he growled, still laughing.

Her own laugh choked, and her eyes went very wide and did an involuntary flick down his body and back up.

Merde, he had just been a damn beast again. What the fuck had he been thinking? He wanted to tell her he didn't mean what she thought he meant, but then, of course, if by any chance she liked the idea, he *did* mean it, and then—fine, it was time to blame all the dirty ideas on her again. "The cream, Jolie. Try to focus."

"I know we're talking about the cream," Jolie said blankly, her eyes dilated to a thin rim of green. She flicked a little fingerful of the cream off his jacket and tasted it again.

Putain, so hot. He wondered if she really had only been thinking about the pastry cream. It was quite possible his mind might go down that particular sexual track a lot more easily than hers did.

And now he had two visions. One of her sucking warm, golden pastry cream off his naked body. And one that was—well, the other one.

And he was going to be torn in ungodly torment between those images for the rest of the damn day.

Jolie gave herself a shake and blinked several times, turning to focus on the *choux*. "I had better finish filling these."

He wasn't sure she should practice squeezing

things repeatedly in his vicinity, not right at the moment, not when every single motion of her hand seemed to squeeze over some part of his body—his heart, his dick, the nape of his neck where it would feel so *sweet* to have a little hand squeeze the tension, his butt where it would feel so hot and also just damn *nice* against the slight soreness starting from his excessive workout that morning.

On the other hand, teaching her this recipe *was* what he had contracted with her to do. He sighed, leaned his elbows on the counter to try to keep his arms out of trouble, and nodded. "Go ahead." But he just could not repress the slow grin, or the wink. "I'll give you tips on your technique."

By the time Jolie finished squeezing pastry cream into all those *choux* and glazing them, biting on her lip or even the tip of her tongue when she focused, Gabriel was one melting, hot mass of imagined pleasure, and it was all he could do not to bury his face in his arms on the counter and groan.

But because he could do all *kinds* of impossible things, even, very rarely, contain himself, he reached out to help her untie her apron instead.

She pushed strands of escaped hair back off her flushed face and heaved a breath. "Whoo. I just don't know how you do it all day, without ever tiring."

Her face was so full of admiration for him that he actually managed to bite his tongue on a quite unprincely remark about his stamina. Really, it was *not* his fault. She kept giving him these openings.

And then he couldn't get his mind off them.

She was making him as obsessed with sex as she was.

She ran a hand up the back of her neck, lifting her ponytail off it, and made a flexing, twisting motion of shoulder and neck muscles, then glanced at the clock.

Ten-thirty. He helped her out of her chef's jacket, for no other reason than that he really enjoyed taking over undressing her, and picked up her notebook—which was filled with doodles among her notes, including, prominent in the upper right corner, his Rose. She had drawn a heart around it, her pen running over and over the shape, deepening the lines. He hesitated a moment over that heart, then slapped the notebook closed and handed it to her.

Slipping his own chef's jacket off for a moment, he stepped outside into the alley with her, his motives of the most impure. Like pulling her into his arms and kissing her for a long time to get him through the lunch service after all that squeezing. Maybe grinding his hips a little against hers while he kissed, because his arousal was driving him insane with the need for contact. And then—

"Thank you," she said happily before he could even touch her. "That was wonderful."

Aww. See? Just when his mind was happily managing to concentrate on *just sex* for once, she said something like that, and whirled all the rest of his emotions into the vortex. How was a man supposed to keep focused that way?

"Let me get out of your way for the lunch service. I have to go see Daniel Laurier now, anyway."

His hands froze mid-reach for her. She might as well have grabbed one of the ice baths out of the kitchen and dumped it over his head. "You have to do *what?*"

"Daniel Laurier. You know, Le Relais d'Or." She looked at him blankly, as if it was inconceivable that anyone not have heard of Daniel Laurier.

Well, it *was* inconceivable, but still. "Of course I know him," Gabriel said, aggravated. "Léa Laurier is some kind of cousin of mine. His wife." He put some emphasis on the *wife*. A man couldn't be too careful. Women always thought Daniel was so hot. When he went on TV, his TV hostesses practically leaned over and licked *him* instead of one of his plates. He knew just how to handle it, too, with that kind of gentle, amused, *I'm-married* firmness, while Gabriel always got his hopes up that the pretty hostess could actually fall for him enough to put up with him longer than a month, and then got his stupid heart stomped on again. Damn smug *happily married* Daniel. "I helped him make sure his pastry kitchen didn't collapse, after Léa's father died and he found the whole restaurant on his shoulders."

Gabriel had just been fired by Jolie's father and working to get the funding together for his own restaurant at the time, and he could hardly stand around twiddling his thumbs while his third cousin by marriage got drowned in the impossible sucking vortex that taking over a legendary three-star restaurant had been. Daniel had only been nineteen, for God's sake, and not even risen to sous-chef yet when his girlfriend's famous chef father died. Gabriel softened a second into reminiscence, almost forgiving Daniel for the fact that the other man had been married eleven damn years to a woman who thought the sun rose and set on him. Something Léa managed to do even though she could never actually *see* the sun set on him, since he was always in the kitchen at sunset. "God, he was such a skinny kid. So intense."

Just like Gabriel had been, in fact. But Daniel had turned into a real damn prince, elegant and self-possessed in a way Gabriel couldn't even imagine being. He always felt pretty damn good about himself after he finished filming a TV segment—laughing, energetic, dragging the host or hostess into the fun. He felt as if he had reached into the homes of the audience and they were feeling the energy with him. And then he would catch some clip of Daniel, all graceful, contained passion, and just want to sink in his chair at how big he himself was. How out there. Let loose in a china shop, he would never break a single thing, not even a spiderweb spinning between dishes, but people always thought he would.

"Ooh!" Jolie clapped her hands together, excited. "I might interview *you* about him, your memories of that first year. That would be awesome! It's such an incredible story, how he managed to hold that place together."

Gabriel's jaw locked. "You're supposed to be working with *me.*" *About me. Focused all on me.*

"I had to have some kind of cover story to tell my father," Jolie explained.

"Oh, did you?" Gabriel folded his arms, absurdly embarrassed by the way that made his muscles stand out. Daniel always slipped his hands in his pockets. Nobody knew when Daniel was mad.

"And anyway, I need some more chefs from the south of France for this cookbook, and some more savory food while I'm at it. I've been focusing too much on desserts. Daniel Laurier is perfect!"

Gabriel's jaw ground so hard it hurt. Daniel always was fucking perfect. Three stars, carried a restaurant on his shoulders at nineteen, and managed to hold Léa Laurier at the same time, a woman who just poured her whole life out for him and thought he deserved it. "*I'm* supposed to be your"—*dream come true*—"focus."

"Gabriel, come on. You're going to be busy, starting in about five minutes. Since Daniel Laurier is making his sous-chef executive chef, he has a more relaxed schedule and can actually sit down and talk to me about his decision to step back from the day-to-day handling of the restaurant. Can you imagine the story? A chef's decision to yield control? I've already sold at least one big article on it, and I might be able to get more."

"Just how many projects are you working on exactly, while you have that contract with me? Another cookbook, articles on Daniel—"

"That's how I earn a living, Gabriel. Multiple projects. I love cookbook writing, but cookbooks take a long time, and the money for them comes in really slowly."

She could live off him, he thought sulkily. He had more than enough money for two. She'd probably get pissed off at him if he said that, though.

On the other hand—his face brightened—he never had tried dating someone who was financially dependent on him. Maybe that would convince someone to overlook his hours.

"I'm always doing spin-off articles. Things that come up during my research for the books that would make wonderful short pieces. Sometimes it can be just something tiny, like what Gabriel Delange makes for a quick dinner at home."

"Potato chips," he said on a puff of frustrated laughter. "But don't worry, I can come up with a good quick salad to tell your readers."

"Or what Gabriel Delange would make if life handed *him* a lemon," she continued, her eyes lighting with ideas.

"My *tarte citron,* but I could come up with something new if you want me to. Or five things. How long do you want the article to be? Do you want these to be simple, or is it okay to do something no one else can do?"

Her eyes caught his a moment, and then a smile broke on her face like sunshine. "You are such a sweetheart!"

He was? He wasn't just trying to get all the attention off Daniel Laurier and back on him? But he caught the word, the belief, the glow in her eyes, pressing it hard against his middle, which felt as if it had just whooshed right out of him.

Her hand rose and curved around his cheek, surprising him and her both. But she didn't yank it back. He went still under the touch, taking a long, deep breath, soaking in the sensation of it. "Thank you," she murmured.

"For?" Blackmailing her with her father's health to

make her come work with him?

She seemed to search for words, her palm still curved over his cheek. He should have shaved. "For being you," she finally said, as if that covered it.

It sure as hell covered a lot. For being him. He stared at her, immobilized, as she flushed suddenly, dropped her hand, and ducked out of the alley.

Heading off to see Daniel Laurier.

Who had conclusively proven already that he could get women to fall for *him* forever.

Chapter 16

❝ Gabriel Delange mentioned that he helped you the first year after Henri Rosier died," Jo said, following Daniel's lean, graceful, ground-eating stride through the stone building, nearly two centuries old, that had been remodeled by Daniel's wife's father, Henri Rosier, into the famous Relais d'Or. Before Chef Rosier had repurposed it and turned it into the home of his legendary restaurant, the place had been used to extract the oils from the roses, violets, and jasmine the region was known for, and Jo could swear she could still smell the scents when she stood close to the stone walls. Or maybe that was some scent coming from the kitchens. Henri Rosier, a Rosier cousin who had had the audacity to branch out from the family fragrance business, was widely credited with starting the trend toward subtly incorporating flower flavors into dishes.

"That's right." A quick kick of that contained Laurier smile, the one that the cameras caught so well on television, where Daniel's lips only turned up two millimeters but a person felt as if she had brushed close to something glorious. "That was an—interesting time. I wasn't even remotely ready for a three-star restaurant. But I could hardly walk out and leave it on Léa's shoulders. She was only eighteen herself and had her two younger siblings to take care of, too. Her father's pastry chef didn't have the same qualms about walking out on us, though, so we were rather fortunate your father fired Gabriel just then. If he hadn't stepped in out of a sense of family—" Daniel broke off and shook his head, clearly unable to say they would have *failed*, and possibly unable to believe he was capable of failing, but some thought of it flinching across his mind nevertheless.

"Maybe it was lucky for him you needed him," Jo suggested. Would it have done her father a world of good if he had gone to save someone instead of sinking into brooding defeat after he lost his star? "Maybe it gave him something to do besides just give up."

Daniel's smile deepened, not growing bigger or wider, just richer somehow, more feeling compressed into it. "Gabe? Give up? You don't know him very well, I think."

"So you liked him?" Jo guessed. Daniel was a hard read. All the chefs she researched were a hard read, now that she thought about it, each with a persona he hid behind. But Daniel was definitely the hardest. So contained you wondered how his body didn't split from the density of his emotions, all packed in tight like that. That's probably why he poured so many fantastical creations out of him so fast. "Liked working with him?"

A glance down at her, warmth in the gray eyes. "I had never met anyone like him. He was so—out there." And the man known for his contained cleanness, who never gestured extravagantly, whose hands were usually in his pockets when he wasn't working, spread his arms wide, as the only way he could express Gabriel.

Jo grinned.

Daniel's face warmed further in response to her enthusiasm. "Even compared to Henri, who was quite a force of nature, Gabe was huge. He was only twenty-three, and he couldn't keep a kilo on him, he worked so hard. But even back then you could feel that energy in him. You know, that force he has. These days it's grown so big that you know if Gabriel Delange is in a room when you're two meters from the closed door. You can feel him." He laughed, a low, firm sound, nothing like Gabriel's full-out happiness. "Sometimes you can hear him."

Jo laughed, too, a memory of that roar of his burring over her, making her want to ditch this interview with Daniel and run right back to it, so it could rub over her skin some more.

Daniel came out on the busy terrace of his restaurant, hands in his pockets again, looking around in seeming casualness. But Jo knew chefs, and she knew that gray gaze was seeing every single square millimeter in the place, and woe betide the person responsible for getting something a millimeter wrong. Only one small table sat empty, at the far end, clearly reserved for them.

"And he's such a hopeless romantic." Daniel shook his head, a lingering curve to his lips. Jo peered at him, surprised at the depth of liking. It wasn't that common for top chefs to truly like each other. Some part of them always wanted to make sure everyone knew who was really the best.

"Do you really think so?" she asked, her face softening despite herself.

A quick cut from those steel-gray eyes. "You didn't pay any attention to that Rose you put on the cover of your father's book?"

Ow. Steel could have a very sharp edge. But at least—"You know that Rose was Gabriel's?"

"Every chef in the world knows it was Gabriel's. You're only fooling amateur chefs. And those *chefs cuisiniers* full enough of themselves to truly believe everything that comes out of the pastry kitchen is theirs by virtue of creative osmosis."

"So if he put it on his own cookbook, no one would think he was copying?"

"Hardly," Daniel said. "Everyone would respect him for reclaiming his own." He looked at his watch, an elegant, understated titanium that suited his strong wrist perfectly, and glanced around. There was a sense of movement behind them on the stairs, and Jo shifted automatically to make way for waiters, but instead it was a woman with a straw-blonde ponytail, her hand touching the small of Daniel's back.

He turned to look down at her, and his smile changed—shrinking even further but holding even more, something so intense and reined in so tightly that it hit Jo with a physical force. Wow, that was— what must it be like to be loved like that?

She looked at the other woman as Daniel introduced her as his wife. Léa Laurier was peculiarly beautiful, in a way that didn't quite make sense, with the careless ponytail and the rough ends of hair that hadn't been taken care of in a while, no make-up, high cheekbones, bony wrists, and long fingers currently stained with paint. She was like a super model whose angular body seemed awkward in repose, but who turned into something stunning when the camera hit. Only Léa didn't need a camera. As soon as her eyes met Daniel's, her face lit, and that generous radiance gave her a luminescent beauty no trick of camera or lighting could ever imitate.

And everything about Daniel softened, seemed to ease. He led them to the open table, holding out chairs for first Jolie and then his wife.

Léa, too, was tracking everything that happened in the restaurant, Jo saw, and Daniel smiled ruefully, catching his wife's eyes after she finished checking the nearby table for the diners' reactions to the dishes a waiter had just set before them. "We shouldn't eat here," he told her. "Maybe we should try the restaurant next door. Or I hear you've got a couple of cousins in Sainte-Mère who aren't half bad."

She laughed wryly and tried to turn her focus back on their own table.

"So Mademoiselle Manon is interviewing me about the decision to name an executive chef," Daniel said, raising his eyebrows at his wife as if inviting her to comment.

"What did you tell her?" Léa asked instead.

He gave that restrained but somehow enormous smile of his, the one that held so much warmth. "So far, we've been talking about Gabriel Delange."

She laughed, with open pleasure. "Gabe is wonderful. I guess the two of you never could have managed to share this restaurant—he wanted control, and it was yours to control—but he made such a difference, that first year." Her eyes caught Jo's, very warm. "What do you think of him?"

Jo was very surprised to find her own gaze lowering and herself blushing a little bit. Oh, come on. Traitorous cheeks.

Léa, on the other hand, sat up a little straighter, delighted. She caught her husband's eyes just a second, glanced back at Jolie, and carefully kept her mouth shut.

"So about the executive chef decision," Jolie said firmly. "How *were* you able to reach the point when you stepped back and left the day-to-day control in someone else's hands?"

A waiter came up, and she paused to savor the luxury of choices for a moment, and when she finally chose and looked up, Léa had her hand curled over one of Daniel's, and he was watching Jo with a faint, intensely satisfied curve of his mouth, making her glad she had let her delight in the menu show.

She waited until the waiter left before repeating her question about the executive chef choice. Interviewers had to be persistent.

"I didn't have anything more to prove to anyone," Daniel said slowly. "That could be proven in a kitchen." He turned his hand over and closed it around Léa's, without looking at her. One strong thumb stroked over the tendons in her hand, found a spot of dry paint by texture, and rubbed over it gently.

Jo let the silence draw out, an interview technique, waiting for more.

"I wanted a chance to be with my wife," Daniel said, still low and quiet and careful. "And to be with myself. I thought maybe I didn't have to put every single bite of my whole self out there on a plate for someone to eat.

Maybe just some bites would do. And when you reach that point, it's time to let another chef step up."

"Someone who wants to let himself be eaten alive?" Jolie murmured uneasily. Images of her father and Gabriel both flashed through her mind, Gabriel's enthusiasm, her father's grim depression, as if he had been eaten up and spat out again.

"Yes," Daniel said firmly. Léa linked her fingers with his and squeezed once.

"How did you feel about it?" Jolie asked her.

Léa was silent a long moment, that radiance of hers growing quieter and not in a bad way, as if a cloud had gently diffused the rays of the sun. "Deeply happy," she finally said softly. And then, after a moment Jolie let stretch: "It's good. Good to have time to be something else. But you know, don't you? Your father was Pierre Manon."

Jolie tried to hide the profound sadness that winced through her whenever someone referred to her father in the past tense, as if he was either no longer alive at all or, at best, he no longer deserved to call himself by his own name. No wonder her father believed the same thing.

Although . . . hadn't he had some role in getting that attitude started? He was the one who had treated the loss of a star as his own death. He could have come back fighting. He could have shown everyone he was still alive. She brought a hand up to rub the nape of her neck.

"You have to know exactly how much being a top chef consumes everything else," Léa said.

"And everyone," Jolie agreed reluctantly. This interview wasn't supposed to be about her. "Wife, children, friends, himself."

Léa had married at eighteen, in a moment of terrible crisis—the sudden death of her legendary father, two younger siblings to finish raising, and the world-famous three-star restaurant on her shoulders.

So Jo couldn't blame her for getting caught in a cycle—marrying what she knew, another chef, getting sucked into that.

She wondered how long the abnegation of her own life had seemed natural to Léa, or if there was ever a moment when the other woman looked around at all the normal lives she could have had and realized what Jo's mother had taught her own daughter so well: a woman had to be crazy, to marry a superstar chef.

"So you don't need lunch now?" Gabriel scowled at Jolie from his balcony, ready to leap across that gap and strangle her. He had somehow just assumed that she would be drawn irresistibly back into his kitchens when she got hungry and would show up around two o'clock, toward the end of the service, to eat all the different delights he had decided to feed her. "What did you do, eat at McDonald's?"

"I had lunch with Daniel Laurier," Jo said, and his head blew off.

"Oh, you did, did you?" That damn self-worshiping twirp. After Gabriel had saved his whole damned pastry kitchen, too. The Côte d'Azur might not be big enough for both of them after all.

"His wife has such a generous spirit," Jo said. "I wonder how she does it. It's like she just pours herself out there to everyone else as much as he does."

"That's Léa for you," he said, trying to pry his teeth apart so she couldn't actually hear him speaking through them. Daniel had had someone pouring her generous warmth on him since he was *nineteen years old*. Younger, damn it. The two of them had been dating a year before they got married. *Why him?*

Daniel's hours were *worse* than his. He did all those television chef contest shows, and Gabriel mostly thought those were a pain. What did *he* have that Gabriel didn't, that glued a woman like Léa to him with such loyalty? Had Jolie seen it in Daniel, too?

Why not me? Why not me? Why not me?

It made him want to kick something so he didn't have to admit how much it hurt.

"And she's gorgeous," Jo pointed out, a little spark of humor in her eyes.

His arms locked across his chest. "*Fine.* Do you know how much I don't care?"

Jo blinked at him a moment. She had added a pot of Tahitian gardenias to her balcony sometime that day, and the scent wafting across from her side was heady and sweet, competing even with the jasmine. "Meaning I really doubt he's flirting with other women," she explained, with the subtlest gentle amusement.

His arms flung out. "Have you fucking looked at yourself in the mirror ever, Jolie?" *Merde*, had he just admitted how jealous he was? To a woman who thought his jealousy was funny, because she wouldn't have any problem dumping him? Could he not learn to sit on himself *ever?*

She blinked again. And then flushed rosy with pleasure. In fact, she didn't seem to have the slightest idea what to say next, her head bending as she ran her fingers over one of her gardenias, sneaking glances at him across the stupid three-floor drop.

He tested his strength against the balcony railing, making sure it wouldn't cave away from him when he launched himself off it. Because those glances . . . a man sure as hell should not have a three-floor drop between him and responding to those glances.

"Hey." She straightened, holding up a flat hand. "Don't even think about it."

He gave her a sweet smile. "Oh, I'm thinking about it." His smile got meaner, as he leaned into the gap. "What are *you* thinking about, Jolie? Would you care to share some details?"

"If you ever try to leap across that, I will murder

you! You could *die!* You could break your spine and be paralyzed for the rest of your life! Don't you *dare!*"

"You're going to murder me so I don't die?"

She crushed the gardenia in her hand and threw the petals at him. He tried to catch one, but they floated too far out of reach, wafting down to the street below.

"Aww," he said. "Now you're throwing flowers onto my balcony. Isn't that sweet? Do you play the guitar?"

Jolie's fingers curled around the edge of the big gardenia pot in an ominous fashion. He was pretty sure he could catch it intact, but could she throw it far enough, that was the question. He didn't want some passing pedestrian to end up with a cracked skull.

"Come for a walk with me before you do something desperate," he said. "You know you like me better when I'm within reach."

He had to admit he preferred sitting with her astride him, her pelvis riding his and driving him out of his mind as he kissed her, but still, there was something to be said for lounging near her on the stone wall by the *boules* court, shaded by pines, looking down at the spread of population to the sea, in the background the soft *toc* of the *boules* and the rumble of conversation from the older men playing. Was she remembering how successfully and cruelly she had manipulated him with their first kiss, only a few meters down the wall?

"Did *you* eat lunch?" she demanded suddenly.

"Raphaël was inventing something new with a lamb *confit.* I tried that." Was she taking care of him? His mouth curved, and he looked down, rubbing his thumb against his jeans.

She was so damn pretty. Was she willing to consider this a date yet?

"I think Daniel and Léa are trying to wind it down a notch," she said, making him blank. Where the hell was *her* mind? Off at lunch with Daniel again?

"Their marriage?" he demanded, horrified. They had always seemed so happy. It made him bitter and jealous, but, since his heart was so incorrigibly optimistic that way, it gave him a little bit of hope.

"No! No, how much of themselves they put into the restaurant. I think they're trying to create a more balanced life. Have time for themselves, for a social life. Make actual friends they can hang out with."

Gabriel considered that blankly. Hunh. Really? But then, of course, Daniel wouldn't have the same problem Gabriel did, whenever he did try to take a Friday or a Saturday evening off and discovered that he had absolutely no one to spend it with, and the whole stupid evening stretched out before him so bleakly that he finally he went back to work, where he could pour his heart into something. Daniel could pour his heart into his wife. Probably children one day soon, too. Gabriel slouched a little lower on the wall, brooding.

"Maybe we should have them over for dinner," Jolie said. "I liked them. And I'm interested in how he and Léa are going to find that balance."

We should have them over. Like a couple. He sat on his surge of energy as hard as he could, but he was just not very squashable. "Sure," he managed to say. Neutrally enough. "Monday or Tuesday would work best. I'll give him a call."

And then he spoiled it all by bursting into a grin. "*We?*"

Jolie blinked, took a moment to think through the implications in what she had just said, and then looked shocked.

He just grinned at her.

Her gaze slid away but then back, very curious. *He* wasn't the one staring at a man with eyes dilated, then hopping back whenever that man politely reciprocated, so he hoped she was searching her own convoluted soul.

He leaned in, so she didn't search her soul *too* hard, to the point she found doubts, and kissed her. Thorough and hungry and in no hurry.

After all, why hurry, in her head they had time to develop long-term friendships as a couple now. He grinned again, even as he kissed her, and lifted his head before the surge of hunger could overtake him.

Amused comments came from the nearest group of old men playing *boules*. "Try, try again?" one of them called. "You never give up, do you?"

He stiffened and pulled Jolie to her feet, his jaw setting. Damn seventy-year-olds. Nothing better to do than gloat over the younger men, knowing there could be no payback. And damn small hilltowns where everyone had witnessed the fiasco of his dating life for the past ten years, too. Yes, he had kissed a few other women in the past decade, but did they have to bring it up right then?

He drew her down the alley of his now very-favorite stone staircase in the world, arousal surging through him instantly at the memories. If he had been Pavlov's dog, he would have been a damn quick study.

"Try again?" Jolie demanded, bridling. Maybe he could steal all the old men's *boules* or something. That would make them suffer, although not nearly enough. "What did that mean?"

His jaw set. He would have folded his arms, but he had managed to get hold of her hand again, and she wasn't trying to get it back. "You know how you're always dumping men when you get sick of them? I'm always getting dumped."

And wasn't that just a wonderful thing to have to admit to someone you could eat for breakfast, probably every damn day for the rest of your life?

Jolie stopped under a line of three shirts hung high above her, tugging him around to face her. "Women *dump* you?" she said incredulously.

His heart swelled with pleasure, even while it got confused. She didn't understand other women who did the same thing she liked to do?

She took a step into him, her fingertips rising to his chest. "They don't get addicted?" she asked softly, her eyes just eating him up again.

Oh, that—he squeezed her into him in a rushing hug, kissing her until he had to reach out and twine his fingers around the nearest iron staircase railing to remind him that they were in a public street. Breathing raggedly, he flexed his arm too hard around her, driving her into his body, and when he finally forced his head up, she pressed her cheek against his chest, her breathing crazy, too, her hands curled into his shirt. All her weight lay against him. The triumphant, starving joy of it, to be what was holding her up. To have made her that weak.

He sure as hell felt strong. Strong enough to carry her weight in one arm, and break down doors, and rip clothes, and. . . .

He drew a long, shaky breath, rocking them minutely on their feet, trying to calm himself.

Jolie rubbed her cheek against him and curled her fingers more deeply into his shirt, not trying to step away. He could feel her breath in little puffs through the thin knit. Her body was so pliant. He could just swing her up in his arms, her apartment was only a couple of streets away. Everyone would see them, and she would want to crawl out of herself with shame when she recovered and realized, but *he* wouldn't mind.

He would feel rather savagely victorious striding through the street to her apartment with her in his arms in full view of the world, in fact.

He heaved another deep breath, rubbing her back with one hand, every calming gesture for himself he could think of.

Then she finally looked up at him, and before he

could stop himself, he had leaned down to sip another kiss off those parted damp lips.

It wasn't his fault. That face, tilting up from his chest like that—how was he supposed to control himself?

One little kiss, and then another, and then another three, his hand slipping free of the rail, petting her hair back from her face in urgent strokes, her mouth so delicious and so his. He couldn't get enough of it and of her reaction to him.

Madame Delatour's little dog saved him, sniffing at his ankle. He managed to lift his head again, to see Madame Delatour passing, not really looking at them, her face almost neutral except for the little smile that curved her mouth.

"I can't touch you anymore," he gasped. "I might die." Stretching both hands behind him this time, he locked them around the twisting wrought iron bars of the railing. Jolie forced herself to take a step back, but then her gaze got lost on him. Her eyes ran slowly from his hands knotted around the iron, up his corded arms, over his undefended chest.

He squeezed his eyes shut, twisting his head away. "*Non, non, non,* don't look at me like that. Jolie, you have no idea—" She probably didn't. He always did seem to feel things more powerfully than anyone else around him. Out there, unshielded, and subjugated by his damn senses.

He peeked, and Jolie's eyes were brilliant with hunger, the black of her pupils eating up the gold again. She lifted a hand to touch, very lightly, his straining chest.

He snapped, on a quick flick of pure rage. Damn her, she shouldn't *toy* with him like that. Cruel little I'll-dump-you-when-I-please.

"I've got to go back to work," he growled, striding away as fast as he could. And it was a good hour into the evening service before he calmed down enough to want to beat his own head against the wall, instead of the heads of everyone else around him. *You idiot. What a stupid moment to lose your temper.*

She was clearly getting addicted.

Chapter 17

I t was amazing how much energy and pleasure surged through Gabriel on his walk home at midnight, when that walk was in the same direction as Jolie's apartment. Even knowing that if he tried to redirect his path enough to show up at her door instead of his own, she would probably hit him over the head.

She hadn't come to the restaurant that night. It pissed him off. *Come on, you love this, and you're only here three and a half days each week. Don't* waste *it.*

He had almost called her to beg her to come by, but that had pissed him off, too. He had kept hoping she would forgive him for being a *connard* earlier in the day and show up on her own accord; and in the end, instead of calling her, he had just had a crappy, high-strung night, always checking the back door in the hopes to spot her coming down the alley. Always turning away in crushing, growling disappointment.

He lived so much too much on all his emotions. He wished sometimes that he could flatten himself out, be all even and self-possessed—like Daniel, *merde*—but then he gave up on it, because it felt horrible and two-dimensional when he actually tried. Who wanted to live life like a sheet of metal?

But, *merde*. He stood for a moment under their balconies, looking up at Jolie's. Strongly tempted to throw a stone. To sing a teasing little serenade. To whistle for her to come. His grin flashed.

It left him wide open at her mercy, those emotions. Sent to heaven or hell by a touch of her finger or its removal, and *she* held cautiously back.

Well, not so cautiously sometimes, but she *wanted* to hold cautiously back. *No one else moves as fast as you. You need to remember that other people go slower than you do.*

Oh, and if you do get what you want—me—then it's at the price of your own heart, because I like to dump people. Sucker.

He fisted big fists and pushed himself up his own stairway. There was always that leap from the balcony if he cracked later, he promised himself, with a delighted kick of testosterone.

He took a shower and went into his kitchen to find some food. The potato chips were sitting in the middle of the kitchen table, which threw him. In his kitchens, he *always* put things back in their exact place. They were *always* where he wanted them.

Still, she had him pretty rattled. Maybe he had actually forgotten to clean up.

He reached for the bag and realized there was a big white note taping the bag closed. *Mange quelque chose de plus équilibré*, it said. *Eat something better for you.* With an arrow toward the refrigerator.

His chest tightened, so that he almost couldn't breathe. He approached the refrigerator as if it might contain one of those exploding practical jokes, snakes springing out at him or something. No. Two simple glass containers of rice and—his heart beat so hard as he peeled back the lid—something with red lentils. He dipped his head and breathed in the fresh clear scent of cilantro and then the richer, earthy aromas it brightened. Dal.

Something good and filling and healthy that he would never in a million years eat at his own restaurant, where they didn't serve Indian food.

Oh, God. He actually thought he might cry. Had she done this after he stalked away from her like a bastard?

The soft knock on Jo's door came a little after midnight. She could feel him through the door, a dangerous monster in the dark, wanting in. She had stayed up late, then lambasted herself for doing so and gone to bed around eleven-thirty, only to twist and turn under the thin shelter of the sheet, watching the open balcony windows.

She pulled jeans and a shirt on over her pajamas this time. She just couldn't be that brazen, to answer the door nearly naked twice in a row, especially knowing what was waiting out there. A great shadow, leaning into the door. "What do you want?"

His eyes flickered over her rumpled hair. She had forgotten to turn on the light. He was a darker figure than anything else there, indistinct and very large, shadows condensed in him. Danger brought to life.

"Were you asleep?" He was breathing deeply, and it couldn't possibly be from the stairs. Not with the physical intensity of his life.

"A little bit."

"Sorry," he said. And he did sound a little sorry. But he didn't go away. Forearms braced on the doorjamb, he leaned his weight into them, gazing down at her, swamping her. She had a feeling he was trying very hard not to push his way in. "How did you get into my place?" he murmured.

Oh, so he had found her present. Her heart squeezed with pleasure and trepidation. It felt so good to take care of him. Stupid, stupid, stupid. "Raphaël's key."

"Ah, so that's why he looked so pleased with himself." Gabriel leaned more weight onto his forearms. "Why didn't you come by?"

Her face flickered with a smile, hard to keep lit under the thick pressure building in the room. "You'll spoil me, letting me come by every mealtime like some stray alley cat."

"You're not my stray," he said. "And I want to spoil you."

She slipped in closer to him, unable to help it. His forearms, braced high against the doorjamb, his body on offer for her. She wanted more of its heat and strength. She wanted more of that danger and that utter, blissful sense of safety of their kisses in that alley.

"If I kiss you, will you not throw me down on that bed because you're sure I want it?"

Eyebrows plummetted, and just for a second that aggressive, take-what-I-want face was wide-open with shock and hurt. "I wouldn't do that. *Putain*, you really do think I'm a beast." He pulled his weight back off his arms, straightening away from her.

"I didn't mean—" She shook her head and put a hand on one bunched shoulder. He stilled. Then slowly let his weight settle back against his forearms. "I didn't mean that. I wouldn't open the door to you, if I thought you would hurt me. But I don't know what I'm doing here. You're bigger than anyone I've ever met in my whole entire life. You fill *every* inch of space. Just because you're right, that I want you, doesn't mean I'm going to take you."

He shook his shaggy head. "It's like a diet, isn't it? I hate diets."

Her fingers spread unconsciously on his shoulder, seeking to feel more of him. That shoulder tightened under her hand, more pressure going against those forearms holding him off her. Her fingers shifted, tracing the effect of that effort farther, seeing what other muscles came into play. His back, his abs . . . his biceps, his forearms themselves. . . .

"They're evil," he breathed. "Diets. Sado-masochistic."

"But sometimes you do need to pay attention to what you put in your mouth," she said, as she curled her hand behind his neck, lifted herself up, and kissed him.

All his muscles strained against the doorjamb as he took her mouth in return, long and hungrily. He didn't lower his arms. He didn't try to touch her. Just his mouth, his neck straining to bend low enough for her, while her hands slid from his nape to frame his jaw as she kissed him longer and longer. He was so intensely—everything. She couldn't get enough of him.

He made a little groaning sound when she finally fell back onto her feet. And then a low, dangerous growl that licked heat all through her.

She forced herself to take a step back and drop her hands away from him, trying to get her bearings.

The muscles on his arms corded, fists clenching above the doorjamb. But he kept them there. "It's biology, isn't it? Women are programmed to select, to make sure the man would be a good—partner." His mouth twisted. "And you don't think I would be one. That's why the invisible fence. Right?"

"I just don't know what I'm doing," she repeated softly. "You're so big."

He shivered, locked against the doorframe. "You're killing me."

"Will you keep your arms on the door?" she whispered.

"Oh, *putain*, you're so mean," he breathed. And lowered his head to her so she could take his mouth.

She dragged her hands through his hair and over his shoulders, pulling herself into him as she kissed him and kissed him, struggling to get closer all by herself, struggling to press her body as tightly to him as she wanted without his help.

She couldn't do it. She went wild at the frustration, kissing him harder and harder, wide open, dragging her hands over all the bow-taut muscles of his back, his sides, sliding them back up over his chest to dig into his shoulders again and try—try and fail, try and fail—

to get enough of his heat.

He didn't touch her. He locked his arms against the doorjamb until she thought he might break through the frame, and he gave his all to the kisses, a desperate claiming.

He had promised, and he let her. Do everything she could to him, without taking over. The self-restraint undid her in a different and even more profound way than the feel of his body.

The years of yoga hadn't left her weak, not by any means. She could pull herself up into him. She could wrap her thighs around him and hold herself there in a long, strong grip, taking her time, in for the long haul. She could tighten herself to him until the clothes between them seemed as if they should burn away in their heat, no space left for them.

But she still couldn't get close enough.

She twisted against him, thighs locked around his hips, still kissing, kissing, kissing, while he hung there. Wild. Crazy wild.

"Jolie. Jolie." He was begging, her name a plea. His body was so taut, it felt as if his muscles might just snap, fling him apart. He fought her for her mouth, fought to make her lose her mind.

No, he had already won that battle. Why wouldn't she let him take his hands off the door?

She wanted them around her back. She wanted his hands digging into her butt. She wanted the two of them wild and tangling in her bed. She wanted him to take her like that, driven crazy.

If she wanted to establish a long, happy, fruitful working relationship with someone, this was sure as hell not the way to go about it.

That he was aroused, that he was starving aroused now, was unmistakable. But beyond her name, he didn't ask. He bunched and clenched under her frantic clutching, he arched his pelvis into hers, he kissed her mindless. But he didn't take his hands off the door.

She slid down at last from his body, like some mud slide caving helplessly off a mountain, that was how destroyed she felt. She was shaking all over.

She literally fell against his chest, swaying forward, unable to hold herself up for the shivering, hot hunger.

"Jolie." His voice was so hoarse she could barely hear it. She petted his chest in frantic, trembling touches. "Please say I can take my arms off this *putain de porte.*"

She slid her head up and down in agreement against his chest, shaking all through her, unable to look at him, so desperate for him to crack.

He picked her up by the hips, just lifted her straight off the floor, and kicked the door closed behind him as he strode straight down the hall to her bed. He stilled with her held vertical just above it. "And throw you down on it? Because I'm pretty sure you really, really want it."

"Yes." She groaned it like a curse, twisting in his hands. "Yes, *please.*"

He did throw her. Tossed her onto the mattress and came down on top of her like an avalanche, ripping her shirt over her head.

He laughed, rough and despairing, when he discovered her little white cami under that shirt and nothing else. He wrenched her jeans open instantly to check for the lace-edged boy short. "*Bébé,* when I told you I would treat you right and *not* like a beast, I didn't expect this much provocation. You *want* me wild."

"I do." She flexed into him, pressing her hips up hard. "I do."

"*Bordel.*" He yanked her jeans off and threw them somewhere. "Well, you've got me that way."

Her hands slid over his forearms and stopped to run over the deep red indentations left from the door frame. "I'm sorry, I didn't mean—"

He dragged his hands over her body roughly to grab and pin her shoulders to the mattress. "If you tell me you didn't mean to go this far, I will lose my freaking mind."

"Well, I didn't," she whispered, running her hands down his torso, finding the clasp of his own jeans. "But don't stop. Please don't stop."

He shivered, digging in the pocket of those jeans. She could be pissed off at him later for showing up at her apartment at midnight with a condom in his pocket. Now, she just tried to help him put it on.

He knocked her hand away as if she had tried to hurt him. "This is going to be bad enough as it is."

"Bad?" Offense prickled, even as he pushed the little boy shorts and the panties under them to the side.

"Wild." He positioned himself against her, fingers forcing the panties and shorts out of the way until their elastic dug into the skin of her hip. "Rough." She arched her hips up involuntarily at the promise, wrapping her thighs around him. He drove into her in one savage thrust, and she moaned with the pure pleasure of that first hard taking. "Short." For a second, he managed to hold still, staring down at her, maybe to let her body adjust to him. What her body did instead was writhe helplessly for movement. "*Putain.* And I'm pretty sure you'll find my manners atrocious."

"No ladies' first?" She bucked her hips against him, managed to make it teasing.

"Oh, *minette*, I wish. You have no idea what you just did to me." He drove into her hard again, making her gasp, her body all his, controlled by pleasure.

"I thought you believed in doing impossible things." She dragged one of his hands off her thigh and to her sex.

A savage grin glinted, even in the dark. "All right, *chaton*. Why don't we try how many impossible things we can do before breakfast?"

She had never in her life had her body worked over the way he worked it. He made her come with him, with a kind of ruthless determination, as he reduced her to a begging mass of desire with his thumb while his thrusts grew harder and harder.

She bit her own thumb to keep from screaming out just before the waves broke, and then she was wrenched apart by them, lost in them even as he grabbed her bottom with both hard hands and drove one last time into her.

He hung over her for a long time, after that. When she opened her eyes, he was just watching her, his expression impossible to fathom in the dark. He stroked her hair off her face and then slipped away into the bathroom. She heard the shower run briefly.

He came back naked, towel-dried, the light from the shower falling across his body.

Her mouth went dry, despite her satiation. It was like seeing a god walk out of heaven into the mortal shadows.

A wild god. An old god. From deep, dark, primitive times.

He really did have a beautiful body. The lean, delineated muscle of a man so physically active that his greatest challenge was to manage to eat enough to keep on weight. The heavy shoulders of his gym workouts. The tight butt. His sex jutting from dark curls.

Jutting again? Already?

He slipped into bed behind her and pulled her back in tight against his body. Before she could relax into the post-sex cuddle, one arm tightened around her upper torso like a vise. The other slipped between her thighs. She made a little sound, her last orgasm still recent enough that it would take very little to send her into another one. His hand pulled back a little, just enough to frustrate. His low growl seemed to nip warning teeth all up and down her skin. "Pace yourself, *minette*. This is punitive. I want you to know exactly what you did to me, there in the doorway."

Chapter 18

G abriel slept until the sun was high on the horizon, nine o'clock, which must be very late for him. His big body sprawled across her double bed, leaving her almost no room. If she didn't want a man to take up her space, had she ever picked the wrong man to let in.

All her centered, happy existence tilting toward him like he tilted the cheap mattress. It made her feel as if she was scrambling to stay up as a cliff crumbled out from under her.

She tried to wiggle out from under his arm, and he groaned at her efforts, his eyes opening reluctantly. From close to her face, she could see all the striations in the blue.

She blushed fiercely and twisted away. Just as her body was escaping, his fingertips made a grab, too late, and she stood.

"*Merde*," he said from behind her. "Please tell me those finger-shaped bruises on your butt are not from me. No. No. Don't tell me that. I don't like the other possibility, either."

"They're not from anybody else," she said dryly, hunting for something to cover herself. Only lace-edged boy shorts immediately presented themselves to her eye, and she just couldn't go there, not with the bright sunlight beating through on what they had done during the night. She made a beeline for the bathroom.

When she came back out, a long, hot shower later, in a towel because she still had to dig through her carry-on for clothes, he had a pillow over his head, locked firmly there by powerful forearms.

She snuck closer. He had bruise marks, too. In lines, diagonal across his arms, the shape of a door frame.

He pulled the pillow off his head and looked at her. Deep in his eyes, there was something wary, careful. "I'm sorry I was rough. I know I told you I would treat you right. I meant to."

She smiled a little. She couldn't help it. Embarrassed though she was, there was something about how wild she had driven him that made her feel like a cat with cream.

Some of his wariness faded. But he still watched. Stuffing the pillow under his head, he stretched an arm to her. "How about a little early-morning cuddle?"

She hesitated, not sure if she could bare herself any more to him, after that night. Her sense of intimacy needed time to adjust. "I think you're late to work."

His arm drooped back to the bed. She realized only as it faded that there had been a profound sense of contentment in him, and she had just stomped on it. The wariness came back, lurking deep in the blue, like a little sea monster no one would ever believe existed.

She could have kicked herself for mentioning work, too. If for once he stopped working, for God's sake, let him. No matter what it did to her sense of space.

"That will confuse them, all right, me coming in late. I should warn Raf at least." But he lay there gazing at her with guarded eyes, showing no inclination whatsoever to move.

She tried to get clothes out of her carry-on on the floor, only to realize that the benefits to unpacking included having clothes in drawers. Higher up. Where she didn't have to bend over in this really skimpy towel to get them.

She started to bend, hesitated. Shifted so that her butt wasn't toward him. Saw his eyes follow her butt as it turned away from him. Started to bend again. Saw

his gaze glide with a lazy pleasure over her cleavage as more of it started to show. Straightened again. Considered squatting. Which would part the towel and.
. . .

She gave him a frustrated look, wondering if maybe he would go into the bathroom in a second or something, so she could get dressed in comfort.

He rolled to sit on the edge of the bed, started to stand, and instead just let himself sink down, down, past the edge of the mattress, until his butt hit the floor. "I think I might need to call in sick. You *used* me." A little leap of exultancy on the *used*. He rolled his shoulders and stretched his neck, feeling the muscles.

That little smile started to lurk more irrepressibly around the corners of her mouth. She sure had made someone happy.

"It's going to be tricky calling in sick to my own restaurant, too, in this size town. Someone will be bound to spot me, and then everyone will be complaining among themselves about how the chef does whatever he wants, but if ever I catch one of *them* doing it. . .grumble, grumble. I'll have to hide out in your apartment all day." He tried to look in desperate need of asylum, but the blue of his eyes gleamed too bright.

"Tell them you're dealing with negotations for a cookbook deal this morning and that Raphaël and your sous-chefs will have to handle things, just like they would if you were a guest on a television show or off judging some *concours.*"

"Sure, that would work," he said with lazy amusement. "I like the way you negotiate. How does it work out? Whoever has the fewest orgasms gets the highest percentage of the royalties to make up for it? You're not going to be making much out of the deal at that rate." He grinned.

And she had thought he was arrogant and self-satisfied *before.*

"It's too late, though," he said. "We already have an ironclad contract." A sudden, surprisingly dark glance, a subtle emphasis on *ironclad contract.* "You can't renegotiate the terms."

"You mean you can't," she retorted. "You're the one trying to steal my royalties."

"It's not my fault you're easy," he grinned, entirely full of himself, and she gasped and took a step back.

His eyes caught on her face. "What did I say? Oh, no, I didn't mean—Jolie, I was just *teasing* you about how many times you—*merde.* I didn't mean—" He smacked his head against the heels of his palms.

He was so expressive. So—she smiled—out there. Every bit of him extended into the world.

He groaned into his arms and lifted his head with a sudden self-assertion. "Just because *I* can do something doesn't mean it's easy to do. I bet no one else has ever made you come five times in one night." And he grinned again.

If she had a pillow to hand, she would smack him on the head with it until the room was full of feathers. Unfortunately, she would have to go through him to reach the pillows, and she didn't think that would work out for her the way she planned.

She threw the wet towel—what the hell point *was* there of trying to hide your body from a man who had given you five orgasms, anyway?—and turned her back on him, reaching for bra and panties. He made a low rumbling sound of pleasure, watching her, and in the mirror, she saw him gather the damp towel in his fists and sneak a deep breath of it.

Of her scent.

That man. He melted her. He made her want to do anything for him. But what kind of insane person fell for a top chef? You enjoyed their work. You *loved* their work, all the creative, magnificent, ruthlessly driven spirit they poured into it, but that was *all you took from them.* You never tried to fit yourself into their nonexistent private life.

Nobody fit into something that sliver thin.

And this particular chef was her father's adamant enemy. He was *blackmailing* her into being here with him instead of with her father where she should be.

She suspected he was about as capable of enforcing that blackmail as kicking a kitten, but she refused to admit that out loud to herself or anyone else. Otherwise, the guilt for being here would be too great.

"*You* don't feel too used?" he asked suddenly. And there it was again, that wariness.

Gloriously so. "I like my body. It's nice somebody got some use out of it." She grinned at him.

He looked a little confused at this attitude, as if a woman enjoying him using her was a whole new concept. What, were all the women in the south of France complete idiots or something? But then he slowly grinned back at her. "Any time you want to feel your body is, ah, useful to and appreciated by someone besides yourself, you just let me know. In fact, I'll do my best to make sure you don't even have to ask."

She laughed.

And then thought, *Good lord. Does he think this is the start of a beautiful affair?*

Is *it the start of a beautiful affair?* They had, at a minimum, a year of cookbook work to do together. But she didn't do year-long affairs. Men were just so invasive and clingy, draping around her life like some heavy, wet cloak she just had to shrug off.

She bet Gabriel would not be very shruggable. The very idea made her mouth curve wryly. On the other hand—he didn't really drape much either, did he? Too full of energy. Nothing about him yet felt likely to weigh her down. Quite the reverse. He suffused her life with exhiliration.

Pulling a sea-green knit shirt over her head, she turned and looked at him for a second. She would have said he was a man who didn't let anyone "do" things with him. Too aggressive, too arrogant, too big. But he had locked himself in that doorway the night before until she knew what she wanted.

So . . . what was she going to do with him?

Gabriel made it to the shower with a lazy, easy smile on his face, and then he turned on the water full blast and slowly let his back slide down the wall, until he was sitting with his legs crunched up by the opposite wall. The water beat down on him, streaming into his eyes.

What had he done?

No sudden movements. He had *known* he shouldn't make any sudden movements with her hand gripping his heart like that.

And sure enough, she had ripped it right out of his body, and now she was standing there looking at it as if it was icky and bloody and she wasn't sure where to put it so that it didn't mess anything up.

He sank his head forward into his hands, the water pounding on the back of his head. His chest felt torn wide open, one gaping, terrifying hole, and no one was handing her heart back across the way to fill the spot.

What the hell had he just done to himself?

Chapter 19

The argument exploded as soon as Jolie referred to her train trip back to Paris, Gabriel's outrage immediate.

"You haven't even stayed a full three days here! You didn't get here until Tuesday and then we spent all of that day getting you set up in your apartment. I should get Friday this week."

"Gabriel, don't you have a flock of César-winning actors coming up from Cannes Friday night for some big banquet? When do you think you'll have time to see me?"

Gabriel shoved his toe against the nearest counter in something suspiciously like a kick. "At night," he muttered.

Jolie folded her arms. Not that she minded the *at night* as much as all that—especially if he still had some energy left—but a woman had to draw the line.

"And at five in the morning." His expression was wistful until he looked up and caught hers, and then he folded his own arms defensively. That did such hot things to his biceps. "Well, what?"

"At five in the morning, I would be heading down to Nice to catch the first train. No. This will just have to be a short week, as we *agreed*, because I had to have Monday to get everything organized with Papa's therapists."

The usual conflicted expressions on his face when she mentioned anything pertaining to her father's stroke—pity, some flash of fear, and outraged frustration at both feelings. As well as jealousy, resentment, and a powerful old hatred, his knuckles digging into his arms.

"If you stayed, you could come to the kitchen and watch and get something to eat. And do an article or something, about a 'Feast for the Stars'," Gabriel urged. He didn't really know how to lose something, did he? He kept bouncing right back with more arguments.

His ideas sounded fantastic—far better than watching her father roll a rolling pin on a table as if life had nothing left. "Gabriel," Jolie said desperately, tightly. "Stop it. Don't *cling* so much."

He took a step back, his expression blanking.

"Sorry." Jolie scrubbed her face. "I didn't mean that exactly, I just"—she drew a breath, her voice dropping—"don't make it harder."

Again a war of expressions on his face, one of which was sudden bright pleasure. "It's hard?"

Jolie glared at him.

"*Pardon*," it was his turn to say. "I just meant"—the brightness crept back into his face, irrepressible—"hard to leave *me*? Or just hard to go back to"—his tone darkened—"Pierre Manon?"

He always said her father's name in the same tone as *that bastard*. Sometimes it was *that poor bastard*, but *bastard* was always in there.

"Look, I don't want to talk about this anymore. We had an agreement—"

"And you're not meeting it," he said promptly. "We agreed on three full days a week."

"And that means Friday through Sunday in Paris," Jolie spoke over him determinedly. "So I'm leaving tonight. As we agreed."

"*What?*" Gabriel's arms flung out in outrage. "*Tonight?* Why can't you leave in the morning?"

"Because then it won't be three full days in Paris," Jolie said between her teeth. Like, what, she would rather be on a night train back to deal with her father's depression than curled up late typing her notes for the day in comfort, near a three-star restaurant where she could stop by whenever she wanted a snack, all while waiting for a man who knew how to give a woman five orgasms in a row?

"How *late* tonight?" Gabriel sounded rather panicked. "I thought—*putain*, Jolie."

"I thought I would catch the train at five," she said. After his afternoon break finished.

"You're not even going to stay and eat?" he asked sulkily.

Damn it, that was such an unfair temptation. He was *impossibly* irresistible. "*Stop it!*"

"You could catch the train at nine. You'll get in too late to see your father until the morning anyway."

Jolie hesitated. "I would get in too late for the Métro. I suppose there will be taxis at the station, though, even that late at night." Would there be? She had never actually gotten into a Paris train station that late.

Gabriel began to frown. "Where is your apartment exactly? Is it a secure building? Damn it—it will be three in the morning, won't it? I don't—never mind." He growled, and her skin prickled everywhere, and most particularly in her nipples. "Just—fine. You can catch the five o'clock train. *Putain.* Maybe you should leave at four."

He scowled down at his feet, the biceps in those folded arms bulging with frustration.

"Thank you," Jolie said awfully, "for your permission."

He shot her a quick, feral look and snarled.

Wow. That snarl was *so* hot. And he was concerned about her safety, too. Hot *and* sweet. And extremely demanding.

His fists clenched and unclenched in the fold of his elbows. "So are you going to be back by Monday this time? Like you're supposed to be? As per, you know, *our contract.*"

"I'll catch the first train out Monday morning," Jolie promised. And wasn't that going to be a thrill, dragging herself to the station by five a.m.

"But then you won't get here until nearly noon! The restaurant is *closed* Monday!" Gabriel sounded like a child who had just had Christmas wrenched away from him.

Was spending the morning with her Christmas? Jolie thought with a spark of joy. "Well . . . I could come late Sunday. It's a five and a half hour trip, so if I left at eight, I would get in at . . . one-thirty in the morning." And then have to drive up here, negotiating those narrow, impossible streets in the dark, tired.

More scowling. "Why not Sunday afternoon?"

"Because then that's only two and a half days in Paris? Did I mention that my father just had a—"

"Stroke." This time the shove of his toe against the counter was considerably harder. "Yes. I got it. I got it." A pause when she thought he was going to let it drop. "But why do *I* have to get all the half days? I only have two full days. Why does he always get first choice of everything?"

Jolie gaped at him. Outrage surged. "I'm sorry, who exactly do you think my days belong to? I'm not a candy bar you're splitting between you!"

He growled again. And hung his head. And then sighed slowly, at least some of the tension relaxing out of his body. "*Pardon,*" he muttered. "You're right." He reached for her, pulling her into his arms, his muscles still too taut but the gesture soothing her, nevertheless. Until he spoke again: "You're much more special than a candy-bar. You taste better, too. I'll make you something sometime, to show you what you are."

For someone who made everything in life seem possible, he sure as hell was hopeless. She thumped her head against his chest. "And I'm the one spending eleven hours on a train every week! Not to mention all the time getting to and from the station!"

He sighed again, very heavily, and wrapped her more tightly in his arms. "Damn Pierre Manon," he muttered, so low and grumbly she almost didn't catch it. And maybe wasn't meant to.

Gabriel might be the hottest thing since molten sugar, but he wasn't exactly without his issues.

Chapter 20

" *Salut, Papa,*" Jolie said cheerfully, bending down to kiss her father's cheek.

"How was he?" he asked. "Daniel Laurier?"

"He just promoted his *second* to executive chef, if you can believe it. He's taking a step back. Trying to find more family time." She snuck a sideways glance at her father's face, not quite sure what she was looking for or why she didn't want him to know she was looking for it. Some regret, for the fact that he had put his own restaurant before his family? Some reflection on it?

"Daniel Laurier?" her father said incredulously. "What happened, did he hear a rumor that the restaurant was going to lose a star? He wants to make sure that gets blamed on someone else?"

"I don't think so, Papa." Jolie turned away, oddly saddened. Whatever she had been looking for, she hadn't found it. "Have you thought any more about that invitation from Luc Leroi?" she asked carefully, not looking at him.

Her father stood from the couch and walked over to the window, a little slower and heavier on the left side than the right, but not too bad. Jolie liked his physical therapist. The woman didn't put up with much.

"Remember, when I was interviewing him last week, he said the Leucé would be delighted to host us for an event in honor of the cookbook," she said. "He offered to have himself and his chefs make a selection of the recipes to serve."

The Hôtel de Leucé was *only* one of the most famous restaurants in the world. But, of course, the

Leucé had climbed up in the world while Pierre Manon's restaurant at the hotel's rival, the Luxe, had fallen. Back when her father had three stars, the Leucé only had two. Now their situations were reversed—or rather, her father had no stars, really, since he had quit, but everyone knew that under his leadership the Luxe had both gained its third star and lost it.

"Why?" Pierre Manon asked harshly. "Pity?"

Jolie bit her lip. The energy and cheerfulness she had absorbed in Sainte-Mère wavered, struggling to hold up against the heaviness in this apartment. "I think it was for my sake," she said cautiously.

Her father clenched his fist—his left fist—slowly and carefully and hard.

"Because I'm working with him, Papa. I think he's offering it as a friendly gesture." Even when she was working on other books, did her father still see her as only that tiny font name?

"Five years ago, when those idiots were taking away one of my stars, they were *giving* one to that kid. And *he's* going to make my recipes to help me? You may not think it's pity, but I know pity when I see it."

Jolie was silent a long moment. "I think it was to help me," she said again. "He's actually a very nice guy, under that intense self-control of his. I think he likes to help people live their dreams."

Her father snorted. "The amount of people who have interviewed Luc Leroi can't even be counted. It doesn't make you important enough for him to organize an event in your honor."

Jo's jaw set. Tears stung, sudden and bright, but she blinked them back. "All right, Papa. Come for a walk with me in the gardens? We'll stop and eat in the bistrot at the corner." Her father never felt threatened by the homey bistrot.

Settling into the seat on the TGV south to Nice

three days later was like exfoliating the soul. First the guilt and then the worry, slowly washed away by the inexorable swift roll of the train, to reveal the bright hopefulness, clean again.

It wasn't so bad, really, having a five and a half hour commute. She typed up notes from her kitchen testing of recipes and from the work with Philippe Lyonnais that Friday. How to process his macarons into a recipe a home cook could approximate was a challenge. She watched Youtube clips of Gabriel demonstrating a dessert for this or that TV station—big, fun, pulling everyone into his energy. She drafted some behind-the-scenes stories to post over the next week on her blog. She scrolled through the weekend's texts from Gabriel. There were a lot, photo after photo of different savory and sweet plates being produced or tested in his restaurant, with which he wanted to tempt her. Once in a while a word thrown in: *Hungry yet?*

Oh, yeah. He made her hungry. And he made her smile.

She grew happier, with each mile closer. Except when guilt tried to sneak back for the fact that she had slipped out Sunday afternoon after all, after having spent the day with her father. She wasn't entirely sure that her father knew what to do with her around the whole weekend, anymore than she knew what to do with him, but she still cringed at the thought of leaving him alone.

And yet here she was, leaving him alone. Trying to convince herself she was doing it to protect him, when she knew perfectly well that Gabriel would never really do anything to hurt her father. Her soul got lighter and lighter, more and more eager, at the rate of over five kilometers a minute. And yet guilt twisted through it uneasily, unsettling everything, making some part of her long for freedom that no human with a heart could ever truly have.

She got into Sainte-Mère at eleven at night, while Gabriel was still working, and slipped a message to

Raphaël. He came out as soon as he could, diners turning to eye him as he passed through the white-arched *salle*, murmuring to each other, *Which one is that?*

"This is going to make Gabe's night," Raphaël said with something of his brother's grin. Raphaël looked as if he should have been a seafarer, a pirate, or in this day and age just someone who busked his way around the world. Despite a clear resemblance in facial structure and height to his brother, his shaggy hair was a little darker, his eyes gray-green, and he looked more—windblown and exposed to the elements, as if he got his non-cooking exercise windsurfing. "What can I help you with?"

Jolie felt herself grow a thousand pounds lighter just at his confidence that Gabriel would be thrilled. "Can I have your key again?"

He grinned, fishing in his pocket. "Why don't you just ask him for a copy? You know he would give you one."

Did she know that? Jolie thought, on a hiccup and a sudden, whooshing slide. Whoa.

Did she *want* to know that?

Well, yeah. In a way, it made her heart all fuzzy with delight. And that fuzziness terrified her. *Never, never, never get involved with a chef,* her mother said. *They'll suck everything out of you and never give anything back.*

Don't you dare fall for one of my chefs. Her father. *Or any chef. Find someone you can make a life with.*

Careful, some part of her said, slinking away, wanting to protect itself. *Don't let a man suck the life out of you. Don't let a man claim your happiness and then crush it out like a weight.*

And yet, big as he was, greedy as he was, Gabriel never felt like a weight. Or a vacuum.

"We've got some late tables, so he probably won't be home until after midnight, just so you know," Raphaël told her.

"Yes," she said. "I know how it goes."

Raphaël wiggled a key off his ring and looked at her a long moment as he handed it to her, and for an instant his grin faded. "Be careful of my brother, Jolie."

Uh-oh. She wasn't sure she knew how to be careful of Gabriel.

"Don't . . . *merde*. Don't—make him fall even harder for you, if you're going to drop him when you get bored."

Bored? Of Gabriel?

And—happiness lodged in her like a purring cat in a lap it was not about to get pushed off of—*make him fall even harder for me?*

"He's not very boring," she said.

"I need to meet a cookbook writer," Raphaël informed the heavens very firmly. "Let's say, when you get frustrated, then."

Jolie burst out laughing. "I've been frustrated with him since before I even met him."

Raphaël sighed. "This intervening in someone else's love affairs doesn't really work, does it? Just—don't do anything mean, all right?"

Like *don't break up with him*. Because he *needed* her, right. Just like her father needed her. Jolie waited for that uneasy sensation of someone else's weight on her life to descend, that familiar sense of a man sucking more out of her than he was willing to give back.

She was still prodding curiously, trying to figure out where that feeling was hiding, when she let herself into Gabriel's apartment.

Then she forgot all about it, laughing in anticipation as she rinsed the day off her in his shower and slipped into her little white cami pajamas. His favorite.

She was reading a book when she heard his feet on

the stairs, and her body immediately thrummed with adrenalin. She ran across to open the door and grin up at him. "Surprise!"

Gabriel's face just *lit*. Tiredness vanished in a burst of delight, and the next instant, she had disappeared in a bear hug.

"*Pardon*," he said, when he finally released her. "I know I need to take a shower." But instead, he framed her face and kissed her, deeply. "Jolie. That just beat Christmas. I'm never going to walk home to my apartment with quite the same attitude again. I'll always be hoping."

He was so big. With how much he felt, with how little he hid it. She bounced on her toes, face still framed in his hands, beaming up at him.

His fingers flexed into her hair before he dragged them reluctantly away. "Let me go take a shower. It was a crazy day."

"I made you some more dal," Jolie said, following behind him.

He stopped in the hallway so suddenly she ran into his broad back. Then he turned, cupped her head, and kissed her very hard again.

"It's simple," she said, a little embarrassed, since what *he* fed *her* received international awards. And he had yet to repeat himself, in anything he offered her. "And the ingredients were leftover from last time."

"Are you apologizing?" Gabriel asked incredulously. "Jolie." He kissed her again, fierce and hard. She was backed up against the wall now. "Let me go take a shower before I crack, okay?"

He pushed off the wall and strode away, fast, stripping off his T-shirt as he went. A smooth, muscled back was revealed for half a second before the bathroom door shut behind him.

Mmm.

She gave him a couple of minutes while she stood where he had left her, pressed against the hall wall, listening to that shower run over that beautiful, indefatigable, irrepressible body.

Then she walked into the bathroom and right up to the edge of the spray. He had no bathtub but a tiled shower walled with glass, so that she could just step between the panes of it.

He froze with one arm stretched up, one hand full of soap lather sliding over his ribs.

"I couldn't wait," she said and stepped in under the water with him.

Her little white cami and boy shorts turned instantly transparent, clinging to her skin. He made a sound as if he had taken a battering ram to the stomach, and the soap slid out of his hand and hit the floor.

"Oh, *merde*," he muttered, in a frantic, drowning voice. "Jolie—you're going to *kill* me."

She stiffened, flushing all over her wet body. It was the first time in her life she had ever stepped in on a man in a shower, and she had been expecting a hot and happy reception. "Sorry." She tried to step back, and his hand lanced out and grabbed her in a grip of steel. "If you're tired," she said stiffly, pulling at that grip, not in any hope she could break it, but just to show him her resistance.

"I'm not tired, I'm terrified. Jolie." Still holding her by one arm so that she couldn't get away, he brought the other, soapy hand to cup her breast through the transparent wet cotton. "You're incredible." His voice thickened. "Jolie. I *promised* to treat you right, and then you do this to me. I'm so happy I don't even know what to do with myself, and then you layer sex on top of it. I can't even remember my name." His hand flexed helplessly on her breast, and she made a sound in her throat, as pleasure ran through her. "You turn me into an animal." The hand holding her arm slipped from it and cupped her other breast. He squeezed them up and toward each other, lost in the view. "And then the next day you're not sure you want me," he muttered, so low and far back in his throat she almost couldn't hear it.

Before she could figure out what to say to that—who *did* know what to do with someone this big in her life in the morning?—he slipped his hands down the clinging wet fabric and gripped her butt, lifting her to ride against his nakedness, and she lost coherent speech. There might as well have been nothing between his hard sex and hers. Nothing but that annoying, frantically arousing slip of transparent wet fabric.

He twisted her against him, sliding her back and forth over his sex. The shower rained down over her face. He stared down at that, fascinated, his own head well above the spray, sliding her harder, watching her pure helplessness to the elements in which she was caught: him, the water, her own desire.

His own face flushed, his arousal turning him into something—animal. Feral. Dangerous. He twisted suddenly to protect her face with his body, pushing her back against the wall of the shower, and she blinked wet lashes up at him, feeling absurdly grateful for being rescued from what he had submitted her to. "I'm going to last thirty seconds." His voice was guttural. "I might come right here. You have *no* idea what you look like, or what you're doing to me."

"I like it," she admitted again in a whisper. "I really like driving you wild." She twisted her hips, the wet fabric dragging against her clitoris, the lips of her sex struggling to cling to him through the cloth. "Make me come in thirty seconds, too."

"Oh, no." He dragged her up the wall, closing his mouth around one of her breasts through the cloth and suckling so hard she whimpered. "*You* I'm going to torture for at least an hour. But I think that's going to have to come second."

It didn't, though. In a sudden change of resolution, he dropped to his knees and pulled her thighs over his shoulders, so that she was riding on them. Tilting his head back for one long look up at her, while the water streamed into his face, he waited for her to realize what was coming and to twist and writhe in a sudden panicked conflict of embarrassment and desire. His hands gripped her thighs hard, so that she couldn't get away.

And then he brought his mouth to her, suckling her straight through the cloth. She made a little screaming sound, her hands clutching in his hair, pulling it too hard. "Twenty-nine more seconds," he said. And bit her with exquisite gentleness, as if he was tasting some tiny fragile chocolate. "Twenty-five." He sucked her clitoris slowly again, through the cloth, elusive and thorough as if he wanted her to melt on his tongue. Which she did, whimpering, her hands writhing in his hair. "Twenty-two. Twenty-one. What's your name?"

"Gabriel," she moaned, bucking helplessly, held like iron.

"Oh, good, you've forgotten yours, too. Twenty. Ah, Jolie." Her body was starting to shake uncontrollably. Her head fell back in the waves of pleasure. When they took her over, she could have drowned under them, drowned in the shower, for all she knew, but as the world came back to her, it was a world made of his body. He was holding her again, pulling off the wet boy shorts.

"I think that leaves five seconds for me," he said roughly and thrust deep into her, once, and then again, and again, as if he couldn't stop himself, he couldn't slow down. "*Ma belle*, you are so . . . so . . . " Words seemed to fail him. He dragged himself out of her and found finally a word to describe her as he drove hard again: "Mine."

His body pinned her to the wall in one deep, final thrust as he claimed her, her own body clutching helplessly around him.

Chapter 21

G abriel sprawled again. His bed was much bigger than hers, but he still took up most of it. She had woken lying on her side, curled toward the edge of it, her knees thrust past the side. An arm was snug over her waist, keeping her from falling. She twisted slowly, carefully toward him. As before, he slept so heavily she had the impression his body would leave its imprint on the bed forever.

She could hear the sound of his breathing, close and soft and intimate. The warmth and weight of his arm pressed her to the soft cotton sheets.

She had at least one idea of what to do with him in the morning. She curled up against him again, throwing her leg over his, and fell back asleep.

When she woke up again, Gabriel was still sleeping like the dead. His body hadn't even moved. It must be close to noon, which made her mouth curve wryly. Was this what he had been so determined not to miss Monday mornings? Sleeping? Or had he just thought that with her around, he would skip what must be his weekly recuperation from his short nights?

She did that, too. Slept short nights all through the week—working or reading late, her quiet time, then up early because she loved the dawn hours—then recuperated in one slothful, indulgent morning.

But she finally couldn't stay still any longer and slipped into the bathroom. Trying to comb her hair after her shower made her eyes water. Gabriel didn't have any conditioner, and his hands had left her hair in a mass of tangles. She tucked a towel around herself and went to the door, comb in hand, to see if he needed the bathroom space while she tried to get those tangles out.

He was lying on his back now, arms crushing the pillow on either side of his head, one knee bent as he stared at the ceiling. God, what a beautiful body. Her gaze drifted over the six-pack abs, the faint tan that suggested he did some kind of beach sport sometimes on his days off, the paler line at his hips, around that intimate part of his body that never saw sun but was all exposed to her.

Heat ran through her, and pride. That he wanted *her.*

It was enough to make a woman walk straight across the room and sit astride him to take possession again, if she could only get this blasted comb out of her hair.

His stomach muscles flinched. "*Putain.* What did I do to make you cry?" he asked, and she looked back at his face to find him watching her warily.

"You are so hot," she said helplessly. "It's probably a bad idea for me to keep telling you that."

He rolled over onto his side and propped on one elbow, an eyebrow going up. "It feels good to me."

"Yes, but you're already so arrogant."

"You keep saying that. And here I am, putting myself humbly at your service, trying to do everything you want me to do. No matter how unreasonable the demands." He looked smug.

He was the most infuriating man in the world. She yanked extra hard on the comb to punish herself for being that damn obvious about what she wanted him to do to her.

"*Now* what did I say? Jolie, please. Don't just stand there crying at me. Tell me what I did."

"It's my hair," she said between her teeth. "I'm not crying over you, you, you—arrogant—*animal.*"

He sat up, swinging his legs over the side. "That is completely unfair, to walk into the shower in that little, instantly-transparent outfit like some porn film fantasy and then complain a man is an animal. I'm doing my damned best. Come here." He tossed a pillow down between his spread feet.

She halted abruptly, giving that pillow and his spread legs a suspicious look.

His eyebrows went up, and then he grinned. "Honestly, you never think of *anything* but sex when I'm around. Are you sure you should be casting stones about me being an animal? I'm going to help you with your hair. And it's cheating for you to give me ideas about the way *you* could occupy yourself while I do it."

She narrowed her eyes at him.

He laughed out loud and pulled a prim sheet over his hips, tucking it firmly under his butt to hold it there while giving her a look like a stern nun. "Sit here. *With your back to me,* Jolie. Thank you." She curled her knees under her, strongly tempted to nestle her wet head back against that pseudo-puritanical sheet. But before she could, one strong hand took control of her head, pressing her forehead against his thigh, and the other delicately worked the comb free.

She didn't even feel a sting.

As the comb began to work through her hair, all the muscles in her back slowly undid, and she sank limp against his knee. He was so careful. This man who always seemed so big, so full of life he would break things just by the force of energy coming off him, and yet who every day, in the midst of his roaring, handled non-stop such exquisite, fragile, complex things. The man who went so fast toward what he wanted, and yet who took, every moment of his life, as long as he needed to get those delicate things just right, without breaking them.

She never felt a sting once. He used two hands for the more complicated snarls, but she could almost believe that even then, he never broke a single strand of hair.

By the time he finished, shifting her head to the other thigh when he needed to change sides, she was in a state of pure physical bliss, boneless.

"You know, for a beast . . . " she murmured dreamily, caressing her cheek against his thigh.

He slid those strong hands under her arms and picked her up, drawing her down on the bed, her back against his chest. "I know how to be gentle, Jolie." He closed his hand around hers and stretched her arm out, turning it to expose the most vulnerable flesh of her inner elbow and wrist. A little stream of air blew over that sensitive skin, as if he was blowing gold dust over something delicious. "Haven't I ever shown you?"

He dusted her all over in gold, with his breath, with his barely skimming touch. He was in no hurry himself, having had quite a night, and he made her feel so special she actually cried a little.

He sipped the tears off her cheeks, looking as if he didn't know what to do with that particular flavor.

Gabriel sat over warm, golden eggs, soft and fluffy and with just the right touch of butter and dollop of cream, a little blend of cheese, a sprinkling of sea salt. She was good in a kitchen. Not good like him. Just confident and content. It made him terrifyingly happy just to watch her, scared his stomach off somewhere out of his body to imagine breakfasts like this every lazy Monday and Tuesday morning, maybe with some little kids clinging onto their legs or clamoring for more.

Oh, *putain. Kids? Will you the fuck learn to sit on yourself* ever?! *How hurt do you want to get?*

"Do you know you're the first woman besides my mother who has ever offered to cook for me?"

She gave him a puzzled look. "You know, I'm quite a selfish person, but—"

"No, you're not."

"I am, really," she said earnestly, as if she just had to confess herself.

It pissed him off. "Shut up, Jolie. You don't know what you're talking about." Selfish. Her.

Pouring out all her enthusiasm and sense of wonder on everything he did. Giving that body of hers—God, how she gave her body. Making him supper. And breakfast. Because she wanted to. Running back and forth between Paris and Sainte-Mère to please the demands of two insanely greedy men.

He looked down at his eggs. How the hell self-absorbed were all the other people in her life, to beat him? And leave her thinking *she* was the selfish one?

"Do you really eat this for breakfast in the U.S.?" he asked, to escape his own thoughts. "Eggs? I could get used to this." *Putain.* Could he bite his tongue? Of course he could get used to it. That was his damn problem. He could get used to it so easily, and she could waltz on out and never even notice his world crashing down when its center disappeared.

It was her defense against self-absorbed people, maybe: her ability to leave them.

Or maybe her father lays such a weight on her life that she can't carry anyone else, too, and he always wins.

Or maybe, just maybe, she clings to that idea of being able to dump someone the way a woman might cling to a life preserver going over the Niagara Falls, because it reassures her even though it's not going to do a damn bit of good. He wished *he* had a life preserver.

Jolie's eyes flickered, and she gave him a searching look, then refocused on her work. Now she was adding some American pancakes to the mix, laughing, teasing him about getting used to an American breakfast—getting *used* to one—and every time she flipped the pancakes with a little expert jerk of the skillet, he felt as if it was his heart tumbling in freefall through the air.

He held his breath each time until her skillet dipped neatly under the whirling pancake and caught it. And then he let it out again, absurdly reassured by the little *smack* the pancake made hitting the pan. She was pretty good at catching spinning, freefalling things, wasn't she? At least it wasn't on the damn floor.

He couldn't believe he was looking for positive signs in the fact that she could flip a pancake.

"I was going to say, I'm pretty selfish, but—"

"Will you *stop* saying that? *Merde.*"

"*But* it kind of sounds like the other women you've dated have been real pieces of work. Did they ever look at anything but themselves in the mirror? I mean, is that why you picked them up, because they were pretty and you love to pour yourself out for people, and they were happy to let you do that without ever giving anything back?" She smacked the skillet down too hard on the burner. "Without ever getting their heads out of their own assholes," she muttered.

He stared at her, wondering suddenly if she had just been beamed down to him from some alien planet. Maybe he needed to check the Web to see what the real, human Jolie Manon was supposed to actually look like. "I *am* Gabriel Delange. It's natural they would assume I would do all the cooking." Had he been doing the same thing Matt was doing all this time? Dating women who couldn't see him, who only wanted to be seen?

Shit, how had he gotten lucky enough to meet *her* then? She saw him. She looked straight into him all the time and smiled at what she saw, too. Oh, God. This was so fucking scary.

"Really? Natural it would never occur to them that you might be *tired* when you get off after thirteen hours of merciless physical activity? Or *hungry,* as in, you know, that kind of thing *burns calories?*"

Why, she was pissed off, too, he realized, wonderingly. At least as pissed off as he got, when she said she was selfish.

"Why do you really get dumped, Gabriel? Tell the truth. Some woman gets all bitchy because you can't take her out for drinks because you have the *President of France* helicoptering in to dine here with half the leaders of the free world, and so you have to work that night *at your dream*, the thing you've *dedicated your life to*. And she just wants you to drop that. Because, you know, she can't figure out how to read a damn book by herself and maybe talk some of her friends into doing things Monday nights with you guys instead."

Gabriel was gaping at her. Wow. She had picked up a lot more kitchen language than one would think through the glass walls of her father's office. That was quite some attitude she had going there, too. "I, uh—"

"Eat your pancakes," she said, sliding a golden one out of the pan onto his plate. "And we need some maple syrup in this apartment. I'll pick some up at the Grande Épicérie when I'm in Paris."

As in . . . supply his kitchen with things she might need on a long-term basis?

At least the other women he had dated had only left behind a few hair products. If he had to discover bottles of maple syrup in his cabinets months after she had dumped him and remember this morning, he didn't know how he was going to survive it.

She slid him a jar of rosemary honey in place of the maple syrup and sat down across from him with her own pancake, just one and a little helping of eggs compared to his starving-man's plateful of them. Her eyes met his across their plates, bright and warm, and he gave a little sigh of despair. Maybe the aliens had sent her to utterly destroy him.

"Speaking of Monday night, I talked to Léa," he told her. "She said they would love to come over."

Jolie looked pleased for just a second, before a sudden realization hit her, and she brought her hand to her mouth, eyes rounding. "Oh, no. I'm going to be cooking dinner for Daniel Laurier?"

Gabriel had kind of figured *he* would be cooking dinner and Jolie would be setting the table. Maybe they could do the cooking together. The idea seized him too hard. It sounded so damn—warm. Wait a minute. He stiffened. "You cook dinner for *me*. Why should Daniel Laurier unnerve you?"

"Because if I screw up with him, I can't redeem myself with great sex," she told him witheringly. And laughed.

Yes, there was no way around it: if he couldn't convince her that his heart was worth holding onto, it was going to leave one hell of a shitty, awful hole in his chest when she dropped it and walked off.

Chapter 22

G abriel and Jolie had such a fun time in the kitchen—between laughter, butt pinches, threats to make someone regret interfering in someone else's recipe, a couple of growls, and Gabriel pressing her back against the counter with his big body and acting menacing more times than she could count—that Jolie forgot any thought of nerves.

Until they opened the door to see Léa smiling up at Daniel, who was saying something to her. Both the Lauriers turned at once as the door opened, dropping their exchange automatically, but Léa's expression stayed with Jolie.

How did she *do* that, pour so much love and support out for her husband that it was as if it was his lifeblood? Did he give her that much of himself *back*? Was it worth it?

Was there something wrong with Jo herself, that she couldn't seem to properly nourish her own father with enough love and enthusiasm, that she was afraid to offer that unstinting love and support to Gabriel, who so clearly deserved it? Was it some selfishness she had learned from her mother? she thought, with a lash of anger so old she hadn't realized the emotion still existed: that rage and pain from her childhood, when their mother had divorced their father and taken her and her sisters to the other side of the Atlantic so that they almost never saw him anymore, the rage that had grown up, that had learned to accept her mother's side of it as valid. More valid.

All of her flinched at the thought of changing, of becoming Léa, the person who gave all of herself up to the people she loved. And yet there was no denying that Léa's generosity of spirit made her extraordinarily beautiful. Even Jolie wanted to bask in it, despite a certain flicker of resentment at the woman for being a better person than she was.

(Why was she better? that resentment thought stubbornly. Why did the ability to give herself up without stinting make her *better*?)

She glanced up at Gabriel and caught a flicker of wistfulness on his face as he looked at the other couple, before he pressed the wistfulness away and bent down to kiss Léa's cheeks.

Sometimes, she just hated that French cheek-kissing tradition. She knew Gabriel and Léa were some kind of distant cousin, but last she checked, nothing prevented a man from being in love with his third cousin and wishing to hell he had won her for himself.

Gabriel straightened, shaking Daniel's hand so briskly the other man barely had time to finish kissing *Jolie*'s cheeks, and pulled them into the apartment.

Jolie enjoyed watching the two chefs together. Despite his earlier expressions of jealousy, Gabriel seemed very happy to see Daniel, and it was soon obvious that he still felt an affectionate, older-brother style pride in the younger man, which must date back to their days when Gabriel stepped in to help keep his pastry kitchen running and probably gave out all kinds of advice that saved Daniel's untried neck.

Daniel had such a contained elegance to him while Gabriel's energy was so expansive, just filling the whole room, that Jo had the whimsical impression of a black hole and a supernova trying to sit down to dinner together while still respecting each other's space. She wondered what Gabriel's impressions of the contrast between her and Léa were. Selfless versus selfish? The generous mother goddess versus the stubborn mortal?

He had said she wasn't selfish, but he could hardly

miss the contrast, could he?

At the end of the meal, she sighed, told herself not to be ridiculous, and then went into the bathroom to double-check her lipstick anyway. Because Léa had forgotten to put on lipstick, and she could at least have *that* advantage to being self-absorbed: she could manage to make her lips look more tempting.

"You're nuts, you know that?" Gabriel murmured from the doorway, and she looked from the mirror to him, her heart brightening instantly.

"I know," she said ruefully. "But you've got to admit she's gorgeous." When Léa looked up at Daniel, she was.

"Of course she's gorgeous," Gabriel said, amused and maybe a bit annoyed. "What do you think you are?"

Jolie dropped her lipstick and walked right up to him, wrapping her arms around his waist. He just picked her up and kissed that lipstick straight off her. "I love you," he said, dropped her back on her feet, and went back to the guests.

Leaving Jolie clutching the sink, staring at the space he had been as if nothing could ever fill the imprint he had left on it.

Putain. It was all Gabriel could do not to groan aloud and break one of those geranium pots on his balcony over his head or something. Could he not sit on himself *ever?*

How many million times had he told himself to go slow, to be careful? And there you go, just blabbed right out like that, because she was so cute, and she wrapped her arms around his waist like it was a perfect place to be, and she looked up at him with that smile, and it was so ridiculous for her to worry about Léa.

Look at Daniel, he thought with anguish, as his old protégé gave that slight smile of his down at his wife. There was a world of love in those gray eyes, in the angle of his head, in the way his fingertips rubbed just slightly, almost constantly, on her hip.

But he didn't go *jostling* her all the time with all his wants, throwing his heart out there like it was some bouncing ball that would just hop around happily and recover, instead of the fragile, terrified, essential organ it was.

Gabriel hesitated, remembering a bit more about the Daniel he had known at nineteen, when the man barely out of boyhood had just married Léa. Fine, so maybe Daniel *had* thrown his heart out there all unguarded like that, but, but . . . he had been *nineteen.* Gabriel was thirty-four. He should know better by now.

The problem was, when Jolie looked at him like that, she made him think anything was possible, even her.

And when she looked at him the way she did when she finally came out of the bathroom—wary, searching, confused, doubting, wondering—she made his heart lose all its bounce and slink down in him like sludge.

She drew Léa out on the balcony after that, with the excuse of showing her how beautiful the street looked from up there, and that was fine, in a way, because he didn't need her hanging close to him and Daniel, making contrasts between cool elegant princes and roaring uncontrolled beasts. But whenever he caught her eyes on him through the balcony doors, her lips were parted. Like he'd shocked the hell out of her.

Damn it.

He managed to ply her with another glass of the wine Daniel had brought. Given that it was Daniel who had selected it, and in addition as worthy of pleasing another three-star chef's palate, the wine was beyond sublime, so it wasn't like she resisted.

But she *still* didn't throw herself at him and say, *I love you, too.*

And it had been a whole half hour!

Damn it.

"Are you all right?" Léa Laurier asked Jo, in the careful tones of someone not sure she should intrude. The night settling over the old village was lovely, a softening of time, until they themselves grew eternal, two people who could have stood there at any moment over more than a thousand years, who could be here still a thousand years hence. The street, at that hour of the night,was not quieter than the afternoon, as one might expect, but noisier, laughter coming from one apartment, the clank of dishes from another, someone playing the guitar, and a woman's voice, from another apartment entirely, singing along to the guitar player's tune. The guitarist played a love song, and Jo found herself watching the shifting curtains from which the music came, trying to make out if it was a man or a woman who played, if the musician watched the window of the woman singing, if they knew each other or wanted to. "You look as if you've gotten bad news," Léa said tentatively.

"Not bad, no," Jolie said, surprised. *I love you. Not bad.* Scary, though. Overwhelming, when she quite stubbornly did not want to be overwhelmed. But the energy in him was *so* bright. So unutterably tempting.

"You're not in a fight with Gabe?" Léa asked. "We didn't come at a bad time? Because we can go."

"No, of course not," Jo said, really startled now and discomfited. How in the world did the other woman manage to be so sensitive even to a near-stranger's needs? Didn't that get *exhausting*? God, and Jo didn't even want to take care of her own *father's* needs, when they were so grim and desperate. She didn't even want to take care of *Gabriel's* needs more than a couple of hours a day and maybe on the restaurateur's equivalent of weekends, and Gabriel's needs were actually fun, in their greedy way. Why did she need so much time to just do what she wanted, take care of herself? "I was just thinking about something. I'm sorry." *Je t'aime.* For an expression that was only two syllables long, it sure packed in a lot of material for thought.

Down the street, the guitar player shifted gradually from the love song to something merrier, more teasing. The pretty contralto stopped singing in the other apartment, but Jo could swear there was the shape of a shadow against the woman's curtains, as if she gazed across the street from a gauzy hiding spot. Jo wondered if they both knew the song, if there was some joke or flirtation in it that she didn't get.

"How do you do it?" she asked Léa suddenly.

The other woman gave her a look of friendly inquiry.

"The chef's wife thing. Just pour yourself all into him that way. You never get—tired?"

Léa's face blanked a second, and she took a half-step back until her bottom pressed against the balcony railing, as if Jolie had just reached straight into her and hurt her. She didn't say anything, staring down into her wine.

Oh.

Jo looked away guiltily. The guitar song had shifted again, to something slow in a minor key, with a low brush of sound over it, and she realized after a moment that the brush of sound was actually the guitarist's voice. A man, then. Singing so very softly, she wasn't sure even the woman across the way from him was supposed to hear. Maybe he wasn't sure either.

Just for a moment, she was envious of the imagined careful, delicate courtship, a courtship that gave both of them all the time in the world to tiptoe through the eggshells between self and a relationship, to feel their way tentatively toward what they wanted. Gabriel would already have jumped across that balcony, probably. The man had *no* stop button. In fact, she might want to start locking her balcony door just to make sure he wasn't tempted into doing something stupid and getting hurt.

"You do have to be careful," Léa said, and Jolie looked back at her, surprised. She had thought the conversation over, having veered onto too fragile territory. "To keep something for yourself. No man really needs you to give all yourself up to him. Or he shouldn't. I'm, ah, trying to learn that."

Good lord, that look on Léa's face when she gazed at Daniel was her trying to hold herself *back*? She was starting to make Jo feel like the Wicked Witch of the West.

"You have to be careful to let him keep something for himself, too," Léa said quietly. "They have a very strong drive to give all of themselves without stinting, these chefs."

Jolie's mouth twisted wryly. "Sometimes I think *I* am the thing Gabriel wants to keep for himself."

"Yes," Léa said, as if this was the most natural thing in the world. "That's part of the trick. To balance yourself with that need."

Jo studied the other woman as if Léa held the mysteries of the universe. She had, after all, been married to a chef eleven years, and no sign of divorce yet. On the other hand, Léa was only a few years older than she was, right? Why did Jo feel so much more immature?

"It's a beautiful thing," Léa said, and Jo realized she, too, was gazing at the guitar player and the gauzy, dreamy curtains between him and the woman in the other apartment. The curtains that kept them both safe. "To be loved like that."

Jo could hear the other woman's throat tightening, and she closed her hand around the balcony railing uneasily. She hadn't realized how fast her question would lead her straight into a near-stranger's heart.

Léa took a breath, her voice growing stronger again: "But you have to be careful of your—time for each other. And apart. For both your sakes."

Jolie gave that some thought, rocked gently by that

guitar song, and finally shook her head. "I think I must just be too selfish. I want space for myself."

A little silence. "I'm not even sure I really understand what you mean," Léa said, with a tone Jolie couldn't quite place. Not sadness, not wistfulness, not envy. But something—some hint of something of those. "But sometimes I think it wouldn't have hurt us at all, Daniel and me, to grow up a little bit more before we married, to each have had a chance to develop a greater sense of self. Selfishness, if that's what you want to call it. It's a rather delicate process, to start developing it at this stage of our lives instead."

Hunh. Jolie tilted her head a little bit, trying not to too obviously stare at the other woman in the soft night, as if she was examining an alien species.

"I wouldn't knock selfishness, if you've got it," Léa said wryly and lifted her wine glass in a little toasting gesture. Before Jo could toast her back, she realized the gesture was intended for Daniel, through the balcony doors. "A little dose of it could go a long way, when making sure you don't get swallowed whole by the most extraordinary person in your life."

But you wouldn't really know, would you? Jolie thought. *Never having tried it.*

Maybe, when she thought it through, she didn't feel so bad not to be as generous with herself as Léa. Oddly enough, she might even feel rather proud.

Chapter 23

❝ You know, we didn't get any work done today,"
Jolie said, after the Lauriers had left, as she
finished helping load the dishwasher. She had seemed
so thoughtful after she came in from the balcony that
Gabriel had been trying to let her finish thinking, all
the way through to how much she loved him back. *See
how happy Léa is?* She *loves a chef.*

Of course, Daniel was a damn prince. Maybe it was
easier to love him.

"Hein?" They didn't get any *work* done today? What
the hell did that have to do with whether she felt any
love in her hard little heart for him, too? To think he
had told her how generous and unselfish she was.
Gabriel shoved at the dishwasher with his toe as he
closed it. Damn it. She could make a man pancakes
until he wanted to bury his head on the table and cry,
but she couldn't tell him she loved him? What was
wrong with her? Had she been warped at birth?

Oh, shit, yes, she was Pierre Manon's daughter,
she probably had. That man would warp anybody.

"We'll have to focus more tomorrow, or we'll never
get anything done," she said. "I'm not here for very
long, remember?"

As if he could forget that.

"In fact, I should probably go back a little earlier
Thursday, so I can check in on my father when I get in.
Since I left early Sunday."

Gabriel's lips slammed together. "He does not need
more of your life, Jolie! He's out of danger, he has
people checking on him when you're out of town, he

sees therapists, and you see him three days a week!" *I need more of your life.*

For all he took from me, Pierre Manon can give his most precious thing up to me.

And Gabriel would give him a nice little *bras d'honneur* while he took her, too. Maybe with the middle finger thrown in.

Her eyebrows knit, and she stared at him as if he was impossible to decipher.

Yeah, well, if you can't figure me out, you'd better not be dreaming of Daniel. That's how princes get so elegant, you know—by hiding most of themselves.

"Well, I should probably be going," she said.

He gaped at her, so stunned that she managed to walk right out the door while he was still standing there struck to stone.

That's it? I told you I love you and that's all you've got to say back? You've had three fucking hours over dinner to figure out something!

It took her entire descent of his three floors to recover. And her ascent of her three floors on the other side for fury to build until the urge to roar could have silenced four kitchens and a whole town, too. And that damn guitar player down the street, who drove him crazy. *Just go knock on that singing woman's door and introduce yourself already, merde.*

A light clicked on in Jolie's apartment. Gabriel went out onto his balcony. "Are you watching, Jolie?"

A shadow stood still in her living room, just glimpsed through the balcony doors.

He swung up on the two-centimeter wide iron railing and launched himself across the gap.

Jolie screamed, a strangled sound, caught in her throat from pure fear. And then Gabriel was landing on her balcony, heavily, no issues with the gap at all.

Her heart began to beat again in a mad rage, blood throbbing in her head. "You *idiot*. You *imbécile*. You stupid, stupid"—His body hit hers full on, taking her down to the floor, one arm under her protecting her from the full force of the fall.

"Go ahead," he snarled, making her body suddenly feel like a wisp of a butterfly, while his was all big, muscled, dangerous. "Tell me again how stupid I am."

Her adrenalin latched onto those hard muscles immediately, with a soft, eager *ooh*. She fought herself and him, shoving at him and writhing. He kissed her, hard, with a low growl deep in his throat, and just when that had almost undone her ability to try to smack him, he rolled off her. With another snarl.

She jumped to her feet, quite furious about being able to. She had been enjoying that particular bodice-ripper fantasy quite a lot, thank you. "You *idiot!*"

"It's only two meters, Jolie. What, are you scared of heights?"

Conscious of all the open windows the length of their street, she snarled her second scream low in her throat.

He sat up. "That's kind of hot. Why don't you go run so I can catch you some more?"

She narrowed her eyes at him, fulminating so hard she was seriously tempted to kick him. She turned around and stalked into the kitchen. Which had the only light turned on in the place.

She slid a glance back into the shadowy living room. Hesitated just one moment of delicious trepidation.

And turned the light off.

Absolute silence from the living room.

In the blackness, Jolie slipped out of the other end of the kitchen, sneaking down the hall.

"Jolie?"

She hesitated before the doors, her heart beating like a mad thing now that she had started this, wondering where in the world she was going to hide.

"Jolie." The rumble was back in his voice, low, dangerous. "You're asking for trouble."

Well, yes. If he hadn't figured out she liked trouble by now, he must have a very unrealistic view of himself.

Silence again. Her breathing sounded too loud.

A floorboard creaked.

She dove through the nearest door into the unfurnished spare bedroom. Shoot. Nowhere to hide. She plastered herself behind the door.

Silence. She strained for the creak of floorboards, trying to follow him. He moved like a—beast. So big but so light on his feet. So prowlingly graceful. She could imagine that prowl in the dark, his eyes hunting.

Why did she provoke him to catch her? If she was afraid to lose herself, why did she love so much the idea of being caught? Did she want no choice? Did she want him to make it impossible for her to get away?

A little growl crawled through the apartment, raising all the hair on her body and melting her sex. Pleasure tangled through her, mixing with adrenalin, and her heart slammed out of control as he pushed the door open and stepped inside.

Quick as she could, she darted out of the room, feeling the brush of his fingers and the low growl again all over her nerves.

She dove all out for the next room, something big and menacing behind her, coming for her.

She gave an involuntary little scream, of primal fear and primal delight, as he almost caught her.

Almost? There was no way she could escape him in that small space, not with his reflexes. He was *letting her get away*. Playing with her like a mouse.

Just so she knew she didn't really want to.

And he kept doing it until, like the poor mouse, she

was about to go mad with terror. Low wicked laughs brushed over her just as she snuck by. Fingers grazed her, again and again, until she was a mass of adrenalin and desire and deep, delighted fear.

He played with her until she couldn't take it anymore, and finally she cracked, leaping out from behind her door as he came into her room and landing on his back with a loud, "Boo!!"

He jumped at least a foot.

Her adrenalin escalated into laughter, almost hysterical with satisfaction at the coup and the still crazy pressure of heart-thumping hunger.

He began to laugh, too, but lower and much, much more dangerous as he peeled her off his back and carried her to the bed. "Oh, Jolie, you are in so much trouble."

Chapter 24

Well, that had been good for his temper. But she hadn't cried out, *I love you, I love you, you gorgeous sex-god of a man you,* in the middle of any of her orgasms either.

He hated it. It made him so mad. What the fuck was *wrong* with his heart? Why didn't she want it?

She wanted everything else about him.

"I don't understand," Jolie protested, as Gabriel dragged her through the streets the next morning to the parking lot below the walls. "Aren't we supposed to be working on the cookbook at some point?"

"I don't feel like it," he growled. "I get two days off a week, I might as well enjoy them. We can work tomorrow."

She put her hand on her hips indignantly. She might have tried to brace her feet, because he felt a tiny smidgen of resistance, but by the time he paid attention to it, he had already run right over it and had her halfway down the stairs. No sense backing up now. "So you blackmailed me into spending four days a week down here so I can be your sex slave for two of them?"

"If that's what you call four days, you have a counting problem. Four days minus thirteen hours, maybe. And *I* am *your* sex slave. You're the one who only thinks about one thing. No wonder I'm exhausted and need time to get out of town and think."

She glared at him. He unlocked his car and held open her door.

She looked down at the sleek silver car for the first time, and her eyebrows went up a little. "To attract girls?"

"Well—yes." With hours like his, a man had to try whatever he could.

"Does it work?"

"No," he said indignantly. "It mostly attracts men. It's a beautiful car, too. I'll never understand women in a million years. What *do* you care about?"

Her fingers grazed over the back of his hand holding the door, as she slid into the low leather seat, and the touch shivered a little delicate brush of pleasure all through him. She smiled up at him, and he forgot to be annoyed at how easy she found it to make him her sex slave. "You're so cute. You, of course. If you've been dating people who care about something else, that explains your problem."

Which flummoxed him into silence for the whole winding trip up into the high hills. They wound through *garrigue*, the tangled mass of Mediterranean brush and herbs spotted with yellow flowers, on roads that seemed narrower than the car and where he could only manage to pass cars coming the other way by nearly hanging two wheels off a cliff. The top down, they soaked up scents of thyme, lavender, rosemary, and pine, the intense, unforgettable, sun-baked scents of the *garrigue*.

He drove all the way to a tiny, old village, so high above the sea one could almost forget the population crowding the coast, just them, the ancient stone, the deep blue of the Mediterranean, and the dark green of the hills. A haven of peace, with its old church and its little stone fountain rippling quietly, the village so empty of people at this hour of a workday that it felt almost deserted.

Be a nice place for someone to say, *I love you, too,* he thought and sighed heavily, leaning back against the church and sticking his hands in his pockets the way Daniel always did. Was he just going too fast again?

And why did falling in love with him inspire so

much greater caution on her end? Did he look that bad?

Fuck, what if she was always this enthusiastic and hungry and admiring with all those other boyfriends she eventually dumped? *You're so cute. Of course I care about you, but. . . .*

"My mom always said not to get involved with a chef," she said suddenly, sitting on the wall near an old, gnarled cypress, staring out to sea at one of the hazy green islands, so that he could only just see her profile from his sulk against the church.

He stiffened. And slumped against the stone, feeling defeated. Everything that was the best and most wonderful about himself, what expressed *everything* in him, all the energy and beauty and love, the heart of him that he could only communicate that way because every other way people always thought it was such a beast's. Everything beautiful—and women always thought it was what made him the worst. What they couldn't love.

I can't do this, he thought to the village. A dove called a soft, pitying *roucoucou*, but otherwise the old stone village gave the thought the silence it deserved. And his brain shook it off him like water off a duck's back. *I can't do this* just wasn't a phrase that stuck to him very well.

"Maybe your mother didn't like it," he said.

Jolie angled her perch on the wall enough to give him an ironic look. "You think?"

"The obsession with food, and being the best, the emotions and the temperament, the fact that she had to be alone sometimes."

"It destroyed our family. Do you know how little I saw Papa, after I was five years old?"

Gabriel was silent for a moment, searching through his words, aware that he couldn't just say them the first way they popped out, as he often did. "I barely remember your mother, she came to the kitchens so rarely. But Pierre . . . I hate him. But he never changed. He was the same man when I started working for him as he was when he fired me in a crash of pans. So it's hard to believe he was different before he got married. It may be that your mother married him wanting him to be someone else, wanting him to change."

Fuck. If he thought that being dumped after a month hurt, or after six years, what about being dumped after ten fucking years and three darling little girls?

Fuck-shit-fuck. Maybe I can't do this after all. The thought of it, Jolie dumping him like that and stealing their children away to the other side of the world, made him want to curl over his knees under that cypress and vomit.

He took deep breaths, planting his back hard against the stone, staring out at the sea, breathing in cypress and sun and age. An eternity of endurance. *Putain, non. I'm not going to crawl back into my beastly hole of a kitchen and brood over my wounds until I die alone because I'm afraid.* "Maybe your mother didn't like it," he said strongly. "But Jolie—you do."

Her hands curled into the stone wall. She turned suddenly, putting her back to the ocean, and faced him. She looked beautiful that way, half-framed by the cypress, with the sea beyond her. He wished he had a camera. *In case you don't see her this way again?*

"You love food. You know you do. You love coming into my kitchen. You love it when I feed you. And I love to feed you. We could probably build a lifetime on just that, right there. Every day, that happiness."

Her eyes widened at the word *lifetime.* Too fast again, damn it. He would never, ever, ever learn to hold himself back to something other people could handle.

He forged on. "You like my temper. You—*play* with it. You enjoy it."

Her mouth curved sheepishly. "You're like a big marshmallow, Gabriel. It's not exactly scary."

He was a little offended at the idea that he wasn't scary, especially after she had nearly made him hit the ceiling when she jumped on his back out of the dark the night before, but he plowed ahead. "And you like being alone. You've said so. You love to be able to curl into yourself in peace and quiet at least part of every day and sink into the introspective side of your own work. Maybe the balance between my work and yours solves *your* problem with men, your need for space."

The curve of her mouth deepened. Her eyes were very green. "And you don't drape very much," she murmured.

Whatever that meant. In his entire life, no one had *ever* compared him to drapery. "You even like the rhythm, as far as I can tell. I never asked you to get up at five-thirty, and I never asked you to stay up until midnight for me. You just do it."

She shrugged. "I've always been like that. It started as a teenager." Her eyes slid away from his and then back. "When I was visiting my father."

If he ended up owing Pierre Manon for the best thing to ever happen in his life—namely, his daughter— it would be the weirdest full circle.

"So. See?" He held out his hands, palms up, his heart kicking into overdrive again. "*I* think we're a perfect match." Except for the fact that she was her mother's daughter, and her mother had shown her how to dump a man even after ten years, of course. He pushed the treacherous thought away and kept his hands extended, even as his heart begged pitifully for him to close his fists back around it and lock it away somewhere safer.

Did it look all yucky to her again?

Putain, a *marshmallow*? After all the beautiful things he had shown her, that was the best comparison for his heart she had come up with? She was a damn food writer!

"Except for the fact that my father needs me, lives

in Paris, and you hate him, of course," Jolie said heavily and sighed.

Damn it. He was going to have to solve that problem somehow, wasn't he?

He drove them up even higher in the hills, where the spaghetti road turned into angellini and made him think of twisting, turning soars of sugar with which he could grace something delicious. They pulled off in a *parc naturel*, and he lay back on the hillside soaking in the clear bright view of the sky, as he rarely had time to do during the rest of the week.

But Jolie sat with her arms wrapped around her legs. Maybe she was trying to work up the courage to tell him she loved him. She took a deep breath. His heart sparked hopefully despite himself.

"He's so depressed," Jolie said, low, and his heart slammed into a damn wall and thudded to the ground. Damn it. Maybe he needed to put protective gear on it or something. "He was depressed already—ever since he lost that star and resigned, of course."

Gabriel said nothing. He had had a hard time of it himself, when Pierre fired him just a few weeks after the girlfriend he lost while giving his all for his chef dumped him. It had taken him months to get mad enough to pull his act together and come back fighting, although to be honest, he hadn't had time to brood about it nearly as much as he might have wanted to, because Daniel and Léa had been in such desperate straits. A man could hardly sit on his ass, nursing his wounds, while his cousins' restaurant crumbled down on top of them in the earthquake of its great chef's death. He'd admired Henri Rosier, too, after all; the man used to let him come into his kitchens all the time when he was a kid and gaze around in fascination. He'd done his apprenticeship with him, and it had been that training that let him take off like such a rocket in Paris when he got his first job there at nineteen.

Where he had done so extraordinarily well until Pierre Manon fired him. So admittedly, his sense of sympathy when Pierre lost his star had been—entirely absent. Vicious satisfaction described his feelings a lot better. And then eye-rolling disgust when Pierre just caved to the blow. He'd wanted to go up to Paris and shake the man out of it—physically, with his hands gripping the older chef's shoulders—but Pierre had lost the right to be saved by him. He'd tucked his fists under his arms and glowered at the computer which would have let him purchase a train ticket and thought, *Tough shit to you. You don't deserve my help.*

It would be devastating to lose a star, of course. Far worse than losing a job. Gabriel just felt—he might take a year off to safari through Africa or something, but he would still, in the end, come back fighting.

"But now." Jolie sighed heavily. She looked so sad and despairing, as if she just didn't know what to do.

Well, of course she didn't know what to do. She would have to be desperate to be talking to *him* about her father.

"I try to get him interested in things. He's not even very badly off, you know—you should see some of the people who were in his rehab hospital. It makes you want to cry. He could be *fine.* But—it's like he's determined to give up. I can't pit my will against his."

"So what do you do?" Gabriel asked abruptly. "If you don't pit your will against his?" God knew, he had pitted his will against Pierre Manon's before, and all a headbutt of titanic wills got you was a lot of bystander destruction and severe migraines.

"What I did before, with the cookbook. I try to coax him into working on some of his recipes, because—well, I read that it was good for people to revisit what they were proud of. Like a scrapbook of accomplishments. That's what the cookbook is!"

"*That's* how you got started cookbook writing," he said softly. "To give your father your pride in him."

"Well, and I love it," Jolie said, embarrassed. "Finally getting to sink my hands into a chef's world, to be right in the middle of it, it's so *amazing*. But . . . maybe, yes. A little bit of both, maybe."

"And what do you do when he says no? To working on the recipes."

"I don't push it. I don't want to stress him. His blood pressure. . ."

"Isn't he taking medication for that? Because if you have to keep Pierre Manon from getting stressed or losing his temper for the rest of his life to save him from a stroke, Jolie, it's just not possible. He's a *stressé de la vie.*" Everything in life stressed that man. Unlike Gabriel himself, who tended to let all his emotions out, one way or the other.

"I'd like to let a little more time pass, get him a little more stable!"

"Did his doctors say you needed to do that?"

She hesitated. "Well, they said to make sure he exercised and to try to get him engaged in life."

Gabriel considered that, and Jolie. "I think you're babying him."

"He just had a stroke!"

Gabriel shook his head. "It sounds to me as if you've been babying him for years. Ever since he quit like a coward and fled the restaurant scene, instead of at least picking himself back up and making some stunning turnaround with a new restaurant two years later. He's *Pierre Manon, putain.* He doesn't need *babying.* Oh, I'm sure he laps it up. More than fifteen years with his family on the other side of the ocean? Who wouldn't lap up the attention? Certainly not that narcissist. In fact, if you ask me, the depression is partly his way of making sure he keeps getting attention. What happens to him if he gets better? You stay down here in the south of France where you're happy, that's what." He just went ahead and said that as if it was a given, because one thing he had learned in kitchens before he was even nineteen—to speak with authority about anything he wanted to make happen.

Jolie folded her arms, scowling at him. *Bon sang*, she was copying his expressions. And it brought out the family resemblance to Pierre vividly. "Are you trying to twist the way I take care of my father after a stroke into whatever suits *you* the best?"

"Look, Jolie, we're not running a nursery school in a three-star kitchen—"

"Yes, I noticed how much of a chance you were willing to give to a new hire," she said, with dudgeon.

"If they don't have the absolute will to be the most perfect, most beautiful out there—""How do you know I don't have that will?" she demanded indignantly. "You didn't give me a chance!

"I mostly fired you so I could ask you out," Gabriel reminded her.

"Sexual hara—"

"Can we just remember that you were not actually working for me at the time! Anyway, if they don't have that will, and Jolie, no one who likes to have long periods of time in quiet solitude like you do should work in a three-star kitchen, then they're gone. Are you trying to get me off the subject of your father on purpose?"

She frowned and looked down.

"Well, I'm not going to baby you either. Not in this. It won't help you. Your father spent *his life* in three-star kitchens. He rose to the *top* of this field. He fought with people like *me*—and won. You can't engage him in life by wrapping him up in padding. He responds to *stressors*, to urgency, to demand. He responds to the compulsion to be perfect, to create something beautiful, to prove his worth. He responds to people telling him he can't do something and that he needs to try harder, not to people telling him he can and not to worry if it's not as good as it could be. If you want to go around reassuring him that he has plenty of worth and not to

worry about it, and that his daughter will love him
while he sits on his butt not trying, then . . . I don't
know. Maybe he will live a long time without another
stroke. Fine. Forty more years of watching TV. But he
sure as hell won't be engaged with life. Not Pierre
Manon."

He fell silent.

Jolie glared at her feet, but her teeth worried at her
lower lip.

Gabriel scowled himself, before he finally burst out
with just one last word he had to say on the subject.
"And *my* cookbook is not going to be a retrospective
memorial of my life. It's going to be the first tribute of
many to all that I'm still going to do. Since your father's
only fifty-five, I sure as hell hope no one is treating his
cookbook like a memorial service either."

Because, you know, he still hated that man. And it
was nothing but a guilty, ugly feeling, hating a man at
his memorial service.

Chapter 25

J olie was almost looking forward to the train ride. Five and a half hours away from anyone but strangers, no one wanting anything from her except to check her ticket and maybe get past her to go to the restroom. Her initial attraction to Gabriel could be likened to seeing a trickle of water coming from a great huge wall, walking up to it to get a sip to quench her thirst, and having the dam burst on her, carrying her away in its rushing flood. It was exciting, and unlike an actual dam burst it was fun, but since she wasn't going to manage to get that rushing flood to slow down for anything, she wouldn't mind finding a little island of rock where she could sit and take a break while she thought a while. Or just rested quietly with herself. A long train ride worked well.

If only she didn't have her father's depression to face at the end of it.

She winced away from the thought guiltily, but it was too late. Part of her mind was already sinking into the fantasy: her time to herself came not from a train ride but from Gabriel heading into work the next morning while she went to work in her apartment, and they met up again six hours later after the lunch service, to talk or stroll or make love or whatever struck their fancy, and then he went back to work, and she went back to work, and evening fell, and she slipped into the back door of his kitchen and watched his face light up. . . .

If only her time to herself could be framed every day with that brightness, that energy, that delight in his face. If only she could fill *his* time off work with that delight he seemed to take in her. . . .

I love you.

What did that mean to him, exactly?

Everything?

Had he said it a lot, with that buoyant enthusiasm of his, to all the women who had dumped him? Did it scare him at all?

It would be nice to know she was special somehow and not just the woman who hadn't dumped him yet because she was tolerant of his hours.

Tolerant. She wasn't sure she understood his previous girlfriends' inability to entertain themselves while he was working. If they got bored, surely there was nothing more fascinating in the world than a three-star kitchen on a Friday or Saturday night? Especially when it just made the three-star chef's night to be able to feed his girlfriend something special. . . .

Granted, in a long-term relationship, one that—oh, say, just for argument purposes, might include kids or something—it would certainly be nice to have a bit more of the weekend off to spend with the family, but . . . she and kids might have leverage on Gabriel. He wasn't her father, and it was very hard to imagine him not wanting to swing his own kids up in his arms with all the greedy enthusiasm with which he grabbed her. If he wanted the time enough, he could make his sous-chefs handle Saturdays and Sundays, for example. Or he could close Sunday entirely and take the financial hit. Lots of things could be negotiated in a couple, if you were strong yourself and knew how to be both firm and understanding. Couldn't they?

Her parents hadn't managed to negotiate those things, but then, had they actually tried. All she could remember were fights, and her mother's increasing hatred of her father's obsession with his work.

Gabriel, with kids, crawling on all fours, playing growly gonna-get-you games. Gabriel with a couple of pre-schoolers sitting on top of him, pinning him to the floor as they got him back, wrapping him completely around their little fingers.

Whoosh went her stomach, as if she had gone over an innocent-looking hill and found the road just dropped out from under her. That was—where had *that* come from? The only times she had ever even tried to think of a marriage-with-kids vision before, it had been at the man's insistence, and it had made her frantic to get away, back to where she could be herself.

Gabriel, making a little girl's princess birthday cake. That little girl would have the most fantastical wonderland of a fairy cake ever.

Okay, stop it already! she shouted at her brain.

"Philippe Lyonnais," Gabriel said broodingly, watching her while she got dressed and packed up her computer and the things she wanted to take with her. "All Saturday afternoon. He doesn't want to go home and be with his *fiancée*, by any chance?"

Jolie grinned. "Gabriel. I told you he was crazy about her."

"Maybe." Gabriel lounged on the bed like a lion contemplating a fight. "But the last time *I* saw him, women were falling all over him. And you love aggressive men."

"No, I do not!" Jolie said indignantly.

Gabriel cut a glance at her and raised his eyebrows. He was lying naked on his stomach on her bed, braced on his elbows, which provided a really glorious view of his strong, smooth back and tight butt.

"I don't love you because I *love aggressive men*, I— wait."

Gabriel raised his eyebrows, for all the world as if he was just politely inviting her to elaborate, but his eyes had gone brilliantly feral and intent. He rolled on his side, where he could face her more directly and have a hand free for grabbing.

"*Stop it!* You're not *tricking* me into saying— Gabriel."

Anger rose in the feral eyes, a thunderstorm.

"Can you not just hold back, *ever*?"

"No," he said. "I can't. I can persist. I can take rejection and keep going. But I can't hold back to avoid the failure in the first place. I already tried."

She blinked at him for a moment. "With me? *When?*"

He scowled. "I knew you couldn't even tell."

"You are so *arrogant*! You're worse than every man I've ever dated, times ten. You think you can just *take over my life* to suit yours."

He flung himself out of bed and hunted for pants, incensed. "You know what? That's right, Jolie. I do take. I'll take every last thing you've got to give. But it just might the fuck be that I might the fuck give you something back in exchange."

He found his pants and yanked them on, looking so furious and so hurt.

"That's worth you," he muttered suddenly. "Maybe. You could let me the fuck try."

"Oh, you're worth more than me," Jolie exclaimed involuntarily, stunned he could ever think otherwise. And then she slammed her lips together, on a sudden wave of realization. Was *that* what she was afraid of? That she would just be the tiny font in his great, huge life?

Because she didn't like being the tiny font, she realized, for the very first time. She loved these incredible chefs and all they did, she was delighted to sing their praises to everyone willing to buy a book or look at a blog. But she wanted what she did to be worth something, too. Maybe a quieter worth. But front and firm and center.

Gabriel looked enraged. Half-naked, all mad. Mad was really a glorious good look on him. It tightened all those beautiful muscles. "Don't you ever think that! What I do is for you. The most beautiful thing I could possibly make in the world is only *for you to eat*." He leaned in close to her, said it between his teeth. "To give you pleasure. I was calling to you like a damn firefly, and you found me, and now I think of *you* when I make them. Don't you *ever* say you're worth less than *my best.*"

He bent over her where she sat cross-legged on the bed, his face too close, forcing himself into her space. His eyes glittered like sun off the Mediterranean, a lit blue that almost hurt the eyes. She lifted a hand and curved it against that taut face.

She wanted to check if he had meant it, then, when he said he loved her. But then she thought, *Of course he did, you idiot. It's an insult even to ask it.*

She wanted to say, *I love you, too.* But he was so very big, in every way, and unless she counted all that time she had spent on her father's cookbook trying to write the perfect description for his Rose as an exploration of his soul, she had only known him a few weeks.

She just wasn't ready. He was amazing, but she just hadn't relaxed those inner muscles of hers enough yet to let all this work.

So she sat there staring up at him, not sure what to say, her fingers caressing his cheek in an unconscious tiny motion, just getting lost in those blue eyes.

The tension slowly, very slowly, relaxed out of him, as they held still like that, and as it did, something in her—maybe those inner muscles—responded and started to relax, too.

He really was amazing. She brought up her other hand, framing his face now, pushing back the lock of hair that had fallen over his forehead, gazing into those blue eyes. She started to smile, and just as her lips started to part—

Gabriel heaved a great breath and let his forehead drop onto hers. "I just need more time," he muttered, his arms going around her. "I hate it when you go off to

Paris every week. I just need a way to *know* that you'll come back."

The first fragile breath of those words got blown away, not something one could say unless everything was waiting to hear them. "I've got a legal contract to come back, Gabriel! What else do you need?"

"I know." He squeezed her harder. "I know. But Pierre—" He broke off.

She tucked herself into his hold, a sense of defeat managing to sneak through her, even embraced by so much energy. This thing with her father, this depression, how could she ever overcome it? And this thing between Gabriel and him—how could she keep being the person caught in the middle? Sometimes she had to wonder if the need to beat her father was all that had drawn Gabriel to her in the first place. If she was really just the tiny font in the picture, the bit of debris caught in the flood and soon destroyed by it, when she was so busy deluding herself it was all for her.

"Gabriel?" she whispered into his shoulder.

"*Oui, chaton?*" he whispered back to the top of her head, the gentlest of breaths on her hair.

"Will you make me your Rose?"

Silence, the muscles that held her stiffening. He pulled away. "Jolie." He turned his head away, his profile rigid. "Don't ask me that."

No. And it was absurd to be that disappointed. He had moved on from that dessert, that was all; it held too much pain for him. It wasn't as if he had ever held back from her, or—she remembered uneasily his statement *I tried*—not that she had noticed. She didn't know why she felt that if he made that Rose for her, she would be able to trust him with her. Maybe it was because it would feel as if he was trusting her at last with the most vulnerable part of him. That for all the ways he wanted to push his way in, take over her life, grab it for his, he would invite her into this most fragile, most precious part of himself.

She sighed and pressed her forehead a moment against his shoulder before she pulled herself together and to her feet. "It's probably a bad moment to mention this, but I need to get moving, if I'm going to catch the train," she said.

And Gabriel went to the window and stood there, staring across at his apartment, one fist clenched and his jaw rigid.

Well, there went the life out of his week, Gabriel thought an hour later, watching the train pull away. He curled his fists in his pockets—trying to channel elegant princeliness as hard as he possibly could—and wondered, abruptly, how badly the life went out of *her* week.

When the train pulled away, and she settled into that six-hour commute to go face her father's depression, did she feel all her energy being sucked away? Did it convince her that was what men did, suck the life out of anyone who let herself love them?

Did every kilometer back toward that depression make her more wary of love in general and of loving chefs in particular?

He couldn't even share the commute with her, because if she knew what he was planning, there was no way she would let him take over her life like that.

He really, really wanted to be a prince for Jolie. But he was afraid that what she needed was a beast.

Chapter 26

Pierre Manon wasn't quite as tall as Gabriel, but he wasn't small, and he had always had that Russian KGB look to help him seem bigger and tougher. He had let himself go, about the way you could expect of a man used to burning through thousands and thousands of calories a day who suddenly stopped working and went off to sulk for years. But the slight drag at the left corner of his mouth wasn't nearly as bad as Gabriel had feared. Fortunately. Otherwise, even Gabriel might not have been able to go through with this.

"Gabriel Delange," Pierre said flatly, when he recovered from the shock of seeing Gabriel on his doorstep. "Come to gloat?"

"Yes," Gabriel said and shoved his way in, bumping the older man out of his way and striding into his living room. He could have gotten past Pierre without bumping him, but he wasn't here to make friends with his old chef, or to baby him, or to pamper him into feeling better about himself in any way whatsoever. In his pocket, his phone rode reassuringly against his butt. He'd texted Jolie a couple of hours ago from the train, just to make sure her session with Philippe Lyonnais was still on for this afternoon, and she had texted him back a photo of one of Philippe's beautiful desserts just being offered to her by the man to tease him.

It had done more than tease him. He'd had a strong desire to punch the other man, but he supposed he was going to have to get used to that, since Jolie was a food writer. So he just channeled that extra dose of aggressive energy into what he had come here to do—be the damned beast.

He could hear Pierre's outraged gasp behind him. *I bet that woke up some old instincts, didn't it? Let's see how long you put up with me.*

He turned and looked Pierre over with a sneer. "I told you when you fired me you were going to regret it. Look at you now. You're pathetic."

Pierre Manon went rigid with fury. "You try having a stroke."

It made him feel sick with dread to even imagine it. He shoved the compassion away. "Well, if you're still alive when I do have one, then *you* can gloat. If you still have a gloat in you, the way you're going." He upped his sneer. "But you were pathetic long before you had the stroke. You've never been worth anything without me, have you? Even your cookbook had to have my Rose on the cover to get any attention."

Pierre's eyes had gone brilliant. Funny, for all the times they had glared at him, Pierre's eyes had never stuck in his mind, but they were the exact same color as Jolie's. "Without *you*?" the older chef sneered right back. "You're nothing but a *pâtissier* with delusions of grandeur!"

"Yeah, all three stars' worth," Gabriel said.

Pierre's mouth firmed. Even that stricken left corner of it pulled tight into line.

"Did Jolie tell you she's writing *my* cookbook next?" Gabriel forged ahead, before the other man could speak.

"She's *what*?"

"Oh, you fell for that Daniel Laurier story, did you?" Gabriel said derisively. "What's the matter, are you so out of touch that you didn't even remember what other top chefs were around Nice?"

"I remembered the memorable ones," Pierre sneered, in his turn.

Ooh, nice one. The man would be back to his old *salaud* self in no time, at this rate. "And I bet the cookbook she does for me sells *well*. Since the name on it won't be some has-been. *I'll* be glad to demo and do signings with her until she thinks the sun rises and sets on me."

A flicker in Pierre's green eyes. *Yeah, we all like the idea of Jolie's hero worship, don't we? We'd all like to be the fucking prince in the scenario. Not—this.*

Damn it, did his eyes have to look so much like Jolie's?

"It's too bad you haven't bothered training any new chefs in years. Maybe if you had at least been able to land a few consulting jobs, there would be someone around who still respects you enough to host a promotional event for you. A few people willing to act as your *sous* for the demos."

"I never tried to land consulting jobs!" Pierre Manon hissed.

Gabriel laughed. "I can't believe *you* just used *not trying* as an excuse. And I thought I didn't have any more respect to lose for you."

"And I have respect! Luc Leroi is begging me to come to the Leucé for an event."

"Really?" Gabriel raised his eyebrows. "That's the first I've heard of an event for your cookbook. It didn't get much attention, did it?"

Pierre Manon's lips slammed together again.

"Wait. Luc? Luc Leroi? My old *sous-chef* at the Luxe? You can't tell me he has fond memories of *you*."

Pierre glared at least as hard as the time Gabriel had gotten fired. "I made that kid," he said between his teeth.

Gabriel snorted. "More likely he wants to impress your daughter." *Merde*, and Luc Leroi looked like a damn god had decided to walk out of the Fires of Creation and make sure Earth got built up to his standards. He made an elegant prince look like a step *down.* Gabriel's heart tightened anxiously, because it couldn't help it, because the damn thing was always yanking his emotions around like that.

"More likely he wants to impress *me*," Pierre Manon retorted. "Hugo Faure is retiring next year. They'll need the best to replace him." Hugo Faure was the head chef de cuisine at the Hôtel de Leucé, and Gabriel thought it extremely unlikely the Leucé would replace Faure with a chef known for losing a star for their rival hotel, but Pierre locked eyes with him, with a hard defiance, when he said it, so Gabriel contented himself with sneering, to give that hard defiance a little nourishment.

"You tell yourself that, Pierre. In fact, tell me again why your daughter has to do all the commuting back and forth while she's working on the Côte d'Azur? What's the matter—you can't even land a consulting job in the south of France anymore? Is that because you've been sitting on your butt for so long?"

Pierre's eyes narrowed. He didn't say anything else at all, but that green glittered and burned.

"Well, I just came to gloat." Gabriel glanced at his watch. Yeah, he wanted to give himself plenty of time to get out of here before Jolie finished up with Philippe. "By the way, just so you know. That Rose you stole from me? My girlfriend? My life? I don't even give a fuck. Because *I've* got something better. *I've* stolen *your daughter.*"

And he turned around and walked out of the living room—and straight into Jolie.

"Oh, fuck," he said on a gasp, sick.

She was standing stark still in the hall, a purse slung over her shoulder, her face white, her fists clenched. He hadn't even heard her come in.

"Jolie." He reached for her shoulders.

She wrenched them away. "This was all about the two of you, all the time?"

What?

"All that time you were screwing me, it was really

just to screw him?"

Gabriel made a low sound, as if someone had just gutted him. He couldn't believe she had just said that. All the times they had made love, all that beautiful, hungry happiness—*screwing her*? In some vindictive game against her father?

How could he feel that wonderful, ready to do anything for her, ready to risk even her—for her—and she find it so easy to think he was so horrible?

Yes, she had caught him essentially ripping out a kitten's entrails, but couldn't she at least stop to wonder why?

When he held out his heart to her, what the fuck hell had she seen? Why did people always think his heart must be so damn ugly?

"You bastard," Pierre said from the living room doorway, and Gabriel looked up to find the older man staring at him, both fists clenched, eyes glittering. "You really went after my daughter? To get back at me?"

"Fuck you," Gabriel told him, *va te faire foutre,* and grabbed Jolie's shoulders again, dragging her out of the apartment. He locked her back against the door, his arms on either side of her head.

"It's still all about you two, isn't it?" Jolie said bitterly, and even though her mouth twisted and her jaw set hard, the gold-and-green eyes started to fill with tears. "I can't believe even you came all the way up here just to hurt him, through me."

Even you?

Even? She was supposed to *know* that he was—better than this. Her prince. *Merde.*

Maybe the problem was that what he had just done *was* in a way some of the best of him—the ability to be ruthless to reach an end.

"You—I *knew* some part of you was just using me to get back at him! I knew it!"

All the color drained out of Gabriel, as if she had

unplugged some great hole in his soul. "Oh, you knew that, did you?" he said between barely parted lips. "Nothing I ever did made you think any better of me than that?"

"Well, if it did, it was because I was as stupid as my mother!" she spat at him.

He spoke each word as if it cut his mouth, precise and perfect. "The mother who dumps a man for being who he is, after ten years? Was that how stupid you were? Who destroys a *family* because it's easier than sticking with someone?"

Jolie stared up at him, her face very white.

Gabriel pressed his face down close to hers and spoke between his teeth. "You go back in there, and you tell your father how much I hurt you. And you see what happens." He straightened away, because he suddenly hurt so much he couldn't stand it, and strode toward the elevator.

He had only gotten two paces when he turned back. Anger was a deep, powerful, protective thing. Almost like putting protective gear around his heart. "Jolie. I know you heard me say it. But I still can't understand how you could believe it. Damn you. Deep down, you always did think I was just a beast, didn't you?"

Jolie let herself back into the apartment, feeling lifeless, as if everything around her had turned to shades of white and gray. Maybe it was something like what her father felt in his depression. Maybe.

Her father, who had just been horribly, verbally abused by the man who claimed he loved her. *I've stolen your daughter. Ha, ha, ha. How's that for payback?*

"I always told you not to fall for a chef," her father said softly. Pitying *her.* "We're self-absorbed bastards. The last man in the world I would want you to get involved with is someone like me."

That wasn't entirely true, though. The thought came slowly through Jolie's fogged white-and-gray brain. The last man in the world he had wanted her to get involved with, at least these past few years, was someone *other* than himself. *Of course he laps up the attention. So would I.*

She walked to the window. Gabriel was halfway down the street below, eating up the distance with angry strides.

"He can't help it, you know," her father said, an unusual gentleness in his tone. It reminded her of the times they would lounge on his couch at two a.m., discussing the world. "He can't help thinking of beating me first, before he thinks of you. It doesn't mean he doesn't care about you at all."

Jolie's jaw set against tears, her nostrils stinging.

"But if he thinks he's going to steal you out of my life like your mother did, he can go fuck himself," her father said abruptly, descending into kitchen language as if Gabriel had woken it in him. "I can make a place for myself in Provence. I can have restaurants on the Côte d'Azur begging me to come consult with them. I'm *Pierre Manon.*"

She looked away from the street, blinking. Her father's face looked—cleaner, the muscles tighter. He was opening and closing his left fist.

"When did Luc say he wanted to host us for the cookbook demo?" he asked sharply, in a tone she hadn't heard from him in five years.

"Next weekend," she said slowly. "At least, that was the original idea."

"Then we need to start running through how we're going to do it," he said firmly. "I want it to be a show-stopper."

Jolie turned her head swiftly to look back at the street. But Gabriel had already disappeared around the corner.

Chapter 27

G abriel sank back against the alley door to the kitchens, the last one to leave, and stared at the opposite wall, so close he could punch it. If he wanted to break his knuckles on stone.

He tilted his head back to gaze at the thin sliver of stars through the narrow gap of buildings above him. Then he closed his eyes. He felt—defeated. He felt like he needed that year's safari in Africa, far away from anyone or anything but elephants and wildebeest. He had known he was taking a huge risk for her, but part of the way he had managed it was to never truly acknowledge the possible negative consequences.

How he did most things, really.

But just right now . . . the negative consequences of holding his heart out there one more time were far too obvious. His heart still felt like someone had bludgeoned it with rolling pins.

Something touched his arm, and it flew out in reflexive testosterone, slamming into a small body. He saw who it was a half-second too late, Jolie, knocked back against the wall.

"*Putain.*" He dropped on his knees to check her ribs and because he sure as shit did not want to loom over her after he had just accidentally hit her. "Are you all right? Jolie, *bébé*. Oh, fuck, you should *never* sneak up on a man in the middle of the night like that. And what are you doing taking the train at this hour? I told you— oh, fuck, I'm so sorry. Are you all right?"

Jolie began to cry. Just burst into tears.

"*Putain.*" He sat on the old cobblestones and pulled

her into his lap, fingers checking her ribs , stroking the whole length of each one, compulsively. "I'm so sorry, *bébé.*" He rocked her, like a child.

"I'm all right." She ran her hands over his hair and face and shoulders, digging her fingers into the shoulder muscles to clutch him hard. His whole body responded to the touch in startled relief. He had not really thought he would feel that again.

Well . . . maybe his heart, huddled in wounded self-defense, had nevertheless already been starting to come up with a little plan that might show her he was not a beast, but—

"I'm just so glad to see you," Jolie said. "I didn't—I ran after you, as fast as I could. But you were already gone."

"Really?" Now he could feel those tight-furled petals around his heart blooming open, in startled wonder. "To . . . make up? Was that just a bad fight?"

"I shouldn't have said that about—screwing me," she said, on another burst of tears. "I love you. I didn't mean it. I can't believe I even could say that. You're so wonderful."

His heart stopped. Those last petals clutched tight around it. He couldn't understand why they gripped in such panic. Hadn't this been what he wanted? To hear her say *I love you*?

Except they were—they were only *words*. Anyone could say them.

His old girlfriend had said she loved him, too. Several women had said they loved him, in fact. They'd meant it at the time, too. If you started believing in that kind of thing, you left yourself wide open when they decided they didn't really love you enough to love . . . *you*.

He stared down at her. In his arms, she felt small and entirely his. A man could fall so easily for that feeling. A man could give up his whole damn heart for it and then wake up one day to discover someone had gotten tired of his heart and fed it to the dogs.

He had pressured her and pressured her to say those words, until anyone would think he was almost *trying* to leave her no other choice than to bash him over the head and run away—afraid to let up on her in case she shut him out, afraid to slow down in case she softened and let him entirely in. But she hadn't run away. She'd still kept looking at him as if she found him entirely enticing.

He had run away, this afternoon. And she—*she* had come after *him.*

He rubbed his hands against her ribs again, surreptitiously checking that he wasn't imagining this—that she was right here. Saying she loved him.

She was. Those were her slim muscles, and that was her softness. That was the scent of her, stale from a train ride. And those were her unfamiliar tears, cried over him. Cried over them.

Now he had to make a choice. Now that he had her, he had to actually believe in her.

No.

It was harder than that.

With nothing held back, with nothing kept safe, with only her own guarantee because life had none, he still had to make the choice to leave himself wide open to her.

Her gold-brown head rubbed into him, rubbing her tears against his chest.

Yeah. As if he had ever had a choice.

He bent and kissed her, full out and wide open, putting all of him into it, because—that's what she deserved. And that's what he always did. He always did think people deserved better than he could manage without trying.

He kissed her until she settled against his shoulder happily, tears still tracks down her cheeks. He kissed her until even he relaxed a little, believing she was there again. He kissed her until he couldn't kiss her anymore, until he had to lean his head back against the stone wall behind him and breathe.

He put some effort into it, the breathing, gazing rather awestruck at the stars. Had they always been that beautiful? That close and that scary?

"Anyway," she mumbled against his shoulder, "I was yelling at you about the wrong thing."

Uh-oh. He angled his head, trying to see if he could catch her mouth again before this went any further. The kissing had been *so* nice.

"Isn't it funny how people do that sometimes, focus on the wrong thing in a fight as some kind of cover for the real problem?"

Oh, God, this didn't sound good. He took a deep breath and tried to remind himself of his decision five minutes before to believe in her.

"Gabriel!" She lifted her head and held his eyes, which put her at the perfect angle for his mouth to silence hers, before she could start talking about problems.

He almost did and then it occurred to him that if she had come all this way to tell him she loved him, after that fight, maybe he shouldn't take over the moment and turn it into what he wanted. Maybe he should let her talk.

He took a firm grip on himself, one of those many, many moments when she never knew how hard he was working to contain himself.

"Will you think two seconds about what you just did? You horned into *my father's* life, *my father's* health, without even talking to me about it, because you're so determined to get what you want all the time."

"It's not like he was some stranger, Jolie! I know him better than you do, *merde.*" Actually, he knew Pierre a lot better than he knew Jolie, too, when he thought about it. The two men had worked together for sixteen brutal hours a day for four years. And then the man had dumped him. Shit, and all this time, he thought he had been scared she would act like her *mother*. She got the dumping genes on both sides.

"Gabriel! *I don't care.* You need a damn *stop button.*"

"It worked, didn't it?" he said indignantly.

"That doesn't mitigate your gall in doing it! He's *my* father, Gabriel."

"Yes, but he was *my* chef."

"You could have stressed him right into another stroke! Just because you were so convinced you knew better than I do!"

"And did I?"

"No, you stressed him into calling Luc Leroi to set up that demonstration and into contacting a few would-be starred chefs down here in Provence to see how they would like to learn how to reach that next level," Jolie admitted.

Meaning maybe Gabriel *did* know her father better than she did, but Jolie didn't go ahead and admit it. It probably hurt to admit something like that. He damn well wanted his own kids to know him.

"Gabriel, I'm going to beat you over the head. You're not even guilty or apologetic!"

He tried to figure out what a guilty or apologetic look would feel like on his face. They weren't emotions he was familiar with much. If you were going to do it, there was no point feeling guilty about it. "I'm sorry you're upset," he finally offered. He was, too. It had been like raking claws through his own organs, forcing himself to handle her father, when he knew how angry she would be when she found out.

Jolie thunked her head against his chest in despair. "That's not the same as understanding that you were in the wrong to do it in the first place."

How could he possibly be in the wrong, when it had turned out to be the right thing to do? Sometimes she didn't make any sense at all.

"Oh, for God's sake," she said, peering into his face. "I'm not getting *anywhere* with you, am I? Are we going to be fighting about your inability to contain yourself for the rest of our lives?"

His heart brightened right back up. "Oh, I hope so."

She stared at him a moment, caught between indignation and surprise, and then her mouth softened. "You are hopeless," she said affectionately.

He really thought *hopeless* was the exact opposite of what he was, but he didn't think he wanted to talk about it too much. It was the kind of hope she might accidentally stomp on, in her current precarious temper, even if she might regret it later.

"Even if you did mean well," she muttered, reluctantly.

"Oh, so you've stopped believing I *wanted* to stress him into another stroke for revenge?" he asked, a dry bitterness leaking back into his voice, because that one might hurt for a long time to come.

"It did sound terrible, Gabriel." Jolie petted his shoulder, a healing gesture he liked much, much better than her fussing at him. He still wanted a lot of healing, after being told he was *screwing* her. "I didn't really think you wanted him to *die*, but—"

"I know it sounded terrible, but why did it sound *plausible*?"

"You know part of you was always happy to be stealing me away from your worst enemy. Admit it, Gabriel."

"Part of me was always *worried* that he had the strongest claim on you. He always gets the most beautiful things in my life for himself. Even when he doesn't start with the advantage of being that most beautiful thing's *father*."

"You didn't really want to gloat over him?"

And that was when he realized what really scared him. He stared down at her for a long time, quite still. She felt so good in his arms. His heart thudded hard and slow and shamed, telling him to shut up. Not to let her know this. And he thought about spending the rest of his life waiting for her to realize that he was no damn prince. A hard, reluctant breath struggled through his lungs. "No, I think I can see why you believed it. Because every single word was true."

She stiffened and jerked back against his hold.

But he didn't let her go yet. "That I think he's being pathetic, that I think he needs to get off his butt, that I gloat over being the one to have you. I do, Jolie."

She stopped straining against his hold, her eyebrows drawing together. She was studying him very intently.

"I love you, though. And I'll do all kinds of beautiful things for you. I thought I had already tried." It hurt him still that all his best, what had seemed so beautiful to him, still didn't outshine his darkness. "But I can't manage to never be a bad person for you, because part of me—just really is a beast."

She gazed at him. He wanted to hide his ugly soul from that gaze, but it was too damn late. And then, to his utter surprise, she started to smile a little. "You're amazing," she said.

He—what? His heart hiccuped and then just stopped, and he couldn't figure out how to get it started again.

"I love the combination of roaring and"—she brought his hands up and kissed the palm sides of his fingers—"sweet. I love you."

Really? Even knowing that? He curled the fingers she had kissed around her face, tracing the shape of her with his thumbs. *Really?* She really loved him?

"You did it for him, didn't you?" she said softly, and he stared at her incredulously. "All this time I thought you hated him, but really inside . . . marshmallow."

"Jolie." His hands, the hands that had never been going to risk getting burned by her again, tightened and pulled her in. "For one . . . you're a damned food writer. Find a better comparison than a marshmallow. And for another—I'm sorry to continue to be the beast in your fairytale, but did you listen to what I just said? I would *never* do *anything* for Pierre Manon."

She raised her eyebrows, challenging. "You mean you really did do all that just to gloat?"

"It was a nice secondary benefit." One that had made him feel sick to his stomach. "Jolie. I did it for *you. Putain.* How could you possibly imagine anything else? I'm not subtle!"

"For me?" she said blankly. "I thought this was all about you chefs."

Now *he* wanted to beat his head against something. "He made you sad," Gabriel said finally, simply. "He drained all your happiness, as if going back to Paris was some sea monster that kept dragging one side of your ship under. He made you think you had to be by yourself if you didn't want to be weighed down. He made you feel like you were selfish, because he was sucking so much out of you that you didn't have any other way to protect your own self. And I was getting fucking tired of it, and I wanted you all for me, so—"

"So it was really just all about you, is that right?" Jolie said, one corner of her mouth turning up wryly as her eyes held his.

She could think what she fucking liked. Gabriel scowled and wrenched his hands away from her head to fold his arms.

She reached up and curved her hand around his cheek, the way she did sometimes that made him want to rub his face against it like a puppy. *Merde*, he hadn't shaved for days. He would probably sandpaper her skin off.

"You saved me," she said very softly. "You made yourself be the bad guy so you could save me."

His breath shortened until his chest hurt so much. Did she finally understand him just a little? Would she ever understand what it had cost him to risk that way she looked at him, to risk *her with him*, to save his worst enemy . . . for her?

"I love you," she said, and his heart just went pitter-pat with helpless delight. *Son putain de coeur.* Life would be so much easier if he didn't have that heart. But it wouldn't be nearly as *happy.* She pressed a kiss against his jaw. "You're impossible, but there's something beautiful about how impossible you are."

That one hit him like a lightning bolt straight to the heart. There *was?* She really thought that?

"I love you that way. And I think you wanted to help Pierre Manon more than you admit to."

"No," Gabriel said forcefully, kissing her hard. "I did not. And when we do our cookbook, I want your name in the same damn size font as mine. So you'll get used to thinking of yourself as front and center in the picture. And not the tiny secondary reason for anybody's actions."

"The publisher will never agree to that," Jolie said so ruefully that he kissed her smile, just to remember what it felt like against his lips. "They'll want yours to sell the books, and mine will end up getting squeezed small."

"They'll agree to whatever I ask them to or we'll go somewhere else. We can share the last name so it won't take up that much more space."

She gasped, then wrenched her mouth away from his and buried her face in his chest, laughing helplessly—or was she crying again? He frowned, twisting his head to try to see. "Gabriel, you are hopeless. You will *never* learn to slow down."

"What? Jolie, you know I'm not going to let the name *Manon* be on *my* cookbook. You've been asking for this ever since I first brought up the idea and you kept repeating, 'I'm Jolie *Manon*,' over and over like you were begging someone to change that. I just wanted to make sure the sex was good first, that's all."

Now she was laughing out loud, the sound rippling into the dark, relaxing everything in him as if he had been brushed with a night breeze. "I love you," she said again, and that night breeze ran all through his hair like slim, caressing fingers. "But there is no way you could handle Pierre Manon as a father-in-law."

"I already *am* handling Pierre Manon as a father-in-law," Gabriel said between his teeth. "You just don't like the way I do it."

"In fact, I don't know how you're even going to handle him spending half his time down here on the Côte d'Azur trying to train all your rivals to beat you. Did you think that challenge through?"

"Yes," he said very evenly. "I did. I thought about your twelve hours of commute a week, I thought about your face every time you had to get back on that train and go deal with him, all alone, and I thought about how much I didn't want to spend half of every week without you for the next year, even to avoid dealing with a *putain de salaud de beau-père* in close proximity."

That got him a hard, sudden squeeze and a kiss against his neck. But it didn't get him a yes. "Look, let's just see if you two can avoid killing each other for a while and—"

"No," he interrupted. "You and me does not have anything to do with whether your father and I kill each other. Quit thinking of yourself as the tiny font in the picture. Besides, if I can handle it, you can."

"You think?" Jolie said very dryly.

"*Putain*, Jolie, you can't tell me trying to buck your father out of depression for years by yourself was *easier* than dealing with a couple of men yelling and throwing things at each other. My way is a lot more entertaining."

She began to laugh again and put her head down

on his chest, which he liked quite a bit. "Gabriel. I am not going to be rushed into saying *yes*. We've only known each other for a few weeks. Unless you count me watching you make that Rose from my father's office when I was barely in my teens. I appreciate the— assumption of marriage—but you are *not* going to get me to say yes, for, I don't know, at least a year."

"You think not?" Gabriel tilted his head back and regarded the sliver of stars thoughtfully. Then he hauled himself up off those uncomfortable cobblestones and carried her through the streets toward his apartment, just as he had always wanted to. "Well, we'll see."

Since she kept saying he didn't know how to slow down, he was determined to prove her wrong by waiting at least a week.

Chapter 28

J olie hugged herself excitedly as the first demonstration for the cookbook got underway. At last! It was like her father had lost ten years of age. Or rather, returned to being fifty-five again, instead of the old man with nothing left for him that he had been acting for years, ever since he lost that star.

She wished Gabriel were here to grin at her, in smug *I-told-you-so*, but of course that would make his head blow off. Plus, she didn't really want him and her father to start throwing pans at each other in the middle of the demonstration, no matter how much publicity that might bring.

She had been in Paris for over a week now, something Gabriel sulked about every night on the phone, while she worked with her father in increasing delight as he grew more and more invested in the demo preparation in the Leucé kitchens, training the *sous* who would demonstrate his recipes until they had them exactly the way he wanted them. Pierre had wanted to get Luc's *second*, Patrick Chevalier, to do the Rose, a challenge pseudo-surfer-boy Patrick had seemed quite intrigued by, but Jolie had put her foot down. "No," she said, flatly but with a secret sense of deep loss. "We're not going to do the Rose."

"Jolie, you're the one who insisted on having it on the cover!" her father argued. "Now we have to do it. Everyone loves that dessert. It's one of my best ones."

One of *his* best ones. Some things never changed. But it was worth the frustration, just to see her father re-asserting his right to dominate whatever came out of his kitchens.

Still—"No!" Jolie snapped. "I mean it, Papa!"

Her father growled, but he either had some degree of guilty conscience or didn't want to give Gabriel's desserts the honor of being in his demo, because he yielded.

The idea for the event was two parts: a cooking demonstration for the number of guests who could fit into the kitchens to watch, followed by a tasting event in one of the hotel reception rooms, for a larger crowd.

The guests were excited to be behind-the-scenes, and her father was playing the top chef to the hilt, letting Leucé sous-chefs do the actual demonstrating while he talked to the guests and just added the final fillips to a plate before turning them toward the gathering.

Jolie demonstrated some of them herself, in her role as the amateur who could prove how effective the recipes in the book were at teaching an expert's techniques. And she talked to people, lighting up. She hadn't known if she would be good at this, but it turned out it was easy, smiling at people, engaging them, answering questions.

Luc Leroi appeared beside her, in the stylized white shirt he favored when working for the cameras. Black-haired, with a face that was exceptionally perfect, every detail of bearing and expression so extremely controlled as to seem inhuman, he made the ideal foil for his sous-chef Patrick Chevalier on the other side of her, all golden and dishevelled, with a boneless air about him as if he'd just been making love under a palm tree. Or maybe it was the other way around; maybe Patrick was the foil for Luc.

Either way, not too many women would object to standing between the two of them with a smile on her face for a few minutes, while cameras flashed. Patrick grinned for those cameras, a long, lazy grin, like a lion about to stretch himself out on a rock for the afternoon. Which, to be honest, if you didn't have that adrenalin response to being on camera that some chefs did, a demo really was a relaxed way to pass the time for these guys—lazy and easy, compared to the brutal intensity of making a hundred of the same dessert in five minutes, and five different others, too, during dinner service.

Luc gave that brilliant, intense dark look of his, first down at her and then at the cameras. About thirty cameras went *click* in the same instant, as if they just couldn't help themselves. Luc didn't even seem to notice, although he *must* be playing to the cameras, surely. The angle of his jaw was just too perfect. "It's a pleasure to have here with us today the legendary Pierre Manon and the woman who could make sense of his genius to the rest of us," he told the gathered guests. Her father stood on the other side of him, in pride of place. "Patrick Chevalier and I had originally offered to demonstrate a couple of the desserts in his cookbook, but fortunately, one of this cookbook's authors has a certain pull on someone even better suited to show them."

Jolie looked up at Luc quickly at that and then, already, *felt* that energy filling the space. As if a subsonic roar had just made everyone in the kitchens vibrate to alert. She turned as Gabriel appeared and came forward, in his chef's jacket.

Several people in the crowd gasped. And then everybody burst into applause.

Gabriel smiled wryly, as he took Luc's place between the Manons, his eyes meeting her father's only for one packed second before they focused on Jolie. "Whatever else I can say about my relationship with Pierre Manon, and I can say a lot," he told the crowd, to a rumor of laughter. The group was full of food critics and experts in the French restaurant scene, many of whom knew the Manon-Delange story quite well. "He always pushed me to be my best. So . . . it's an honor to demonstrate one of the recipes I developed under him. At one point, it was the most photographed dessert in France. And"—he picked up the nearest display copy of the cookbook and held it toward the crowd, with a little quick grin sideways at Jolie—"my girlfriend really likes it."

Jolie bit her lip, gazing up at him. Her father had placed both his hands on the counter and was eyeing his former chef pâtissier, body rigid. It was amazing how much good *anger* did her father, not a bitter, brooding anger, but a healthy urge to beat out all challengers, that driving need to compete re-awakened. *Don't forget this lesson, Jolie: if Gabriel ever goes into depression one day, put him in the company of his rivals and do something to provoke a fight.*

"So, Jolie. This is for you." And Gabriel stopped smiling.

Stopped playing the audience. Stopped even noticing them. That bubble of concentration that he could create no matter how many people and how much pressure surrounded him—the knack of anyone who had spent his life in top kitchens—descended around him and enclosed her with it, shutting out the rest of the world.

As if she didn't know already that it was for her. He would never have done it for her father, and he would never have done it for the world. The only way he had managed to drag this back out of himself again—this Rose that represented so much that he had given of himself and so much that had been stolen from him, so much he did not want to risk again—was for her.

He worked so quickly and so beautifully, his face somber in concentration, in a way she had never seen on any of those Youtube videos showing his other demonstrations. His work itself was like watching a miracle take place: the breath of gold dust across the plate, the red- and pink-streaked chocolate petals he loosened from molds. He must have slipped in last night sometime and prepped the whole thing. When he called her last night, complaining she was spending too long in Paris and that they had an ironclad contract, had he been standing here in this very kitchen, grinning in anticipation of his surprise?

A small torch flamed in his hands. Nitrogen vapor rose around his face. Hot, liquid chocolate was poured into a small round shell of hardened chocolate, the whole tucked into an aerated mousse of white chocolate and raspberry that was heartsblood red, that mousse dipped into the nitrogen and out and completely covered with gold leaf, and all of that within ten seconds. Because what was hot had to stay hot, what was cold stay cold, until it reached the mouth that would savor it, all of its heat and coolness shielded in the heart of that half-bloomed rose.

A very tiny smile from Gabriel to her, nothing like his usual big grins. And he adjusted the last petals.

"I changed it, just a little, for you," he murmured and slid it in front of her. Facing her and not the crowd.

Near translucent fragile petals . . . opened. Just enough. The gold heart that had, in this dessert's original form, been tucked like a secret inside them, was now revealed, although not to the crowd. Just to the person right in front of it. Just to her.

Unprotected. Beautiful.

From this great, aggressive man who didn't know how to stop going after what he wanted . . . the most romantic, most fragile dessert Jolie had ever seen.

Dimly, she was aware that people were taking photo after photo, but it didn't really penetrate. It was more as if hers and Gabriel's intimate bubble of concentration was lit with little sparkles.

"Why?" she whispered. Why now? Why so publicly and for his enemy, acknowledging her father's claim on the dessert even as he re-affirmed his own?

"I thought you deserved it," he murmured, looking down at her with a little smile. So quiet, for Gabriel. So wary and hopeful and tentative. He touched one of the innermost chocolate petals very lightly with his thumb, where the gold heart gleamed for her. "I thought I deserved it, too."

She could feel her face lighting. *He* deserved it? To offer her this?

This thing. The one thing he had allowed to be crushed out of him. The one thing that he had loved so much, that had meant so much of his heart, that he just could not risk it again. This one thing—he now offered, in public, to her.

The one man he hated the most—he paid tribute to. For her. In fact, he barely even seemed to care her father was there anymore.

With the thumb that had caressed the curve of the chocolate petal, he now caressed her lower lip. "I'll trade a rose for you," he said softly, certainly.

His thumb flicked up and caught something under her eye, smearing the teardrop gently against the fragile skin there.

"Maybe you'll excuse us," he told the crowd and wrapped one arm around her, picking up the plate with the Rose on it as he led her away.

Hushed, delighted murmurs filled the space behind them, but they were like echoes in a seashell, coming from far away.

"Always trying to steal the show," Pierre Manon told the crowd very dryly, as they disappeared into the walk-in that was kept at fifteen degrees Celsius, that and the even colder refrigerator being the only private spaces in the whole kitchens. "That hasn't changed." From her father, that was, in its way, almost an acceptance. He had chosen Gabriel for his chef pâtissier; Gabriel had reached up into the heavens and caught a star for him. Despite the impossibility of two such powerful personalities coexisting in peace, somewhere he, too, had to realize Gabriel's worth.

Gabriel double-checked the release on the inside of the walk-in door and then pulled it closed behind them. "You had better eat it now," he said. "Otherwise it will be ruined."

"Is there a ring in there?" Jolie asked, low. It would be so exactly like him.

He sat them cross-legged on the floor of the storage room and set the plate in her lap. "I didn't want you to choke." He pulled a small box out of his pants pocket. "You can have this one any time you want, though. Or something else if you prefer."

It was an exceptionally beautiful ring, red gold twining through yellow, the ruby set deeply into the pattern of leaves and petals delicately etched around it, a secret rose.

Jolie stared at it, her lips parted. He smiled, setting his arms on his knees in an attitude of deep, infinite patience. "Eat, Jolie. I can wait."

The first bite of the Rose tasted so good it almost made her cry. Just the fact that she had to eat it—that there was no way to save it forever—made her want to cry. And then the flavors hit, and the textures, the cold and the hot, a texture like new-fallen snow, a thin shell that barely resisted teeth, and then the warm, dense ganache inside it, rushing over her tongue. Everything blended together into a marriage of flavors and sensations so perfect, so enticing, so many ways deliciousness could be packed into one small bite. How could *anything* be that wonderful?

And Gabriel watched her, a profound satisfaction growing ever larger in him with every bite.

"I think I might have found something better to compare your heart to than a marshmallow," she said.

"Well, it was about fucking time," he said. "You're lucky I'm so patient." He reached out and drew one thumb over the shimmering toenail peeking from the totally inappropriate-for-a-kitchen shoes she had worn because she wanted to be glamorous for such a luxury setting. He was smiling a little. "Jolie." He proffered her the ring again. "I really think we know this is going to work out."

She gazed at it a long time, thinking about space.

The thing was, she *wanted* to share her space with him. She *wanted* to give up part of her life to him. He took so much. But he gave so much.

Maybe she hadn't ever wanted to give up part of herself before because no one else had deserved it.

"You have the most beautiful heart I've ever seen," she said softly.

He took a sharp breath, and his hand lifted to cover that heart, as if it suddenly felt fragile. "Not a marshmallow?" he managed, but the attempt at dryness in his voice was a little rough.

"It's so big," she said. "It fills all of you. It fills everyone around you. And yet inside"—she touched the flecks of gold left on her plate—"I think there's this precious center that, if I'm careful, if I show you can trust me with it, you'll give only to me."

His hand shifted helplessly over his chest. His lips had parted, and she noticed with some astonishment that red was streaking his cheeks. "You think my heart is *beautiful?*" he managed. He sounded as if his voice was being dragged through a rough tunnel.

"Doesn't everybody?" she asked blankly and spread her hand over his own larger one against his chest.

He didn't say anything. He was staring at her with that look he had gotten once before, over scrambled eggs and pancakes, as if she had been beamed down from another planet.

She wiggled her fingers in under his palm and found the ring hidden in his belated attempt to protect that glorious heart of his. Too late now. She worked it out and looked at it a moment, then up into his face again, her smile feeling so tender and strange. Yes, she could share her space with this man. The fight to keep him from taking over might be an infuriating trial their entire lives, but nothing about him dragged her down.

"Yes," she said. "I think we really do know this is going to work out. But Gabriel—you have to give me time."

LAURA FLORAND

He looked down at the ring, balanced on the tip of her finger, and then back at her. "Another week?" he asked cautiously.

"I was thinking more along the lines of sixty or seventy years," she said softly, letting the ring slide down to her knuckle. "Quit rushing things, Gabriel."

He took a deep breath, watching that ring stuck above her knuckle. "About kids—"

Her breath hiccuped in shock, and then she gave a half-laugh, half-groan and thumped her bare hand against her forehead. "Gabriel, you are *hopeless*."

"I think it's the opposite," he said carefully. "About the hope. But I was going to say—you're eight years younger than I am. We don't have to rush it. I can wait a few years."

"Thank you," Jolie said awfully. "For your patience. Since, you know, *I* would be the one pregnant."

"It's all right," he allowed magnanimously. "I kind of want you to myself for a few years."

On the point of saying something very sarcastic about his generous permission, Jo took another look at him and stopped. "You kind of want to make sure I won't dump you first, don't you?" she realized, softly.

He flinched. "I just—I really couldn't handle that, Jolie. What your mother did to your father." *Or my father, in a way, did to you.* "I just—I might honestly die."

She brought her bare hand to rub his hand against his heart, soothingly. After a moment, she nodded slowly, solemnly, without speaking. *Understood.*

His gaze moved back to the ring, resting at her first knuckle. He watched it with a kind of wary compulsion, as if it might be the one ring to rule them all. "You know how you're always saying I go after what I want and don't know how to hold back? I didn't know how hard it would be, letting you say *yes*."

"I know you gave me your heart without question," Jolie said very softly. "But do you think you'll learn to

226

trust me with it one day?" She was sorrier than she could say that she had ever been stupid enough to brag about dumping men easily. She'd just been trying to protect herself, and he had always seemed so big, so sure. Why hadn't she thought of that Rose before she spoke and kept her mouth shut?

"It might take me a while," he said low. His hand shifted to curve over her left hand, thumb playing with the ring, back and forth against her first knuckle. "Sixty or seventy years. I'll try. It would help if you could reassure me you love me on a daily basis. You don't have to say it, just—do it. Look at me that, that way you do sometimes. You know, with that—smile."

"I promise to smile at you at least twice a day except when I'm on vacation," Jo told him, bringing their hands to her mouth so she could kiss his knuckles. "I'm planning an annual beach retreat to get away from a demanding husband for a week each year. I don't think letting you know I love you the other fifty-one weeks will be that hard." She smiled. "And if I ever yield to the urge to bop you over the head, I promise to use a foam sledgehammer."

His thumb nudged the ring a tiny bit farther down her finger. "Do you really think my heart is beautiful?" he asked, barely above a whisper.

"It's adorable," she said. One of his eyebrows went up a little at that. He looked dumbfounded. Which was just a damn tragedy, that a man with as extraordinary a heart as his should be surprised that anyone else realized it. "And yes, it's incredibly beautiful." Her voice went very soft. "Thank you for sharing it with me."

"I don't think that's what is defined as 'sharing'," Gabriel said, with cautious wryness. "It suggests I'm keeping a part for myself."

"Léa did warn me about the importance of being a little selfish," Jolie told him. "Of keeping something for yourself."

"Can you be responsible for that part of the relationship?" Gabriel asked. "I just don't know how to do it. I know how to grab for all of you I can get—I know how to be selfish *that* way. But I just don't know how to hold back. And I—don't want to learn. I think it would take something too terrible to even contemplate, for me to learn."

She leaned forward and wrapped her arms around him to give him a strong hug, just a little pre-emptive strike against anything in life that might ever happen to him that would be too terrible to contemplate. Especially since she suspected that the terrible possibilities that grazed across his mind, the ones he couldn't stand to contemplate, would have to do with *her*.

His arms went around her immediately, too, and it was the most wonderful warmth against the chill of the walk-in. "Really?" he said after a moment, his voice with that odd strangled sound again. "Really beautiful?"

"Oh, Gabriel." It made her want to smack pretty much anyone he had ever dated, that he had such a hard time believing her. But then, she had wanted to smack all those women anyway.

"You're not dropping my ring, are you?" he asked, his voice sounding muffled, even though she could not possibly be squeezing him too hard for his big body to breathe.

She brought her left hand out from behind his body and showed it to him, her finger a little bent to keep the ring from falling off the tip.

"I don't mean to rush you, Jolie, but could we at least slide it down one more knuckle? It's going to fall off if you try to keep it like that for the next sixty or seventy years."

"Gabriel," she said suddenly. Because something had finally hit her—how terrible it must feel, the person ready to give all your heart, to always be faced with someone pulling back, not quite sure. "I don't doubt you, you know. I know how incredible you are, how amazing, how beautiful." Her mouth curved, and she tucked her head against his shoulder to whisper: "It's more like foreplay. I can know how big and amazing you are and still need some more time to adjust."

He gave a little crack of laughter. "Jolie. I just love how obsessed with sex you are. Here we are, in the middle of a proposal of marriage, in Luc Leroi's walk-in, with a crowd of people and your own father out there, and you still can't keep your mind off it." He grinned. "Of course, I *am* big and amazing."

She bit the side of his neck, very gently.

He made a little rumbling sound of approval and shifted her into his lap. Which felt good, too. No more space, but it had been darn awkward trying to reach across both her space and his to hug him.

"And beautiful," she said. "Don't forget that."

"I should have made you that Rose before," he decided definitely. "I had no idea it would have this effect on you."

"Yes, you did. You just weren't ready." She smiled against his throat. "I didn't want to rush you. Some things take time."

He angled his body enough to make her own fall back against his arm, so that he could look down into her face. Whatever he saw there made his own face brilliant with happiness.

He picked up her left hand. "I'm just going to go ahead and slide this all the way on, okay? Just so it's more comfortable."

"I wish you would," she murmured. "When it comes down to it, there's no point doing something like this halfway. Never choose half of anything just to be safe, when you have a chance to have something whole and *perfect*."

"*Bon sang,* you actually listen to me occasionally," Gabriel said. As he worked the ring down to the base of her finger, everything inside her flowered into happiness to let herself go with this at last. To stop trying to hide behind boundaries that she had always wanted to open to him, from the very first.

"Besides, you know how I like the idea of a long-term binding contract," Gabriel told her, closing her fingers into her palm and then his hand over hers, to keep that ring extra-securely on her.

She nestled her fist into his palm. "It does sound nice.

* * *

THANK YOU!

Thank you so much for reading! I hope you enjoyed stepping into the world of Provence and meeting some of the extended Rosier clan.

If you're curious to know more about Daniel and Léa's story, check out Laura's novella *Turning Up the Heat*.

And you'll be able to meet more of Gabriel's Rosier relatives in *A Rose in Winter*, coming later this year. Make sure to sign up for Laura's newsletter at www.lauraflorand.com to be notified when it's released!

Meanwhile, you can always find Laura and other readers on Facebook for regular temptations of fantastic French chocolate and other kinds of fun.

For a list of Laura's other Chocolate books and a sneak peek of the upcoming *Chocolate Touch*, please keep reading.

OTHER BOOKS BY LAURA FLORAND

Amour et Chocolat Series

All's Fair in Love and Chocolate, a novella in Kiss the Bride

The Chocolate Thief

The Chocolate Kiss

The Chocolate Rose (also part of La Vie en Roses series)

The Chocolate Touch

The Chocolate Heart

La Vie en Roses Series

Turning Up the Heat (a novella)

The Chocolate Rose (also part of the Amour et Chocolat series)

A Rose in Winter, a novella in No Place Like Home

Memoir

Blame It on Paris

THE CHOCOLATE TOUCH (EXCERPT)

" She's back."

Dom straightened from the enormous block of chocolate he was creating, gave his *maîtresse de salle,* Guillemette, a disgruntled look for having realized he would want to know that, and slipped around to the spot in the glass walls where he could get the best view of the *salle* below. He curled his fingers into his palms so he wouldn't press his chocolaty hands to the glass and leave a stain like a kid outside a candy shop.

She sat alone as she always did, at one of the small tables. For a week now, she had come twice a day. Once in the morning, once in the afternoon. She was probably a tourist, soaking up as much French artisanal chocolate as she could in her short stay in Paris, as they liked to do. But even he admitted it was strange that her soaking up should be only of him. Most wandered: him in the morning, Philippe Lyonnais in the afternoon, Sylvain Marquis the next day. Tourists read guidebooks and visited the top ten; they didn't have the informed taste to know that Sylvain Marquis was boring and Dominique Richard was the only man a woman's tongue could get truly excited about.

This woman—looked hard to excite. She seemed so pulled in on herself, so utterly quiet and contained. She had a wide, soft poet's mouth and long-lashed eyes whose color he couldn't tell from that far away. Hair that was always hidden by a hood, or occasionally a fashionable hat and a loosely tied scarf, like Audrey Hepburn. High cheekbones that needed more flesh on them. A dust-powder of freckles covered her face, so many they blurred together.

The first day, she had looked all skin and bones. Like a model, but she was too small and too freckled, so maybe just another city anorexic. When she had ordered a cup of *chocolat chaud* and a chocolate éclair, he had expected to see her dashing to the *toilettes* soon after, to throw it up before the binge of calories could infect her, and it had pissed him off, because he loathed having his chocolate treated that way.

But she had just sat there, her eyes half closed, her hands curling around the hot cup of chocolate caressingly. She had sat there a long time, working her way through both éclair and *chocolat chaud* bit by little bit. And never once had she pulled out a journal or a phone or done anything except sit quite still, absorbing.

When she had left, he had been surprised to feel part of himself walk out with her. From the long casement windows, he had watched her disappear down the street, walking carefully, as if the sidewalk might rise up and bite her if she didn't.

That afternoon, she was back, her hands curling once again around a cup of his *chocolat chaud*, and this time she tried a slice of his most famous *gâteau*. Taking slow, tiny mouthfuls, absorbing everything around her.

Absorbing him. Everything in this place was him. The rough, revealed stone of the archways and three of the walls. The heavy red velvet curtains that satisfied a hunger in him with their rich, passionate opulence. The rosebud-embossed white wall that formed a backdrop to her, although no one could understand what part of him it came from. The gleaming, severe, cutting-edge displays. The flats of minuscule square chocolates, dark and rich and printed with whimsical elusive designs, displayed in frames of metal; the select collection of pastries, his *gâteaux au chocolat*, his éclairs, his *tartes*; clear columns of his caramels. Even the people around her at other tables were his. While they were in his shop, he owned them, although they thought they were buying him.

The third afternoon, when the waiter came upstairs with her order, Dom shook his head suddenly. "Give her this." He handed Thierry the lemon-thyme-chocolate éclair he had been inventing that morning.

He watched the waiter murmur to her when he

brought it, watched her head lift as she looked around. But she didn't know to look up for him and maybe didn't know what he looked like, even if she did catch sight of him.

When she left, Thierry, the waiter, brought him the receipt she had left on the table. On the back she had written, *Merci beaucoup*, and signed it with a scrawled initial. L? J? S? It could be anything.

A sudden dread seized him that *Merci* meant *Adieu* and he wouldn't see her again, her flight was leaving, she was packing her bags full of souvenirs. She had even left with a box of his chocolates. For the plane ride. It left a hole in him all night, the thought of how his *salon* would be without her.

But the next morning, she was back, sitting quietly, as if being there brought repose to her very soul.

He felt hard-edged just looking at her restfulness, the bones showing in her wrists. He felt if he got too close to her, he would bump into her and break her. What the hell business did he have to stand up there and look at her? She needed to be in Sylvain's place, somewhere glossy and sweet, not in his, where his chocolate was so dark you felt the edge of it on your tongue.

She needed, almost certainly, a prince, not someone who had spent the first six years of his working life, from twelve to eighteen, in a ghastly abattoir, hacking great bloody hunks of meat off bones with hands that had grown massive and ugly from the work, his soul that had grown ugly from it, too. He had mastered the dark space in his life, but he most surely did not need to let her anywhere near it. He did not like to think what might happen if he ever let it slip its leash.

"She certainly has a thing for you, doesn't she?" his short, spiky-haired chocolatier Célie said, squeezing her boss into the corner so she could get a better look. Dom sent a dark glance down at the tufted brown head. He didn't know why his team persisted in treating him like their big brother or perhaps even their indulgent father, when he was only a few years older than they were and would be lousy at both roles. No other top chef in the whole city had a team that treated him that way. Maybe he had a knack for hiring idiots.

Maybe he needed to train them to be in abject terror of him or at least respect him, instead of just training them how to do a damn good job. He only liked his equals to be terrified of him, though. The thought of someone vulnerable to him being terrified made him sick to his stomach.

"She must be in a hotel nearby," he said. That was all. Right?

"Well, she's not eating much else in Paris, not as thin as she is." Célie wasn't fat by any means, but she was slightly more rounded than the Parisian ideal, and judgmental of women who starved themselves for fashion. "She's stuck on you."

Dom struggled manfully to subdue a flush. He couldn't say why, but he liked, quite extraordinarily, the idea of Freckled Would-be Audrey Hepburn being stuck on him.

"You haven't seen her run throw anything up?" Célie checked doubtfully.

"*No*, she doesn't—*non*. She *likes* having me inside her."

Célie made an odd gurgling sound and looked up at him with her eyes alight, and Dom replayed what he had just said. "Will you get out of my space? Don't you have work to do?"

"Probably about as much as you." Célie grinned smugly, not budging.

Hardly. Nobody worked as hard as the owner. What the hell did Sylvain Marquis and Philippe Lyonnais do with employees who persisted in walking all over them? How did this happen to him? *He* was the biggest, ugliest customer in the whole world of Parisian chocolate, and yet in his own *laboratoire*—this was what he had to put up with.

Célie waggled her eyebrows at him. "So what's wrong with you? Are you sick? Why haven't you gone up with your—" She braced her shoulders and swung them back and forth, apparently trying to look macho and aggressive. She looked ridiculous. "We could cover for you for a couple of hours."

She tried to treat it like a joke, the way Dom could walk up to a woman, his aggression coming off him in hard edges all over the place, and have that woman get up and disappear with him for a couple of hours. But a profound disapproval lurked in her brown eyes.

Dom set his jaw. His sex life was really *nobody*'s business, even if it was infamous, and, well—"*No.* Go start on the *pralinés* before I make you come in at three a.m. tomorrow to do them."

For a wonder, Célie actually started to move. She got three steps away before she turned back. "You haven't had sex with her already, have you? Finally broken someone's heart, and now she's lurking here like a ghost, snatching at your crumbs?"

Dominique stared at her. "Broken her—ghost—crumbs—what the *hell* do you guys make up about me when I'm not in earshot?" He never had sex with women who had hearts. Not ones that beat for him, anyway.

"Nothing. We contemplate possible outcomes of your actions, *chef*, but I think we're pretty realistic about it." Célie gave him her puckish grin and strolled a couple more paces away. Naturally, his breath of relief was premature, and she turned back for one last shot. "Now if we were *creative*, we might have come up with this scenario." She waved a hand at Dom, wedged in a corner between glass and stone, gazing down into his *salle* below.

Whatever the hell that meant.

He blocked Célie's face from the edge of his vision

with a shift of one muscled shoulder and focused back on the freckled *inconnue*'s table.

Putain, she had left.

Cancer, he thought that night, with a chill of fear. Maybe that explained the hats or hoods or scarves that always hid her hair. Maybe that explained the thinness, and the way she seemed able to just sit still forever, soaking up his life.

He started preparing her plates himself, arranging whatever she had ordered to his satisfaction and then adding in little surprise presents: a miniature tower of three of his square *bonbons*, for example, fresh from the ganache room where trays of them were scattered on wire shelves, waiting to replenish the displays below.

He went to his secret spot, in the corner of the glass walls above the *salle,* to see her reaction. She didn't smile. But she bit into them slowly, taking her time, eating the tiny morsels in two, sometimes even three bites, as if she wanted to savor every aspect of his flavor. The texture of him on her tongue.

And when she was done with him—with *them,* with the chocolates—she always left. Rising. Brushing crumbs off her lap if she had had one of his famous chocolate *mille-feuilles.* Laying down cash, never once paying with a card so he could know her name.

Was it just his imagination, or was her boniness softening, from the week of absorbing him?

The sixth day, he broke cover, moving suddenly out of his observation post when he saw her rise. His feet sounded too loud, too violent on the polished metal spiral that descended into the room. He was only halfway down by the time she reached the door. She didn't look back toward the sound. She stood as the glass doors slid open for her, and her shoulders shifted in a sigh. And then she was gone, out on the street.

Guillemette and both waiters were eyeing him,

eyebrows raised. He turned abruptly on his heel and went back up into his *laboratoire*.

The seventh day, he almost wanted to open the shop, even though they never opened on Monday, because—what would she do? Where would she go without him?

He resisted his own foolishness and then spent the entire day off roaming restlessly around Paris, sometimes on his motorcycle, sometimes on foot, visiting all the tourist spots, which was ridiculous. Sure, a man should take the time to appreciate his city and not leave it all to tourists, but the odds of spotting someone in the Louvre when you didn't even know if she was there were . . . pretty nearly none. Standing looking up at *La Victoire de Samothrace*, as she soared above the crowds in the Richelieu wing of the Louvre inspired him, though, made flavors and textures shift and flow in his mind, tease his palate, as he tried to think of a chocolate that he could call *Victoire*.

He liked *La Victoire de Samothrace*. The flowing, exultant winged marble would have represented the essence of his soul, if only he could purify it of all its darkness and make it that beautiful.

After the Louvre, he even went up the Eiffel Tower, which he hadn't done since a school trip at age ten. He climbed the first two floors on foot, up and up, taking pleasure in the eventual protest of his thighs, and looked down from it at the whole of Paris. His city. He may once have been this city's outcast, but he had made Paris his.

He liked the Eiffel Tower. All those years it had been shining over his city, and he had never until now realized that. He liked the impossible, fantastical strength of it, the way the metal seemed so massive up close. He liked the fact that it had risen above all the complaints and criticism that surrounded its birth and stamped its power not only over the city but the world. He pulled out the little moleskin journal he always carried with him and stood for a long time sketching the curves and angles of the bolts and metal plates, thinking of designs for the surface of his chocolates.

From the railing, he eyed the tiny figures milling around the Champ de Mars wistfully. He didn't know why he was looking for her. She was too thin and too fragile for him, although something about her conversely exuded strength. He didn't even know what color her hair was, and—her features were quite lovely, with the blue eyes and over-full, wide mouth, too full for her thin face; the thick pale dust of freckles entirely charmed him. But . . . there were any number of women with lovely features in his *chocolaterie* at any one time. There was no reason for her to stand out at all, except the way she sat there, too thin, so quiet, hidden in hoods and draping spring sweaters, pulling all the essence of him into her body as if it was the only thing she wanted to do with her life.

The eighth morning, she didn't come.

His heart congealed. Everything lost its flavor. He looked at his elegant, luscious displays and wanted to throw them all out for their worthless, desperate pretense that he was something other than a twelve-year-old sent by his own father to hack meat off bones for a living. The desperate pretense that the truth of life was not there, in that bloody, stinking, cold place while his father at home kept warm with alcohol.

Something moody and bitter rose up in him, the thing that leaked into his chocolates, made them "dark and cruel," as one critic in *Le Figaro* had called them, apparently in approval, because Parisians eager to prove their sado-masochistic relationship to chocolate had rushed to his *salon* the next day.

When she continued not to come, he couldn't stand himself anymore and flung himself on his motorcycle and cut through the streets, dodging traffic with a lethal disregard for life and limb, over to the Île Saint-Louis. Pretending he needed to see Philippe to talk to him about the Chocolatiers' Expo in a couple of weeks.

This type of event forced him and the other top

chocolatiers and pâtissiers to cooperate, not their favorite thing to do. Dom was well aware that he cooperated worse than any of them. He couldn't stand his rivals. Being around them made him want to start a fight, and pummel and batter his way to the top of the heap of them and grin in bloody, bruised victory. *Yes. I can beat anyone.*

He did like Philippe's little fiancée, Magalie, though. Quite a lot. He liked her smallness and those boots of hers and that impervious center to her, as if she couldn't be touched, and he liked the idea of cutting Philippe out, just hard-edged muscling between them. Mostly he liked the rush of violence in the air whenever he thought about it, liked the fact that it was real and dangerous, that Philippe would genuinely try to kill him, and they could fight with fists and bodies and not just with pastries and chocolate.

He didn't because . . . well, it sure as hell wasn't because he liked or respected Philippe. *Bordel.* It made him gun his motor and cut far too close in front of a car just thinking about that as a possible motivation.

He didn't because . . . *putain.* He didn't because he put a wall of embossed rosebuds in his *salle.* He didn't because, no matter how the temptation might whisper at him sometimes, he could choose *not* to be a man who went around destroying other people's happiness. He could choose to be a man who created happiness, even "dark and cruel" happiness, instead.Still, it was perhaps just as well in his mood that it wasn't Magalie he found hanging out with Philippe but Sylvain Marquis's fiancée, Cade Corey. Who looked at a man as if fighting was such a boring and juvenile thing to do that it kind of took all the fun out of it. She was talking with Philippe when Dom walked into the Lyonnais *laboratoire,* still in his motorcycle leathers. Philippe was doing the gâteaux and *pièces montées* for Cade and Sylvain's wedding, which had been postponed already once due to some issue in Cade's family—somebody who had been in the hospital, maybe? Dom couldn't care less, but naturally, if there was gossiping to be done, his team was on it. Sometimes their chatter even penetrated his concentration while he worked.

Sylvain Marquis would drown himself in his own chocolate before he would ask Dominique Richard to do his wedding, of course.

"Dominique," Philippe said brusquely, not looking particularly thrilled to see him.

"Philippe." Dom didn't try to shake Philippe's hand, which was covered with powdered sugar. "Cade." He kissed the slim, brown-haired woman on each cheek. Cade had once come into his *laboratoire* to try to buy his soul with a few of her millions, and he might have been tempted if he didn't find Corey Bars as vile as he did. After all, he had sold his soul several times before, and the thing had been remarkably stubborn about surviving the treatment. In the end, the poor little rich girl had settled for Sylvain, and Dom always felt guilty when he saw her, for having forced her to stoop so low.

Dom had flirted with her on principle when she was negotiating for his soul but remained fundamentally indifferent to her. That dark, mean part of him woke up often enough, with the beautiful privileged women who came into his shop, and he took advantage of their eagerness to be used by him. There was something intensely satisfying about being begged for more rough sex by a woman who would have thought him worthless scum ten years ago.

But Cade had never shown the least desire to be used by him, and beyond the satisfaction of sex with them, princesses didn't do much for him. Their lives were too facile, too privileged. Plus, for God's sake, *Corey Chocolate*. He wasn't Sylvain; he had standards. How could Sylvain even hold up that arrogant head of his, marrying the heir to a multibillion-dollar corporation that produced such mass-market pap?

He frowned at Cade Corey, wondering what the hell Sylvain saw in her.

"What?" she asked dryly, and he gave her a look of surprised approval. The first time he had met her, she had wanted something from him, and thus had tried to be conciliating. He liked her better today, when she couldn't care less what he thought of her.

Straight brown hair that was relentlessly silky, blue eyes, a steady I-own-the-world look. Odd, he kept feeling as if there was something different about her he should notice. "Nothing." He shrugged and turned to Philippe. "So are you doing the Chocolatiers' Expo? Cade, do you know who will be there?"

"Corey will have a strong representation." She pointed a finger at herself, which, being Cade, might mean that she thought she, by herself, was the strong representation. "Devon Candy. Caillebaut, Kraft, Firenze . . ."

Dominique exchanged a look of mutual confusion with Philippe. "I meant the *important* people."

Cade made a little growling noise of frustration.

"Me, you, Simon, Sylvain, I think those are the biggest names," Philippe said. "Are you going yourself or sending some of your team?"

"Myself." Simon Casset would probably do one of his exquisite, impossible flights of chocolate and jewel-toned sugar. Philippe favored displays that allowed him to showcase multiple *gâteaux* in some elegant effect. Sylvain . . . "What's Sylvain doing?" he asked Cade, since, being new to the Paris chocolatier scene, she might be naive enough to tell him.

She smiled sweetly at him. "Working. Why aren't you? Is business slow?"

Seriously, if Cade got any more annoying, he might actually end up liking her. Or at least respecting her. She handled herself all right for someone who had originally dropped into the ultra-competitive Parisian chocolate scene acting as if she thought she could buy it up and stuff it in her pocket.

Instead of responding, he studied Philippe's current work-in-progress. All roses and pink and cream. A peek into some other, fairy-tale world. How did the man manage it? Was it that privileged Lyonnais past of his? Philippe was one of the few men as big as he was, but Dominique always felt bigger near him, oversized and clumsy. As if all his own edges were too hard and would break anything he ran into. His hands were far too big for his *métier*. Giant, hard laborer's hands. They belonged to his first *métier*, the one his father had thought he deserved, that of a man who hacked meat off bones.

He compared notes about the upcoming event, but it started getting embarrassingly obvious that he was just restless and had no real purpose in being here, so he strode out, looking for other places to invade and be obnoxious.

He came out of the kitchens into Philippe's Beauty and the Beast palace of a *salon de thé*, with its well-dressed crowd sitting among marble pillars under embossed lions' heads and painted ceilings. And stopped.

There she was. The woman who had not come that morning. She was sitting in *Philippe's salon de thé*, with one of those rosy, airy, fairy-tale concoctions in front of her.

He felt stabbed through the heart. Standing there, oversized for this froth of a place, in his black motorcycle leathers, with his shaggy hair and his stupidly shaved face. He, who shaved at best once every four days, had shaved every single damn morning for the past week. Why? For what stupid reason?

She put a spoon to her lips, enjoying *Philippe* on her tongue. She looked as if she belonged there, probably more than in the rough stone surroundings of his *salon*, despite his stupid embossed rosebuds and velvet curtains. She set the spoon down and gazed at her dessert a moment, her face a little sad, tired.

He shifted, accusingly, and she glanced up. Her gaze flicked over him, his size, his leathers, his hard stare. Her face closed entirely, and she looked back at him just as aggressively, until he half expected her to pull out Mace if he walked too close to her table.

Fuck her, he thought, so bitterly and insanely wounded, anyone would think he had just discovered his virgin bride in the arms of another man on their wedding night. He strode out of the *salon*, and did *not* bump into anything or break it, but probably mostly because people and even things just seemed to shrink out of his way.

It was a pure wonder he didn't have an accident as he headed off into the Paris streets again. People kept shrinking out of his way there, too.

COMING AUGUST 2013!

ABOUT LAURA FLORAND

Laura Florand was born in Georgia, but the travel bug bit her early. After a Fulbright year in Tahiti, a semester in Spain, and backpacking everywhere from New Zealand to Greece, she ended up living in Paris, where she met and married her own handsome Frenchman. She is now a lecturer at Duke University and very dedicated to her research into French chocolate. For some behind the scenes glimpses of that research, please visit her website and blog at www.lauraflorand.com. You can also join the conversation on Facebook or email Laura at laura@lauraflorand.com.

CPSIA information can be obtained at www.ICGtesting.com
Printed in the USA
LVOW07s1039010215

425218LV00007B/849/P